Dirty Play

Empire State Hockey Book Four

Lexi James

Copyright © 2024 by Lexi James

All rights reserved.

No part of this book may be reproduced in any form or by any electronic or mechanical means, including information storage and retrieval systems, without written permission from the author, except for the use of brief quotations in a book review.

This is a work of fiction. Names, characters, businesses, events and/or incidents are the products of the author's imagination or to be used in a fictional way. Any resemblance to actual persons, living or dead, or actual events is purely coincidental.

Cover Design: Candice Butchino, @sugarandspicybooks

Editor: Caroline Palmier

Proofreader: Kristen Russell

*For all my people pleasers who put their dreams on hold.
Your dreams are big enough. They are important enough.
They are **enough**. Follow your heart.
Life is too damn short to live for the approval of others.*

Note From The Author

Thank you for choosing to read Dirty Play, I hope you love Cade and Gwen as much as I do. Unlike the previous stories, this story deals with heavier topics that may be triggering to some. I tried to ensure these topics were handled with care, but also wanted to provide a heads up.

Topics include: Death of a loved one (not on page), struggles with grief, strained family dynamics, and organ donation.

While all efforts have been put into research and feedback from others in hopes that this story is as accurate as possible, it is still a work of fiction and I hope you can enjoy it as such.

<3 Lexi James

Dirty Play Playlist

1. Love In This Club ft. Young Jeezy - Usher
2. Last Night- Morgan Wallen
3. Leave Before You Love Me- Marshmello, Jonas Brothers
4. My Type (Little Attitude)- Bryce Savage
5. Villain Era- Bryce Savage
6. Dirty Thoughts- Chloe Adams
7. Devil In Her Eyes- Bryce Savage
8. Addicted- Zerb, The Chainsmokers, Ink
9. Bad Habits- Ed Sheeran
10. Wildest Dreams- Taylor Swift
11. Some Things I'll Never Know- Teddy Swims
12. Like You Mean It- Steven Rodriguez
13. Always Been You- Jessie Murph

Prologue: Cade

Ten Years Ago

Beep. Beep. Beep.

That's all I can hear among the chaos. That and the screams, but I couldn't tell you where they're coming from. The smell of antiseptic mixed with hand soap and desperation hangs thick in the air, clinging to my nose. An unwelcome reminder of why I hate this place.

Nurses and doctors are moving around the room at a speed I can't follow, as I stand here staring at her, like somehow my presence will make this all go away. Like somehow I'd be able to go back and change the past—fix this.

I vaguely notice someone's hand gripping me, trying to move me.

I don't move, though. I don't do anything except stare. My whole body is heavy as the feelings of anguish and heartbreak hit me like a freight train, slamming into me like a blindside collision on ice. They warned me I should be bracing for this, preparing myself for the worst.

I refused to accept it—refused to believe I couldn't fix this.

I promised her I would always take care of her—that she'd be okay. I told her I would keep her safe and protect her, always. She even made me pinky promise, saying that was the most important part.

Obviously not, when I haven't held my end of the deal.

Everything around me starts moving at lightning speed, more medical staff rushing in and people moving in every direction. Suddenly I'm being pulled back, and I hear my dad's voice whispering in my ear. But I can't concentrate on anything, overwhelmed by the realization my entire world is crumbling around me.

Standing outside the hospital room, knowing that in just inside, I'm losing my best friend. It has to be the worst feeling in the world.

I'm wrong.

The moment the noises get louder, just before the beeping flat lines, everything stops. I know what's happening even before the doctor walks out of the room, a look of grief on his face as he approaches us.

I feel myself slide to the floor, my bad arm still held in a sling as my dad moves to stand by my mom and help console my little sister, Kylie. Vince, my brother, sits in the corner with tears sliding down his cheeks, but he doesn't say anything. My father keeps looking between Vince and me, his eyes solemn, almost urging me to come to him as he wraps his arms around my mom and sister like he can protect them from this—protect them from what's about to happen.

Which is why I don't move.

It's why I can't.

They all deserve so much better. They deserve each other, without my poison. I don't deserve their hugs, their words of affirmation, or their comfort.

Because at the end of the day, it doesn't change our reality.

She's dead.

My sister is dead, and it's all my fault.

Chapter 1

Cade

"Would you get your ass out of my face? I'm busy," Miles grumbles to Harris, who decided to do squats as close to Miles's face as possible, the little shit starter.

You can tell Harris is a younger brother. He loves to push people's buttons and is overjoyed when he gets the reaction he's hoping for.

Reminds me of the way my younger brother and I used to be when we were growing up. It drove me crazy —his incessant poking and prodding, all to get a reaction out of me. But as we grew older and got closer, I started to enjoy that side of Vince.

It took a long time after I left to stop missing it so much.

"You could at least say thank you. I mean, I have an incredible ass. But if being this close to my perfect behind makes you uncomfortable, I guess I can move,"

Harris says with a smirk, walking over to where the squat rack is actually set up. Turning back, he looks over at Miles who's currently flexing in the mirror instead of starting another round of bench press. "Besides, Miles, I wouldn't exactly classify you sending sweaty thirst traps to your flavor of the week as being 'busy'."

"Fuck off or I'll send one to your mom."

"Tell her I say hi." Harris winks before starting another set of squats. He may be a shit starter, but Harris works his ass off—it just takes him a while to get started.

There's a reason he's one of the best defensemen in the NHL. Not only does he help make my job a hell of a lot easier, he's also the leading scorer amongst the league's defensemen. He's always been that way, even back when we were kids playing on the only team our parents could find close to our small town, which was still an hour away. That meant we had lots of time to crack jokes and make each other laugh in the back of one of our parents' vehicles, whoever got stuck driving us that day.

"Can you two shut your faces and finish your workouts? I'd have been done half an hour ago had I come on my own," I grumble before picking up my weights again. Being a goalie, my workout program is quite a bit different than these guys. I spend a lot of time focusing on my flexibility and keeping my mobility up, whereas these guys spend most of their time with strength training and cardio. That being said, as annoying as they are, it's nice to burn off some frustration with them when our schedules align.

We pause our workouts when Trevor comes over with post-run sweat dripping down his face. I have no idea how he runs inside on a treadmill. I love to run, probably more than I even realize, but I need my feet hitting that pavement to make it enjoyable.

"You guys remember Ellie's surprise party is tomorrow, right?" Trevor asks as he towels off his face.

"Of course, I've been counting down the days until we have an evening off," Harris says with a smile. "I've been needing a night out."

"We've gone out, you've just been too busy for us these last few months," I grunt, finishing my last rep before reracking my weights. I'm exaggerating a bit. He's bailed on us just a couple of times, but has never told us why—so obviously, I'm giving him shit. I'm a nosy bastard. "But I agree, it's time to let loose. It's been a while since I've had a wild night out."

"You mean, besides when you had your little sleepover with Gwen? Did you get to let loose then?" Miles asks, wagging his eyebrows like a fool. I immediately feel everyone's eyes on me, while he just stands there looking damn proud of himself.

I tell myself it's just their attention that causes my cheeks to heat, not the mention of Gwen or *that* night. Harris and Miles have been giving me so much shit lately, trying to get me to come out with them after a game, but the idea of going to a bar just to spend time with puck bunnies never sounds fun so I've turned them down each time—if I want a quick fuck, I can easily find one in my phone. But for now, my hand and I are doing just fine on those nights I need a release.

"Fuck off," I grumble, glaring at them before turning away and busying myself with stretches.

They've always bugged me about Gwen, pretty much since the first time I met her, and they had to remind me to pick my jaw up off the ground... multiple times. They just don't realize after that day I've shoved down any attraction or feelings, deep down. Just because I think she's hot doesn't mean I want anything to happen between her and me. Well, it doesn't mean I'd ever let anything happen between us.

Well... mostly.

But they've never given up. It definitely didn't help that one night she had two tickets to a concert out in Philly and ended up having one of her friends bail on her at the last minute.

That would have been fine if it hadn't been the Morgan Wallen concert that I'd listened to her drone on about for months. It was insane how much planning she did, figuring out how to get tickets before they sold out, where to stay and how they'd get there, only to have her friend cancel the day of.

When she called me, obviously upset, and asked if I wanted to go with her, I knew I had to go. It didn't matter that I had a million alarms blaring in my

Dirty Play

mind, all encompassed by red flags and flashing lights, telling me I should keep the distance between us. I couldn't. Not when we were home on a break between games and didn't have practice for two days—I had no excuse. I knew she would be devastated if she didn't get to go, plus the excitement in her voice when I said I could go, hell, that was fucking worth it in itself.

But, I mean, every guy wants to see their friends happy... right?

At least that's what I keep telling myself.

"Is that really all we're going to get? Aren't you ready to finally share the juicy details of your little getaway?" Harris jokes while Trevor quietly watches everything unfold, a playful look in his eyes.

"I'll share when you do," I deadpan, watching his eyes widen in shock.

"Next subject please," Harris says as he pulls his sweatshirt back on, and I just smirk.

He's been acting weird lately, bailing on us more than usual or sneaking off early into the night claiming a headache or whatever. Plus, he's just been a little different lately, hot and cold. I don't think the other guys have noticed it yet, but I've known him for almost our entire lives—I've noticed it.

"There has to be something going on between you two. I've seen the way you look at each other, I mean, just the way you bicker... I don't know. It's tense as fuck. But like, in a good way... like, I feel like I need a cigarette if I'm in the room with the two of you for too long." Miles grins.

"You complain about me going to book club with my mom, and you're here talking about sexual tension and the "looks" they were giving each other?" Harris jokes, already back to his usual self.

I'll figure it out one day, but I'll wait till he's ready.

Harris has two older sisters, both of whom have declared themselves the leaders of the book club in our hometown, trying to spice up everyone's life by getting our grandmas reading smut. His mom attends and it's fun watching him squirm whenever she calls to tell him about their recent book choice. At least that's what Harris is always telling us. It's been quite some time since I've been back home to listen to my mom or sister tell me about it.

It's been even longer since I've considered that town my home.

"The book club your mom and sisters are in is a little more... adventurous, than just *talking* about sexual tension," Miles says with a little smirk that tells me he's up to no good. "Since you mentioned book club... what did you say the name of it was? It's after a bird, right?"

I don't think I've ever seen Harris blush before so I almost can't believe my eyes when he avoids eye contact and looks down at his phone, leaving me curious. Thankfully, Miles isn't done.

Dirty Play

"Was it the Robins? The Crows? Maybe the Eagles?"

"The Swallows," Harris replies with no amusement. "That would be thanks to my sisters, Lyla and Emmie, but my mom definitely thought it was hilarious."

I can't help but laugh at his expense. Really, The Swallows?

"Based on the name, they definitely aren't reading Nicholas Sparks level of spice," I chime in, unable to help myself.

"Now, Cade, you're not getting off the hook that easy. Is that really all we're getting? You can't even give us something little?" Harris pokes.

"Yes, that's all you're getting. We went to the concert. It was nice." I roll my eyes, hoping he'll let it go, but of course he doesn't. "We had fun, listened to music, then came home. We're friends, that's all. Now, can we finish this workout? I'm getting fucking hungry and you're somehow even more annoying when I'm hangry."

"Whatever. One day you'll spill the tea," Miles grumbles, shoulders slumped as he turns to finish his workout.

I feel bad they keep asking and I won't give them anything. I'm just not in the mood to have a conversation about Gwen, I never am. They think they know everything about us and give me a ton of shit already. If they knew about all the other times we hung out—the times we hung out away from the group—they'd be insufferable.

That's why I don't mention the times we've bumped into each other and decided to grab drinks, staying out far too late just talking about music. Or the time she needed help setting stuff up in her apartment and didn't know who to call, so I went and hung her TV and built her furniture.

I made her promise to never buy IKEA furniture again unless they fix their fucking instructions.

If the guys knew about all of this, they'd say there was something between us, something more than just friends, and damn, I wish I could tell them they're right. I've always had a crush on her. But I've only ever let myself acknowledge it in the dark.

Outside of that, I just deny it.

Deny, deny, deny.

After a quick shower and a plan to meet at the pub down the street for some food, I'm finally walking out to my car. I feel my phone vibrating in my pocket for the fifth time since we finished our workout. Chances are high it's just my mother again, so I let it go to voicemail like usual; that way I can listen to it and respond by text message. It's easier to decide a conversation is over when you can just choose to not respond to a message.

Over the phone, it's always a lot of questions I don't have answers to and awkward silences that fill the rest of the time, and I'm just not cut out for that.

Especially when anytime I'm talking to my mom or anyone in my family, I want to apologize for what I did, to beg for their forgiveness. But I don't deserve it, so it's just been easier to avoid them all together. This time, though, when I grab my phone to double-check, I see another name flash across the phone as it starts ringing in my hand—again.

Kylie.

My little sister.

Usually, when my parents are trying to get a hold of me, and I don't respond, they get my sister involved. Kylie is my little sister, but she lectures me like she's older and more mature. As much as I want to ignore it and send her straight to voicemail, I promised myself I would never send *her* calls to voicemail. I can ignore everyone else, especially Vince because he never calls, but Kylie knows I'll answer her calls in case there's an emergency.

"Hello," I say into the phone, carrying the rest of my gear in my other hand.

"So, you are alive," she snaps, her tone crisp, annoyance evident. "Do you realize every day you don't answer her phone calls you're breaking her heart a little more?"

Her words hit me hard, exactly like she intended. I hate the way she's upset with me, even though I only have myself to blame. I've caused this entire mess; I can't expect someone else to clean it up for me.

"Yes, Ky, I am. Is everything okay?"

"Everything is fine. Am I not allowed to call my big brother and just say hi?"

I sigh, knowing if I answer truthfully, she'll call me a dick.

"I guess you can," I grit out, getting into my 4Runner and starting her up, getting the heat going. If I have to have this conversation, at least I can be comfortable.

There's a moment of silence, neither of us saying anything. I can hear her breathing on the other end of the line until finally, I hear her sigh.

"Why do you have to make everything so difficult, Cade?" she whines. "Look, Mom and Dad miss you. I miss you. Will you come home for their anniversary party? It's a couple of months away and we both know it's in your off-season, so you can't use that as an excuse.

There's not a chance I'm going back home. I haven't been home in years. At least five years... possibly more. There's nothing for me back there. Just memories and heartbreak. It's better for everyone if I stay far away.

Especially for my family.

"I'm not making anything difficult, Ky. It's just... I'm not coming home. I can't come home."

"That's not true, Cade. It's your home. We're your family. Why can't you just stop running from everything?" Kylie says, her voice softer, filled with sadness now. "Mom hasn't been the same since you left."

"No. Mom hasn't been the same since our sister died. I just make it worse. I know it and I think deep down, you do too," I growl, one hand running through my hair as I wait for her to talk. Instead, all I can hear through my car speakers is her breathing, all but confirming my statement.

When she finally speaks, her voice is so soft I nearly miss it.

"You're wrong, Cade, so wrong. We miss you. Please... please, just think about coming home. That's all I ask. Please, just think about it."

My usual excuses are on the tip of my tongue, but something holds me back. I didn't expect her to sound so... broken. I didn't expect her to sound so upset just because she misses me. It's enough that I can't just tell her no.

"Fine, Ky. But don't get your hopes up, chances are my answer will still be no."

"I'll take it."

"Bye, Kylie."

"Bye, Cade. I love you," she says before hanging up.

I lean back, letting my head hit the seat in defeat.

I love you, too, little sis.

Chapter 2

Gwen

Walking the streets of New York feels nostalgic in a way I can't quite put into words. It reminds me of what I always imagined my experiences would be like.

I didn't grow up with a family who went on walks through the city or out for breakfast just to enjoy a nice day together. No. My parents were either working at the hospital or tucked away in their offices. Even at dinner time, they usually cut it short, opting to bring their plates into their offices to continue working.

Being an only child meant I spent a lot of time by myself, or with a nanny who was preoccupied trying to make my parents' lives easier. So, I started to study... a lot. My parents were thrilled. They loved that I was taking an interest in the medical field, although they weren't exactly happy with my choice to become a nurse. I'm pretty sure it was intentional, though, like I wouldn't let myself follow in their footsteps.

Now, I'm twenty-six and working as a PICU nurse in one of the best hospitals for kids on the east coast. Not too shabby, if I do say so myself. However, my father loves to remind me he finished school a year faster and became an actual doctor in that same amount of time, or whatever bullshit he wants to compete about that day. I started back to school about a year ago and finished one quarter before I said 'fuck it' and dropped out.

I'm not going to throw away my dreams to follow his.

Even though walks and breakfast weren't a part of my childhood experience, I watched enough movies to daydream. I would imagine walking around with a coffee or hot chocolate in one hand and a bagel in the other, window shopping, and enjoying the city with people I love.

Just like I'm doing with Sawyer today.

Although I definitely should've grabbed two coffees because I need all the caffeine—every last drop. I worked at the hospital last night and then headed to the lab when I got off this morning to schedule an appointment... Needless to say, I'm exhausted.

I know working in the PICU is exactly where I'm supposed to be; I can feel it—deep down in my bones, I know this is it. That doesn't mean it's all sunshine and rainbows. In fact, a lot of my days can be pretty rough, and last night definitely falls in the 'rough' category.

It's never easy when a patient's health is worsening, especially one who's been in your care on and off for years. Training tells us to make sure we don't get too close to our patients, so we can remain detached. It's damn near impossible, though, especially when our patients are kids.

"What do you think about getting Ellie a new purse?" Sawyer asks as we walk past the Coach store.

"Honestly, I'm sure she has enough of those. Besides, I definitely wouldn't know what to pick out for her. Bags are a very personal purchase, the pockets have to be just right for what you need or the whole bag is trash," I point out, before taking another bite of my bagel. "I think we should do something fun for her, something she wouldn't normally do. Like an experience or something."

"That's a good idea. Rory has been asking to have Addy over, so that would be the perfect time to let the girls hang out," Sawyer says, biting her lip, deep in thought. "What if we get her a spa day? Like, get her the whole shebang. A full day of relaxation and pampering where the only thing she'll have to think about is what scent of essential oils she wants diffused in the room. I mean, we know Trevor takes care of her, but before he came along, it was just her."

"That would be perfect. Isn't there a new spa just around the corner?" I ask.

"Yeah, I'm pretty sure I walked by there on the way home when they were having their grand opening a few weeks ago," Sawyer says with a smile, her eyes now on a jacket in the window of some tiny boutique—the girl loves to shop.

"Let's head that way. I have an appointment at the hospital later, before the party tonight, but we should go grab lunch first," I tell her.

"You got it. I want to hear all about that date you canceled last week, so lunch is a must."

Too bad I have to go into work tonight, even if it is just the lab. I almost *need* a drink to even want to talk about that *almost* date.

NACHOS AND A DIVE BAR ARE DEFINITELY WHAT THE doctor ordered... or in my case, the nurse. After we got the spa gift certificate for Ellie, it started to rain out of nowhere. Not just a drizzle either—a full-on downpour. After running down the street in our heeled boots, we are both soaked to the bone and tired, opting for coffee to warm us up.

"I'm excited you're able to come out with us tonight. I know the hospital has been crazy, but we've missed you," Sawyer hums into her coffee.

"Me too, it feels like it's been years since I've been able to come out with everyone. It's tough working nights. I'm working while everyone else is sleeping, then sleeping while everyone else is awake. It's brutal and I feel like I'm basically a hermit right now. I haven't quite figured out how to balance these late shifts while still maintaining a social life at the same time," I tell her truthfully, knowing damn well I'm letting work rule my life. But I don't know how to fix it. It's the downside of being a perfectionist.

"Do you have to work in the morning, or do you get to stay out past your bedtime?" Sawyer asks, her little smirk hopeful.

"You're stuck with me all night. I'm still on nights for at least the next two months," I tell her with a wink.

Sawyer starts giddy clapping like a five-year-old, her excitement enough to make me smile. I'm thrilled I'll get to see everyone tonight—it's been way too long since I've been out with the group, and I miss them. I've missed their constant teasing; I've missed Harris constantly arguing with me about music just because he thinks it's funny when I get worked up. I've missed dancing with the girls and feeling carefree, and I've missed conversations with Cade, even if I spent most of the time trying to get him to open up more.

I've just struggled to make time for anything outside of work, and it really, really, sucks. The hospital has been crazy lately—staffing shortages not helping the matter. But none of that matters tonight. Tonight's the night I'm going to take control of my life, grab it by the reins and make it my bitch. Or whatever they say. I'm ready to put my party shoes on, drink with my friends, and maybe, if I'm lucky, find a man to take control of my orgasms, just for tonight.

I bet Cade could do it. I bet he'd have no problem making me come.

Why is he *always* the first person I think about when I want sex?

"Yes! That's what I wanted to hear. I'm pumped," Sawyer says, grabbing her phone and shooting off a text with lightning speed before I can even think to ask who the hell she's talking to.

"Huh?" I ask stupidly, unable to come up with a more intellectual response. My mind is still mush from daydreaming about Cade touching me.

"I texted Cass. She's going to be stoked you're coming out. She was sad because she thought you had to work. Let's get wild tonight, dance until our feet hurt, and then find someone for you to take home and bang," Sawyer says with a wink.

"In my dreams." I sigh. "It's been so damn long since I've been with a man. Even longer since I've been with a man who had a basic understanding of female anatomy."

She knows this dry spell isn't my usual, at least it never used to be. I may not be big on relationships, but I *definitely* enjoy male company. Especially the naked kind. I love sex just as much as the next girl; it's fun, a good stress relief, and if you're doing it right, it can end in an orgasm or two.

I want to blame my lack of time for not getting out

Dirty Play

there, but it's not just that. I've been horny, trust me. On the nights I haven't been working, when I could have gone out and found someone on a dating app, I just didn't want to. Instead, I'm single-handedly keeping Duracell's stock in the green. All because no one has sparked my interest lately, not even a bit. No tingly feelings in my no-no zone from anyone.

It's like my vagina is broken.

"We could always ask the guys if they know anyone," she says with a mouthful of chips. "Although I think all of them, especially Rex, would agree you should just get naked with Cade already."

Cade.

The one man who has always given me tingly feelings, ever since that first night I met him at the bar. A night that is ingrained in my brain—the way he looked when he walked over, his dark brown hair all messy, like he'd been running his hands through it, and all I could think about was what it would be like if I were to run *my* hands through it. His caramel brown eyes were warm from the lights in the bar, and I instantly felt like they were pulling me in. Not because they were warm and inviting, but because they held a darkness that called to me.

Ever since then, he's been the only one I imagine when I touch myself, the one I think about when I make myself come, even if it'll never be a reality. He instantly friend zoned me, and no amount of flirty banter has been able to undo that. Besides, he's never shown any interest in me, outside of our friendship, and I respect that. Although it's still fun to poke him from time to time, see how scrunched I can make his eyebrows while he glares at me.

"Been there, tried that, and we both know how that ended," I tell her. "You remember as clearly as I do. I tried to get him to kiss me, to pretend to be my boyfriend at the bar, and he refused." It wasn't even that I wanted him to kiss me, well... I mean, I did. But I was more embarrassed by the disappointment in his eyes like he couldn't believe I would even ask him.

Then, he looked me dead in the eye and said, "No. I will not kiss you." And that was before he turned away and mumbled the one word that hurt even worse. "Ever."

That word proved we would never be more than friends, and we'd never—ever —do the naked tango.

Since then, we've been nothing if not the most platonic of friends.

"I mean, I don't exactly remember that night clearly, but I see where you're coming from. That being said, I still think it was a lie. That man has secrets—you can see it in his eyes, in the way he listens but rarely talks. I wouldn't be surprised if one of his secrets is just how badly he wants you. I've seen the way he looks at you like he's ready to spread you out on the table and devour you."

"You've been reading too much smut." I roll my

Dirty Play

eyes, trying to force down a smile at the thought Sawyer might be right. I'm refusing to get my hopes up.

"You know I'm right, we both know it. You're the only woman he actually talks to, besides his normal polite conversation. Cassie and I don't count either, we're dating his friends, so he's required to talk to us. It just seems like he actually *likes* to talk to you."

"Cool your jets, woman. I'm talking about fucking, not dating, or liking. Hearts and rainbows and feelings aren't in the cards for me, I don't have the time."

"Gwen—" Sawyer starts but I cut her off.

"Nope. Strictly P in V conversations only. I need an orgasm, not a headache. Emotions only lead to heartbreak, and that's the last damn thing I need."

"Fine. But if you won't go for Cade, we're going on the hunt tonight," Sawyer says, a mischievous twinkle in her eyes. "You deserve a fun night and a hot guy. And who knows, you might just make a certain caveman a little jealous."

Cade... jealous?

I'd pay to see that.

After spending the afternoon with Sawyer, we head back to her place to get ready for tonight, where she proceeds to squeeze me into a pair of skintight jeans that make my ass look fabulous, and a crop top that's making sure the girls are front and center.

If this doesn't get me laid, I'm never going out in anything but sweats and a messy bun. No use in trying if I'm still the only one touching myself.

As much as I hate the idea of walking into work like this, I won't have time to get ready after my appointment, so I don't exactly have many options. Everyone at work is used to seeing me in scrubs, so I feel uncomfortable walking into the hospital all dressed up.

Especially if Dr. Dickhead is there.

He hasn't always acted like a douche, only after I turned him down at the bar before I knew who he was. I didn't need to know who he was to know he wasn't my type. He has the clean-cut, preppy boy look going on, which is fine and all, but mixed with his slightly pretentious attitude, I had to pass.

I knew it was the right call when he said I would regret my decision, all niceness immediately dissipating.

I think it was him who ended up having regrets when he walked into the hospital I work at that very next week, only to realize we'd be working together for the foreseeable future.

Chapter 3

Cade

"What're you having?" the bartender asks as he walks past us, drinks in hand, working both ends of the bar like a boss.

"Just a water for me," I say, looking at Rex who's staring back at me like I'm insane. Doesn't surprise me; they've been living it up tonight. The ladies are currently on the other side of the bar shooting tequila like there will be zero repercussions tomorrow. I was all for a night out getting drunk with the group, until I heard she would be here.

Gwen is the reason I don't drink much when I'm out with everyone, but it's purely a personal choice. Anytime I'm around that woman, I crave her, even if I'm constantly fighting it. Give me a little alcohol and all common sense flies out the window while the desire to claim her increases exponentially. Every second I'm here tonight just brings me that much closer to fucking around and finding out just how sweet she'd taste—consequences be damned.

"Yeah, fuck that idea. I'll take an Old Fashioned and a margarita on the rocks with extra salt, please," Rex says to the bartender before turning back to me. "That girl loves a good margarita, but damn, she gets feisty if they don't give her that extra salt, so I always double-check. For some weird as fuck reason, it's her favorite part of the drink—well, that and the tequila."

"Sawyer likes what she likes, can't fault her for that." I shrug, watching the bartender make our drinks while flirting with the two blondes who've been trying to sneak up to the bar to get a drink, skipping the line growing behind Rex and me.

Spoiler alert: they got two shots of vodka and two long islands before we got our drinks.

Grabbing our drinks, we head back to the group as I do my usual scan of the room to make sure everyone is accounted for. It's hard keeping track of our whole group when the bar is busy, but I always feel like I need to know where everyone is, that I need to make sure everyone is okay. Tonight, it's a little easier since some people have already left.

We're all out for Ellie's birthday, something Trevor had setup to surprise her. They didn't stay too long, though, to the surprise of no one. After some grinding on the dance floor, the two of them high-tailed it out of here like two high schoolers in love.

Dirty Play

Finishing my scan, my gaze stops on a set of bright green eyes and a head full of dark chocolate brown hair belonging to the beauty across the room from me. I home in on her like she's my target, my priority.

You just care that she's safe. Nothing more.

My jaw clenches as I watch the girls out on the dance floor. Gwen and Natalie—who is Ellie's best friend—are out there dancing around, obviously becoming fast friends. Their slight buzz from earlier this evening is slowly evolving into full-on tipsy as they grind on each other to some 90's R&B song by Usher, like a drunk couple in love. I'd be lying if I said it wasn't hot as fuck, but I think just about anything Gwen does is hot as fuck. I'd kill to switch places with Natalie, even for just one night. One hour, even... although I'm not sure that'd be long enough to do what I've been dreaming about.

Rex and Max are both standing around, watching Sawyer and Cassie out on the dance floor, having a good time, just being silly and ridiculous. This is why my eyes keep bouncing back to Gwen, who is rolling her body, practically fucking in the air, and dammit, I feel myself hardening in my pants.

Fuck.

I know I'm not supposed to think about Gwen like this. I promised myself when I first met her I would never cross that line. One thing life has taught me is if you make a promise—especially a pinky promise—

you should always keep it. Even if the pinky promise is only with yourself.

But she's making it so fucking hard. She's having the time of her life—smiling and dancing around—while I'm standing here staring at her like some creep trying to hide his erection. She's having the best night, and I'm jealous. Jealous of how carefree she is, how happy she looks, and jealous of everyone who gets to be close to her. Even Natalie is on my shit list right now.

Most of all, I'm jealous she's having this much fun, without me.

But I can't go out there. She sees right through my armor, my facade. I've spent years building up these walls, and it feels like she's slowly breaking them down. Breaking me down, and dammit, I want to let her, and that scares the fuck out of me. It feels like she sees the real me, but if she saw the scars I've buried deep down inside—if she saw the darkest part of my life—she would never look at me the same. She would see the truth, run for the hills, and never talk to me again.

Which is why I'm keeping my distance, standing here with the guys just watching, and ignoring her presence even if it does calm me. Being around her is the only time I've been able to take a deep breath in the last ten years. Except for when I'm out on the ice, that's always been my space.

Gwen is unique—her personality is a mixture of

hot and cold, a bit of sugar, and a lot of spice. She's like a grown-ass Sour Patch Kid. Starting off a little sour, but once you get to know her, she's one of the sweetest, most genuine people you'll ever meet. Then the second you get comfortable with her, she sucker punches you with her fucking sass.

"So, what are we looking at?" Rex asks as he steps up next to me, his eyes following my gaze until they land right on our girls, specifically on Gwen.

Who is definitely not my girl. I don't have a claim on any of them… but I do care about all of them.

"Wanna share your thoughts with the class, Cade?" Rex says as he looks back at me, a knowing smirk on his face while he sips his Old Fashioned. I'm sure he can read straight through me like he's always been able to. Thankfully, over the years he's been rather accommodating to how little I like to share. "Or would you like me to draw my own conclusions based on the very obvious evidence?"

Except for now.

"Fuck you, old man," I growl, earning me both a slap to the side of my head and a laugh from Rex.

"I would've guessed right, and we both know it," Rex says with a little smirk before walking into the crowd toward them.

What was that? What does he mean by that? And then to just walk away while some bullshit response is still bouncing around in my head. He's already driving me crazy, and it's only been two point seven seconds since he said it.

Irritated, I take off toward Rex, using my six-foot-four height to my advantage, and push through the crowd. Thankfully, I make it over to him before he reaches the girls because I'm able to grab his arm and force him to a stop.

When he turns around, he's smirking again, his eyes a little sparkly like he was hoping I'd chase him. What the fuck kind of fairy dust are they sprinkling in these drinks tonight? That shit better not be in my water.

"So, are we ready to share our thoughts?"

"Fuck off, grumpy, old man," I mutter again as he just shrugs and laughs, walking away for the second time.

Fucker.

As I follow him, I find myself searching for Gwen again, immediately spotting her like always. But this time, I really look at her, really see her.

Her smile is bright—she's out there giggling while dancing around with the girls, obviously having fun. But the smile doesn't meet her eyes, and it feels like a punch to the gut. She should be happy, like really, truly happy. She deserves it. Yet the only thing I can see in her eyes is sadness and I hate it.

"What'd you bring us?" Miles asks with a smirk, as we make it back to our table.

"I brought myself a water. Your drink is still up at

the bar, waiting to be ordered," I deadpan, and Miles and Harris both act offended. "Not my fault you were too busy flirting."

"Miles is always flirting," Rex jokes, which makes Miles smile even wider. He's a huge flirt and he knows it.

"We were not flirting," Harris says, looking up from his phone finally. "We were merely celebrating that we all love music and dancing to that music. Besides, maybe you should've been out there with us. A good lay would probably help take that stick out of your ass."

"Fuck off," I grumble.

"We came back over here a while ago, just been watching the bachelor party that just showed up. A couple of them were eyeing the girls, but I'm trying just to let the ladies enjoy their night," Max says with a shrug, before pouring another beer from the pitcher.

"I'm all for letting them live their life, but if those guys get any closer, then I'm going to have to get up," Rex says, watching Sawyer on the dance floor.

The girls aren't shy—hell they have no reason to be—they're just out there having a good time, ignoring everyone else around them. But damn is it a good show. That is, until some of the guys get closer and immediately try to put their hands on the girls and start dancing with them without so much as a hello.

The girls are not having it, though, and it's actually pretty impressive. If I were on the receiving end of any of their wrath, I'm not sure I'd be as bold as these guys seem to be right now. Is it bold or are they just stupid? Either way, it is rather unfortunate for them. Rex and Max are up first, making their way to the dance floor to grab their girls, who both giggle the second they're swooped off to dance. Harris and Miles head off to go dance with Natalie, who seems more than happy to have the other guys away from her.

Which just leaves Gwen and I. I'll be damned if I'm letting that slimeball continue trying to get his hands on her, obviously not giving a fuck that she firmly said no, which only makes my blood boil.

No is a complete sentence in itself. Nothing needs to be said before or after.

Not a single fucking word.

I immediately step behind her, my hands gripping her slim waist, as I pull her back into me—not thinking about the consequences, only that I need her close to me, and only me.

"Excuse me, we were talking," he says, the slur in his speech evident.

"Actually, she was talking and you weren't fucking listening. So, if you wouldn't mind, we're going to go dance, and you're going to turn around and leave us the fuck alone," I snap, feeling Gwen stiffen, but then immediately relax into my hold. Her ass presses against my groin, and I want to bend her over right here, in the middle of the dance floor.

I half expect her to turn around and slap me,

saying something about me controlling her, but instead, she just glances over her shoulder at me. Both nerves and excitement flare in her eyes, which just makes me feel more possessive. It's like she's daring me to do something, pushing me to make a move. Usually, I give this woman everything she asks for... except for that kiss, but that was for the best.

That's why I can't make a move, and she knows I won't—so, she's fucking testing me. Pushing my limits, seeing just how far she can take this little game, and dammit, I'm not sure I'm strong enough to fight her. I've had just about enough of this push and pull tonight that I just might cave and give her exactly what she's tempting me with.

"What are you doing, Cade?" she asks, a small smile turning up the corner of her mouth as she gazes back to the group of guys. "I was just making some new friends. Those fine... gentlemen were just trying to dance with me."

Anger surges through me. An anger I can't explain. I just... I hate it. I hate them. I hate that they thought they could touch her. I hate that she might have let them... even if it was just dancing. I hate the way they're still looking at her like she's something they can take. They can take her from my cold dead hands. Even then, I'd find a way to come back for her, making sure to haunt them for the rest of their lives. They can't have her.

"I'm aware," I growl, my hands gripping her sides

now, holding her in place. She doesn't flinch, doesn't move away from me. Leaning forward, I stop when my lips are nearly touching her ear and whisper quietly, "But if I recall correctly, I thought I heard you tell those little boys no. I don't hear you telling me no right now... do you want me to stop? Or do you want to stop talking and start dancing with me?"

She pauses, her head tilting in confusion as she stares at me like she's trying to figure out a puzzle, but the joke's on her. It's a giant clusterfuck of a puzzle, filled with every shade of gray possible, a million different shapes, and at least fifty missing pieces that I'm not sure even came in the box. "Well... Mr. Grumps, I wasn't expecting this. But... if you're scaring off my prospects, I need more than just one dance."

It takes everything in me not to pick her up, throw her over my shoulder, and drag her out of this bar to teach her a lesson. She's pushing all of my buttons tonight, only some of them good. If she starts talking to me about fucking someone else, I might actually lose it.

"The whole night," I murmur into her ear as her ass grinds into my now very obvious erection, and based on the twinkle in her eyes, she definitely notices it.

"So... until we leave, or until morning?" she asks, and dammit, I can't tell her no. I could, but not a single part of me wants to in this moment. Right now, I'll give her anything she wants. A car? A shopping spree? The damn moon? It's hers, as long as the only one touching her tonight is me.

"The *whole* night, Tink. Now, can we be done talking?" I growl, nipping her ear in an attempt to distract her.

"What exactly is in it for me?" she asks, her eyes alight with mischief—like she knows exactly what I'm promising—as she bites her lip, the hope evident on her face.

Me. That's what she wants.

My eyes darken, and I feel my cock thicken even further, almost to the point of discomfort, at the promise in her voice. The promise of a night we'd never forget, and I have to hold myself back from pulling her into a dark corner and giving her a taste of what the rest of tonight could be.

But I don't. Instead, I freeze... nerves slowly sneaking back in.

"It's okay, Cade. I'm sure Michael over there wouldn't mind switching places with you," she says, taking a step forward and turning to face me. My hands still hold onto her, unwilling to let go completely, as my fingers slip ever so slightly into her waistband. She has me right where she wants me, and she knows it—she knows damn well I'm not going to willingly hand her over to another man, especially one like him.

"Is that what you want?" I growl, taking a step toward her. Her eyes widen like she didn't expect this.

Well, newsflash: neither did I.

"You think that little boy back there could give you what you need? That he'd be able to keep up with you and give you what you crave? Show you a good time that doesn't end in lies about orgasms that never actually happened? He's probably never even made a girl come, at least not one that wasn't an actress."

"What does that have to do with you?" she asks quietly.

"Me? Tink, I could make you come without even touching you."

Her breath hitches, and her pupils dilate. I realize in this moment I'm well and truly fucked. But there's no turning back—I'm giving this woman anything and everything she wants tonight.

Even me.

With her eyebrows hitched she stares up at me. "I thought—"

"You heard me. It's a yes or no question."

"You haven't asked me a question," she counters, and fuck, I wish I could bend her over my knee right here, right now, and redden her ass in front of everyone.

"Can we just start by taking those stupid shots you've been hounding me about all night?" I force out, trying to keep images of spanking her toward the back of my mind, at least for the moment.

"I thought you said you weren't drinking tonight," she says, her head tilted as she watches me, her dark hair falling in front of her face. She's so fucking pretty I can barely think, let alone manage all of these questions.

"I wasn't."

"So, what changed?"

It's my turn to just stare at her, slowly lowering my gaze down her body, taking in every curve, before making my way back up to meet her eyes.

What the hell does she want me to say? That I'll drink with her if it keeps those guys away from her? That I'll keep up this little game we have going on tonight just to see her smile again? Plus, if it keeps their eyes off her and her eyes on me, I'll take the risk tonight could be. Because she broke me, broke my walls down. Is that what she wants me to admit? That I'd give damn near anything, including myself, because I can't stand the thought of another man with her even for a dance?

Or does she want me to admit the only reason I don't drink around her is that it'll make me struggle to remember the reasons I can't be with her, nearly to the point of saying fuck it every time.

"A lot has changed."

She glares at me, obviously annoyed I'm not giving her more, but at this point, she's getting enough.

"Fine. But you're buying all of it. And going shot for shot with me. Hopefully it'll put your grumpy ass in a better mood, or I'll have to start thinking of more creative ways to make you happier." She winks while grabbing my hand and pulling me toward the bar.

The feel of her hand in mine sends a shock straight through my body, and I'm wondering just what these *creative ways* might be. I can think of about thirteen different ways she can do that, starting with her on her knees, choking on my cock.

What the fuck have I done, and why am I not stopping it?

Chapter 4

Gwen

When Cade interrupted those guys bothering us on the dance floor, I immediately wanted to tell him to go away, that we were fine. But when I saw the look in his eyes as he watched me—his dark eyes full of hunger—all thoughts of sending him away flew out the window. The only thing I wanted to do was to keep my mouth shut and legs open.

It feels like the first time in a *long* time that he's letting out that playful side of himself. Usually, he keeps anything resembling an emotion locked up in a vault. So obviously, I'm testing the waters, seeing how far I can push the limits before he snaps to his senses and reminds me just how bad of an idea this is.

The problem is that I've never thought it was a bad idea.

Luckily, tonight we both seem to be in the frame of

mind that we just want to have fun—hopefully together, based on how he's acting. But now, after being on the dance floor, in such close proximity to him, I need a little liquid courage to keep myself from overthinking everything. Like, why now? What's different today that has him changing his mind—that has him willing to cross these boundaries with me? He's always kept me at arm's length, keeping the line between us well established. But now? Now, I'm not even sure there is a line.

After three... maybe four rounds of tequila with the last of our group, I'm finally feeling ready to dance with the big grump and see just how much trouble I can get into tonight because, dammit, I deserve it.

This is exactly what I need after the shit afternoon I had—a night of fun where I can forget the stress of the real world. The stress of not being in control and knowing that will never change. Working in the nursing field means there are a lot of things I won't have control over, especially when it comes to someone's health.

Looking at Cade across the table from me, I see his eyes drift over to Max and Cassie, who are on the dance floor putting on a show for the entire bar while Sawyer just shakes her head. She's used to it by now, although it took a bit for her to get used to their PDA. It's not long before Cade's eyes come back to me, only now his dark brown eyes are glossed over with tequila and unguarded desire. Mix that with the backwards

Dirty Play

hat he's now wearing and the crooked grin playing on his lips, and he's the bad boy of my dreams.

We've become more and more flirtatious as the night has gone on, but it still feels like we're tiptoeing around it. Nothing obvious has happened yet, just *a lot* of little touches and flirty comments. Right before we came back from the dance floor, he let his lips graze down my neck before pressing a soft kiss against my pulse point that nearly sent me into cardiac arrest. I want him, and I'm not sure what I need to do to make him finally snap.

"He's staring again," Sawyer whispers to me, nodding at Cade, who is chatting with the guys.

I already know, though.

I've been able to feel his eyes on me, piercing my skin with their heat. His usual light brown eyes are a dark, chocolatey shade, like his hair, as desire swirls through them. It's intense in an almost dangerous way —like what I would imagine standing outside of a burning building would feel like. Close to the fire, yet not directly in it. It feels like a warning, but instead of nerves, excitement buzzes through me. I'm eager to run headfirst into the fire, just waiting to get burned.

"No, he's not," I lie.

"Bullshit."

I just shrug and grab my water, hoping she can't tell just how affected I am by this whole situation. It's always fun to flirt around and throw Cade off —it's one of my favorite little games. I'm just not used to him reciprocating, especially so obviously. He knows I think he's hot, and I haven't gotten laid in months. I've made plenty of little jokes about being *well* overdue for a good roll around in the sheets. I mean, the closest I've been to a man in the last twelve months was the night Cade and I went to a concert and stayed in Philly. Between the music, the booze, and the fact that he made sure to protect me in the pit, it did something to me that night. I still remember the feel of his chest pressed against my back while I watched with stars in my eyes, listening to Morgan Wallen serenade me. It was just Cade and I, and that was the one time we almost let things get carried away.

But that was also the night he made it crystal clear he doesn't do relationships or feelings and that he and I would only ever be friends.

Just friends.

I'd fuck my friend, though, so I guess the joke's on him.

When I look back at Cade, he's still watching me, his tongue swiping along his bottom lip, and I can't stop thinking about his tongue sliding down my body. The little grin on his face unnerves me—it makes me believe he knows what I'm thinking. I wonder if he knows that just his heated gaze has already done more to my body than any other man has done, *ever*.

"You look like you have something to say." I set my glass back down, not exactly sure what to add with him looking at me like he wants to eat me. The man's practically oozing sexual energy tonight—not something I'm used to being on the receiving end of.

But the way he's watching me, leaning back in his chair with his glass in one hand and his other arm thrown over the chair next to him, has me about ready to climb into his lap and taste that whiskey he's been drinking.

"You haven't been out with us in a while," he finally says matter-of-factly, no elaboration provided.

"No, I guess I haven't." I shrug.

"Why not?" Cade asks, his deep voice echoing through the noise in the bar, sending tingles down my spine and straight to my lady bits.

"I've been working. The hospital has basically become my second home," I say, glancing around and spotting our friends on the dance floor. Everyone dispersed from our table, leaving Cade and me alone, and I can't help but wish we were out there, too. I wish I could feel his hands on my body again—his body pressed to mine while our friends surround us as they dance.

Fuck, it's so tempting, but I still can't bring myself to be bold and tell him exactly what I want from him.

"You say that like it's a bad thing. The rink is my life, and I love it."

"The difference is that my job doesn't help me get laid, quite the opposite actually. Your job, on the other hand, seems to be pretty damn helpful when it comes to helping you get your dick wet," I joke.

His eyes widen in shock, but he just grins.

"Do you think about me getting my dick wet often?" he whispers, his gravelly voice making me even more turned on. He takes a sip of his drink and watches me like he didn't just ask me if I think about him fucking other women.

"I mean... don't you guys usually have girls throwing themselves all over you after every game? What are they called? Puck bimbos?"

"Bunnies," Cade replies with a smirk, his thumb brushing against his lip, his eyes bouncing down to my mouth, and I can't help it, I stare back.

"Yeah, that's what it is. Puck Bunnies. I bet they go crazy over a guy like you," I say, waving my hand at him.

"A guy like me? What's that supposed to mean?"

"You're one of the best goalies in the league, more saves than anyone else this year, and you're all hot and shit. Girls go crazy for hot athletes, all the muscles and veins, hell, even the sweat. Mix that with the adrenaline that comes from watching you play? It's fucking delicious," I reply, not missing the twinkle in his eyes at my words, even if he doesn't smile.

"So, you're saying you think I'm hot?" Cade says playfully.

"Oh, shut it, Williams. That's like asking if water is wet."

"That's a serious debate, Tink. Bad example," he says with a wink.

Dirty Play

I clench my thighs at the sight, the ache in my core intensifies by the second, and it feels like I'm a simple graze away from coming in the middle of this bar.

I just glare, which makes him chuckle. The banter with Cade when he's in this playful mood is always my favorite, especially when I get to act like a brat because I love watching his eyes flare. But it only makes him broodier, usually. Tonight, it's making him more possessive, like he's almost daring me to test him.

I'm just worried if I do it, it'll all be for nothing. I really don't want to deal with that disappointment, especially because I'm tired of buying batteries to get my orgasms. I'm due for some fun with an actual man —one who actually knows what the hell he's doing— so I swallow down my nerves as I stand up and drain the last of my margarita.

"I'm going to go dance," I announce, the tequila going straight to my head as Cade watches me, his eyes on my cleavage. It's been ages since I've dressed up for a night out, and the confidence I feel in this outfit, with this man's eyes on me, makes me feel sexier than I have in ages.

Scrubs don't exactly scream 'fuck me' unless you watch *Grey's Anatomy*.

"Let's go then," Cade growls from his seat, but he doesn't move.

"To dance?" I question, turning back to Cade as he stands up and makes his way around our table, toward me.

His face has turned to stone; his jaw clenched, while he watches the dance floor. I can see the apprehension in his eyes—the fight he's constantly in to let go, let himself have a night full of fun. But the moment his eyes are back on mine, I can tell he's cracked.

"Yes, to dance, Gwen. If you want to dance, it's with me. There's not a chance in hell I'm letting you go out there to dance with those guys. They are drunk little boys who aren't allowed to fucking touch you."

"And you are?" I ask, unable to stop myself from grinning. "I mean, I thought that broke one of those silly little rules you made. You know, the rules that keep you from touching me like we both know you desperately want to."

The second the words are out of my mouth, I know I've won.

"Fuck," Cade growls before grabbing my hand and pulling me toward the dance floor. His warm hand grips my own firmly as he slides us between others, more smoothly than I'd expect him to be at six-foot-four. When we finally make it to our group, Sawyer turns and winks at me before Rex spins her back into him, not wanting to share her attention.

The first few songs that play are more upbeat, clubby songs, and we end up all dancing as a group before splitting up as the music gets slower. I thought it would be awkward out on the dance floor with Cade, with our friends watching and all, but it doesn't feel awkward. It feels normal.

It helps that he's not weird about any of it, except fully touching me, which is getting annoying.

"Are you saving room for Jesus, or are you just that afraid to touch me?" I say as I watch him standing in front of me. He has his hands on my hips, but he's making sure there's still space between us.

After a moment, I feel his fingers loop into my jeans as he roughly pulls me into him. I fall forward, my hands meeting his firm chest. Before I can say anything, he's spinning me to face away before molding our bodies together, no longer saving room for anyone.

"Does this seem like I'm afraid to touch you, Tink? I was just trying to be respectful," he growls into my ear, the warmth sending chills down my neck.

"Well, stop it," I groan when I feel his erection brush against me.

His breath hitches as I press back against him.

"Stop what?"

"Being respectful," I say, turning to look him in the eye, not wanting him to misinterpret my words. "I'm respectfully asking you to disrespect the fuck out of me."

The man growls. Like, actually growls in my ear before his fingers grip my hips even harder, almost guaranteeing I'll have bruises in the morning, but I embrace it. "I hope you know what you're asking for, Tink," he says, as he grinds our bodies together to

Secretly, I love the idea of him marking me. Of me

having a reminder of what it feels like to have him touch me.

For the next few songs, we lose ourselves in the music and in each other, both of us testing the limits but never going too far.

All I can think about, as his fingers slip past my waistband, teasing me, is how I can still feel him holding back.

"I need to go to the bathroom—come with me," Sawyer whispers in my ear as the song ends, snapping Cade and me out of our little bubble.

I look up at him, and he just nods, his eyes a little dazed like he's in shock.

"We'll be right back," I tell him with a smile.

"We'll, uh, go grab water. Meet you back here," he says before turning and walking away with Rex.

The next thing I know, Sawyer is grabbing my hand and pulling me toward the bathroom.

"What the fuck is happening with you two, and why is the tension at an all-time high?" she bursts out the second we're alone in the bathroom, fanning herself dramatically. Thankfully, the bathrooms here are singles, but Sawyer and I never go alone—I mean, we're girls. It's our M.O.

"I don't really know. I'm kind of just going with it."

"I don't blame you. I mean, it's Cade. He's got that broody hot guy vibe going that I don't think any sane woman would turn down."

"Yeah, he's definitely... intense. Tonight just feels

different, though. It feels normal. I expected it to be awkward, at least at first, but it wasn't. I don't know how to explain it."

"You don't have to. I've watched the whole thing unfold firsthand. You both just seem happy. I love that you're happy, but it's hot as hell watching you two figure this shit out."

"I wouldn't go that far. Like I said, my goal for tonight is to let someone else be in charge of my orgasm for a change, it'll just be an added bonus if it's Cade."

"Then let's stop wasting time and get back out on the dance floor. I want to see what happens when the tension finally snaps."

Hopefully mind-blowing sex that ends in multiple orgasms, but I'd accept just a fun night of hot sex.

Chapter 5

Cade

This woman will be the death of me, and I only have myself to blame.

"Wanna enlighten me on what that's all about?" Rex asks, a stupid grin on his face as we grab our drinks from the table.

The girls ran off to the bathroom, and the moment she walked away, I realized my guard was completely down. That the lines between Gwen and I were blurring—something I promised myself I would never allow, for so many reasons.

Reasons that, for the life of me, I can't remember right now.

"No, because I don't even know what the fuck just happened."

Gwen and I have been friends long enough that I've gotten used to her flirtatious ways; it's always been like this between us. But I've also been good about keeping the boundaries in place. Boundaries I've put in place to torture myself, all for her own good. But tonight, fuck the boundaries. There's not a chance in hell I could sit back and watch someone else dance with Gwen, let alone take her home.

We haven't hung out like this in a long time, not since the concert, but that's because I put distance between us. That was the night everything changed. The night that we almost crossed the line... before I drew that line firmly in the sand. Hell, I didn't just draw it in the sand—I cemented it, made it crystal fucking clear. And in the process, I became an absolute douche to her.

Those boundaries have remained in place... until now.

Tonight is different—there's something in the air. The tension is so thick you could cut it with a knife, but instead of running like I usually do, I'm wading straight into the deep end, praying I don't drown.

"It looks like you both are finally realizing some things. I think you were seconds away from stripping each other in the middle of the bar. I need a cigarette after watching the two of you dance," Rex jokes.

"Nothing is going on," I tell him, my eyes finding the girls who are now making their way back to the dance floor. Rex's whole face lights up when his eyes find Sawyer.

The man is so sick in love. It's adorable.

"I'm gonna go back out there with my girl," Rex

smiles as he drains his drink before looking at me with a raised brow. "What are you going to do?"

Looking out to the dance floor where Gwen and Sawyer have started dancing again—this time, together—all I can do is watch her. Her jeans look like they were painted on. The denim outlines each and every curve of her hips and her ass—curves that are begging to be traced with my tongue. The ass that's been pressed against me for the last hour just asking to get fucked.

I'm rock-hard just thinking about it.

With that, I realize I'm completely, one hundred percent, out of fucks.

Tonight, I need a taste of the forbidden fruit.

Grabbing the last shot left at our table, I shoot it back and stand up, nearly knocking my chair over in the process. But I just shrug and start walking.

"I guess I'm making tonight tomorrow's problem."

I keep walking, watching her the entire way, noticing the way the two of them are dancing, even as Rex grabs Sawyer's hips, snuggling in behind her. Gwen notices and smiles, moving to turn around, and slams directly into me. But I've wrapped my arms around her before she can fall, holding her up.

I don't miss the sharp intake of breath as she realizes it was me touching her, and just how close we are right now.

"Where ya going, Tink?" I say, looking down into her bright green eyes.

"Took you long enough to come back," she says with a smirk, before turning her back to me. With my hands still on her hips, she presses her body back into mine. I'll never tire of feeling her ass pressed against me—our bodies lined up perfectly. "Should I assume you were watching me, or are you always this excited to dance?"

I grin, leaning forward to nip her ear lobe, earning me a squeal that quickly morphs into a moan as I slide one hand up her body, the movement torturously slow, making sure to tease the bare skin of her cleavage as I make my way to the base of her throat. I don't grip, don't press, just hold her in place against me, feeling the way her pulse quickens beneath my hand.

"I've always watched you, Tink. It's this touching thing I'm not quite used to," I murmur against her skin. "But don't get it twisted. I'm *always* this excited to see you."

She watches me for a moment, and I worry I've said too much, that letting her know she's always had this effect on me was taking it too far. She's a girl who likes to have fun; she doesn't want to know I've been thinking about her for as long as I've known her, as more than just a quick fuck. That it's been her name on my lips when I come in the shower, my hand gripping my cock, wishing it were her mouth.

Lifting on her tiptoes, she slides her back up my chest till her mouth is right beneath my ear, her lips brushing along my jaw. "Don't start something you're not going to finish, Cade. Because for once, Cade, I want to finish. I don't want to be teased."

"Who said I'm teasing?"

"I'm just saying," she whispers. "I'm sure plenty of other guys would take me home if you're not up for the challenge."

My eyes narrow, her words burn, but it's her sassiness that's really getting to me. I want to fuck the bratty attitude out of her and punish her for being such a cock tease. Gwen has become something I can no longer run from. I've realized this much. But unless we're doing this in the middle of a bar, she needs to stop talking.

"Close your mouth, Tink, before I fill it with something," I say, my teeth grazing her collarbone. "And for the record, I'm not opposed to doing that right here, right now."

She bites her lip, and instead of stopping this dangerous game we're playing, she turns her body around to face me and presses her hands against my chest. We lose ourselves in the music, in the dancing, and in each other, forgetting anyone else exists.

The next few songs fly by, and when we stop to take another break and grab some water, I'm so wound up I'm sure if she brushes her ass against my cock one more time, I'm bound to come in my jeans like a teenager at prom.

"I think we're going to head out," Rex says, his arm around Sawyer, who looks like she's about ready to crash. I'm not surprised between the dancing and the fact that it's nearly one a.m.

"Do you need a ride home or are you good?" Sawyer asks Gwen, but her eyes bounce between us, eyebrows raised, like the question is actually for both of us.

"I—" she starts, but I cut her off.

"I'll make sure she gets home safely," I say, saluting Rex. "Scouts honor."

"Have fun, kids," Sawyer sings as they turn to walk out.

"You're younger than all of us!" Gwen giggles.

"Whatever." Sawyer just laughs as they leave.

With them gone and Max and Cassie nowhere to be found, it's just Gwen and I left at the bar. And there's not a chance I'm leaving here without her.

"So, what're we doing, Mr. Williams?" Gwen asks, her eyes filled with a mix of excitement and nervousness.

I slip my finger into her belt loop, tugging her into me. Her hands grip my shoulders as I lift her chin up, forcing her to look at me. "Well, Ms. Murphy, I think it's time we take this party somewhere else."

"Do you... do you want to come back with me? To my place?" she asks nervously.

"Deal. Order us an Uber, and I'll go grab us another round and close out?" I say.

I know I'm fucking everything up. I know I should've stopped this whole thing hours ago, but for

Dirty Play

once, I'm letting myself enjoy someone's company as more than just a friend. Well, she is my friend. But right now, she feels like a whole lot more. Maybe she always has been and it's taken my brain this long to catch up.

Or maybe I'm just the right amount of drunk and don't have the energy to fight it anymore.

Needless to say, I sure as hell won't be the one stopping anything tonight.

"Deal."

Chapter 6

Cade

Stepping into her apartment feels different this time. I mean, I've been here before, two, maybe three, other times. But those times were different; I was here to mount her TV and build furniture or pick her up to grab lunch. I've never been here with the intent of fucking her, but tonight, I plan to leave her thoroughly fucked.

"Want something to drink? Bourbon? Water? I think I have some soda, too." Gwen says, rambling a bit, which tells me she's nervous. It's adorable how timid she's acting—the girl on the dance floor was far from timid, and that's the girl I'm going to pull from her tonight.

She's finally getting exactly what she's been asking for.

Me.

"Bourbon, please," I say as I make my way to her living room and sit down on her couch.

From this spot, I have the perfect view of her in the kitchen, where she's grabbing glasses and pouring a heavy amount into each. She's fucking sexy—the way she keeps looking back to check on me, her eyes dark, hungry, but still a bit nervous. By the time she walks over to me, she's turned on some music, the only illumination coming from the fairy lights she has hanging throughout her living room and the window behind me. The dim lighting makes her apartment that much more inviting.

"C'mere." I gesture for her to sit down.

She looks at me for a moment before setting the bourbon on the coffee table and moving to sit next to me on the couch, but that won't do. Gripping her waist with one hand, I pull her on top of me, putting her right where I want her—my lap. She grips my shoulders for support and looks down at me, teasing her bottom lip between her teeth, making me want to bite it. I want to make her scream for me, through both the pleasure and the pain, because she strikes me as the kind of girl who needs both to get off.

But tonight, we'll know for sure if her dirty and depraved fantasies align with my own.

"Where do you think you're going," I growl, my voice raspy with desire, my cock hard as she grinds against me. It's barely noticeable, but, fuck, I'm acutely aware of everything between us. I slip my fingers into her waistband, moving slowly until I get to the button of her jeans, flicking it open with my thumb. Her eyes watch me, but she's not moving—hell, she's not even breathing as my fingers slowly slide her zipper down, revealing black lace against pale skin. Fuck, she's a wet dream come true. My own personal fantasy brought to life. Fuck.

"Is this what you want, Tink?" I ask as my fingers start to play with the lace of her thong, every once in a while swiping beneath the fabric, just enough to drive her wild. "Want me to finger fuck you until you fall apart? Until you come all over my hand, screaming so loud your neighbors call the cops?"

Gwen nods frantically, biting her lip as she stares down at me, eyes wide, as my fingers brush against her clit. "Yes," she rasps, her hips slowly moving forward. She grips my shoulders as she starts to grind her clit against my dick.

Fuuuuuck.

I slide my fingers in further, all the way past the lace, until I'm circling her entrance, my thumb pressing down against her clit.

"I want you, Cade."

"What do you want, Tink? I want to know *exactly* what you want from me."

"I want you to fuck me. I want your fingers, your tongue, your cock until I can't even remember my own name. I want you to test my limits—be rough, take control of my body as you take what you need."

She moans as I slide my fingers in deeper, arching them forward until I press on the spot deep inside that has her squirming against me. Her pussy tightens around my fingers as I begin thrusting them in and out while my thumb rubs small circles against her clit—her moans getting louder and louder.

"You want me to fuck you, Tink? Is that what you want? You want my cock buried so deep inside this cunt you won't even remember any other cock that has been inside of you?" I ask, my free hand gripping her throat, this time with more pressure.

This time, I'm holding her in place, showing her who's in control.

This time, I'm showing her I'm capable of controlling her, just like she desires.

"Yes," she whimpers as I press harder, my circles still slow as I pull her toward the edge. Her body molds to my touch like she craves it. She leans into me, wanting as much of our bodies touching as possible.

"Then be a good girl and come for me—I want my hand soaked with your cum. Only then will you get my cock," I growl against her ear, tightening my grip against her neck, immediately noticing the way her eyes light up, growing wild with lust. The moment I press down on her clit while angling my fingers even further toward myself so I hit perfectly against the spot, she detonates.

"Yes, Cade," she moans.

The second she says it, it's the green light I need,

Dirty Play

and all blood immediately rushes to my cock. It's all I need to hear to throw caution to the wind. With my hand on her throat, I pull her into me, slamming her lips against mine, swallowing her moans as she falls apart. Her orgasm hits her hard and fast, coating my fingers in a rush as her body starts shaking.

"Such a good fucking girl for me," I murmur against her lips, letting her ride out the high. I pull back for just a moment to look at her—her cheeks are flush, her makeup smudged, and I don't think I've ever seen her look so perfect. "God damn, Tink. You look so pretty like this."

She lets out a cute whine as I nip her lip, demanding access, before immediately opening to let me in. Our tongues tangle and teeth gnash as we both take what we need. I can't tell you how long we sit here, her body pliant in my lap, spent from her orgasm. Our mouths explore as I grind her against me until her body stills. She moans in my mouth, her hand sliding into my hair, and I nearly come like a fourteen-year-old boy at the sweet sound. Her hands tug, pulling my hair, as I keep fucking her mouth with my tongue, wishing it was her pussy.

Begrudgingly, I remove my hand, gripping her shirt with both hands, breaking our kiss just long enough to pull it off, leaving her in just a black lace bra that matches her panties.

"Fuck, you're so fucking sexy like this," I tell her, my mouth pressing kisses down her neck as I grip her breasts through her bra, my thumb and finger finding her nipple and pinching firmly until she's squirming above me. "These tits, fuuuuck. I need to see them, all of them. I've dreamed about these fucking tits, your low-cut shirts always teasing me, just asking me to play with them. I knew they would be my ruin," I growl, her eyes widening at my declaration. Unclasping her bra with one hand, I toss it to the ground, staring at her perfect body before me.

I grip them both, tweaking her nipples, rolling them between my thumb and finger as she whimpers, her hips starting to move. I replace my fingers with my mouth, her hands gripping my hair as she holds me in place. I suck and bite her nipples, marking her breasts with my teeth, leaving hickeys to remind her exactly who she belongs to.

A physical reminder of who made her body feel like this.

I've never been like this before. Never wanted to leave my mark on a woman. But with Gwen, I want her to remember this. I want her to remember it was me who made her feel like this. Because I'm pretty sure after tonight, she's going to leave a mark on my heart.

Her hands grip me closer as she squirms in my lap, my teeth continuing to tease her flesh until her head falls back in pleasure.

"These tits are perfect," I growl.

Before I can move, her hands are on me. She grips the bottom of my shirt, pulling it up and over my head, forcing my hat off in the process. She immediately puts it back on with a smirk. Her hands are back on my body without another word, her pupils blown from lust.

"Fuck, Cade," she moans as I slip my hand back into her panties, only this time I slide two fingers through her wetness, coating my fingers in her arousal. Pulling them out, I bring them to my mouth, relishing in the way her eyes widen as I slide my fingers in my mouth, tasting every last drop of her.

"Sweet, just like I knew you'd be," I whisper before bringing my fingers back, pushing in further this time, slowly building up a rhythm. "You're strangling my fingers there, Tink. It's going to be a tight fit when it's my cock. Are you sure?"

"Yes, I want to feel it. I want to feel you," Gwen whimpers as I pick up the pace, my thumb pressing against her clit as I work her closer and closer to orgasm. I lean back, one arm resting on her couch while my other stays firmly inside her, slowly moving, stretching her. She may think she wants to feel it stretch her, but that's before she's seen it.

"What're you doing?" she asks, looking down at me as her hips start grinding against my hand.

"You want to feel it? You want me to stretch you wide as I fuck you for the first time?"

"Yes," she moans, her hips grinding harder.

"Then take me out, Tink. Touch me, see me first, then decide. I'll fuck you however you want me to, give you exactly what you need. That much, I promise. But let's make informed decisions first." I smirk. "Now, use your hands and pull me out."

She looks down at me for a second, her hands resting on my chest as she looks down at my cock with curiosity. With added pressure on her clit, I start working my fingers inside her faster and faster, her face beginning to flush again, another orgasm getting closer and closer.

Perfect. I want to give her at least one more before I fuck her. If she wants to feel it, if she wants my cock to do the work, who am I to take that from her? My cock is already weeping at the thought of being inside this tight, wet cunt.

"Fuck, Cade, I'm so close," she moans as her hands slide down to my belt, opening it with impressive precision before starting on my pants. It doesn't take long until her hand is sliding inside and gripping my cock, pulling it out.

My cock twitches the moment I feel her touching me, my body immediately wanting to take control, but I force myself to leave the choices up to her. For now.

The moment her hand wraps around my cock, I watch as her eyes widen, her fingers unable to meet as they hold me, her surprise evident. Her eyes flash with a tiny moment of uncertainty before she smirks.

"I mean, I guess it's big," she says through a moan as my thumb presses harder, my fingers moving faster. She crashes over the edge, her orgasm pulling

Dirty Play

her under, and it's the most beautiful thing I've ever seen.

"You guess?" I grunt. "I'll show you big." Standing up, I lift her with me, my hands grabbing her ass to hold her in place as my cock rests between us. Her arms wrap around my neck as she holds herself up.

Without another word, I walk us into her bedroom, throwing her down on the bed before stepping out of my jeans, leaving myself fully naked.

"Strip," I tell her, nodding toward her pants that are still on.

Quickly, Gwen lifts her hips, taking everything off in a quick move. Standing there looking down at her, it's hard to believe she's here—with me. Gripping my cock, I just stare at her. She's fucking perfect, sexy as hell, and an even better person. She's the whole fucking package, and she's here with me—a broken-down package, taped up in a million places just to hold me together. And right now, she's looking at me like I'm the best thing she's ever seen.

"Cade?" she whispers, her voice raspy, the sound so erotic.

"Yes, Tink?" I reply as I slowly start to stroke myself.

"Are you just going to stare at me, or are you actually going to fuck me?" she teases.

"Open your legs," I growl, her eyes now watching me touch myself as she quickly drops her knees to the sides, following my instructions perfectly. From here, I can see her beautiful cunt is already dripping wet, just begging for me to fill it. "You're perfect. This cunt is perfect," I tell her as I slide two fingers inside her with ease.

"You're so wet. Is this all for me?"

She nods through a moan as I angle again, hitting her g-spot in the way I already know drives her crazy. Ripping open the condom I grabbed, I roll it over my length while Gwen sits up on her elbows. She's watching me with the same eagerness I feel, the type you only feel when you've wanted something for so long, and you're finally getting it.

I've wanted her for a long time. I've spent years lying to myself, but, deep down, I've always known. So, to give ourselves this, even just this once, fuck... it feels like everything right now.

Crawling onto her bed, I position myself above her.

"You're sure about this?"

"Cade, either fuck me or take me back to the bar so I can see if one of those guys will fuck me instead, but stop treating me like I'm fragile," Gwen spits back.

Her words spur me on, kicking everything into high gear, and without another thought, I line myself up and slide in.

All.

The.

Way.

"Cade!" she screams, her nails digging into my shoulders as I push forward, giving her no time to

Dirty Play

adjust as I stretch her until I'm fully seated inside her. Her body pulses around me, constricting until I feel like she's strangling my dick.

"You okay?" I ask with a wink as she holds me still. "Regretting your decision not to let me give you a few more orgasms first?"

"If you manage to give me one more, I'll get you a trophy. Anything more than two in a night is just impossible," Gwen says, her eyes rolling back as I roll her nipple between my teeth and slide my cock out before thrusting in, slowly and deeply. I start an unhurried rhythm, making sure to slide in deep each time.

"Just one more? You could have at least made it a challenge," I murmur, licking my way up to her collarbone. With my free hand, I grip her throat, holding her still, keeping her attention on me. "Now, stop talking and let me fuck you, or I'll shove my cock down your throat instead."

Her eyes widen as I lean down, taking her mouth in a bruising kiss while her hands grip my ass, holding me close as I piston my hips harder, deeper. Sitting back on my knees, I lift her hips up with my free hand, angling her just right to have her seeing stars within the minute.

Bet.

Our tongues tangle, our bodies turning into a sweaty, hot mess. Never in my wildest dreams did I think she'd actually want to be here with me, and now that she is, I don't want it to end.

"Cade... I'm—"

"You're what?" I tease, her eyes flutter as I pinch her clit, the sensation sending her over the edge without warning.

Her entire body shakes, her hands gripping my shoulder, my hair—anything she can find—as she screams my name until finally, her arms relax down on the bed. I pause, her pussy still constricting, the tiny fluttering nearly sparking my own release. The tingling slowly begins down at the base of my spine, just dying to be released.

Not yet. Not until she's coming with me.

Sliding out, I quickly thrust back in, earning me a surprised look from Gwen.

"You're not done?" she squeaks, her eyes wide with confusion.

I chuckle. "No, Tink, I had to secure my trophy first. You know me, I like to win. Now we'll come together. Just be a good girl and scream my name again when you come all over my cock—that's the sound I want to hear while I'm filling you with my cum."

Chapter 7

Gwen

"Is everything okay?" I ask as I walk back into my bedroom, where Cade is now sitting at the edge of my bed, his elbows resting on his thighs.

I immediately sense something is off. The man that just gave me the best orgasms of my life is officially nowhere to be found. Nope, no, it seems we are back to the usual Cade.

"No, everything is not okay," he growls, his tone angry, filled with frustration as his fingers tug on his hair. "We shouldn't have let this happen, none of it!" he shouts, and I feel like he's just slapped me.

His touch gave me some of the most insane pleasure of my life, but now, his words feel like thorns. His whole demeanor has changed—the fun, playful Cade is gone, leaving me with the moody Cade who doesn't believe in fun.

"Little too late for that realization, don't ya think?" I ask coldly, suddenly realizing just how naked I am. Grabbing an oversized t-shirt from my drawer, I quickly throw it on before leveling him with a stare.

"It's not like we can exactly go back in time and undo what we just did," I say. My tone is no longer sweet as I try to push down the emotions for the moment, not wanting him to see them. I'll deal with my emotional well-being tomorrow, but tonight, I'm just trying to make it out somewhat unscathed, even if it is all for show. I can fall apart when he leaves.

"If I could, I'd have done it already, Gwen. This was all a big fucking mistake," Cade says, his voice getting louder, the anguish evident on his face, but it's nothing compared to what I'm feeling.

My face heats as I do my best to swallow down the hurt and not let him see just how much his words are hurting me. It's hard, though. I trusted him. I trusted that when he made the choice to walk into my apartment, he was doing so because he wanted to. I trusted that he respected me enough not to treat me like this less than ten minutes after fucking me, but apparently that's too much to fucking ask.

I take a step back, realizing just how vulnerable I'm feeling at this moment—used up and tossed to the side, like I'm not good enough to keep around after getting what you want.

"I told you before this couldn't fucking happen, Gwen. I didn't want this, and you still let this happen,"

Dirty Play

Cade says, finally standing up. His fists are balled at his sides, but I'm not afraid of him. He's not actually mad at me, that much is evident. But it's easier for him to take it out on me than to take accountability.

"Well, your cock said otherwise, Cade. Don't you dare put this all on me. If I'm not mistaken, both you and your cock wanted me in any way you could get me, and you said so yourself. Are you going to use the excuse you tripped and fell inside my pussy, over and over and over, and somehow that's *my* fault?"

"That's not the fucking point!" he snaps, his voice angrier, louder, his chest heaving as he stands there, and my heart hurts because I've never seen him like this. He doesn't look mad anymore, the anger rolling away, leaving only a very broken and confused man.

"I've gotta go," he says out of nowhere, standing in front of me with his jaw slack as he just stares at me. Leaning forward, he presses a chaste kiss to my cheek, and then, without a second glance, he turns around and walks out the door.

The sound of the door clicking shut is the final straw.

The floodgates open, and I'm left feeling abandoned and used.

S.O.S.

> I need you.

SAWYER
> On the way.

CASSIE
> Who am I killing?

ELLIE
> Do we need bail money?

"What the hell do you mean he got up and left?" Sawyer shouts loud enough that I'm positive my neighbors can hear her.

The girls came over first thing this morning after I texted them. I didn't even have to tell them everything, basically just that I had the best orgasms of my life—*multiple*—only for him to make a complete U-turn and call it all a mistake before leaving me all alone.

He altered my brain chemistry with his magical dick and then disappeared like fucking Houdini, leaving me high and dry and feeling like an idiot.

I knew he could be a dick, but I'd never personally experienced it until now.

"I don't know how else to say it—we had sex. Really, *really* good sex, and then I went to clean myself up. By the time I came back out, he was dressed and irritated. It was so unexpected and immediately killed my buzz. It was like one minute he's naked in my bed,

Dirty Play

giving me the best orgasms of my life. The next, he's kissing me on the cheek and walking out the door, no explanation, no anything, other than telling me it was a mistake and should have never happened," I say, an unwelcome feeling of sadness settling in the pit of my stomach.

Although Cade is just a friend, this feels an awful lot like heartbreak.

I knew this was a possibility going into tonight, but for some reason, I actually trusted that he'd thought through his decision. That he wasn't throwing away our friendship just to get his dick wet. He knows I don't date, but I've been pretty up-front about my attraction to him while he's always been hot and cold. I play it off that I'm interested in Cade because he's hot and looks like he can fuck well, but I also just enjoy being around him, which to me would be an added bonus for a hookup.

But apparently, he can only have a hookup or a friend, not both. And he chose to leave.

"You're joking, right?" Cassie says, her voice sharp, the look on her face a weapon.

These girls are definitely my protectors, and that's something I'll never take for granted. "I wish I were," I say quietly, the memories from that night still hard to think about.

"That's brutal. What a dickbag. Don't get me wrong, I say that with love because it's Cade, and I love the grumpy ass. But fuck him big right now," Cassie finally says. "If they're going to be dicks after the big O, they shouldn't be allowed to be good in bed. They definitely shouldn't be allowed to have big dicks, either."

"Cassie, he wasn't just good—he was beyond amazing. I saw stars. I'm pretty sure I blacked out and lost actual moments of my life while I floated around in outer space. Don't even get me started on his dick. He's big *and* knows how to use it. It's so unfair, plus his dirty talk could nearly get me there by itself. I mean, I nearly came just from hearing him tell me what to do."

"Oh, I love it when Rex does that," Sawyer says with a smirk. "Although I have a hard time seeing you enjoy someone telling you what to do, even in the bedroom."

"We all knew a man would bring her to her knees one of these days, and we've always hoped it'd be Cade." Cassie smirks.

"Yeah, but we also expected him to actually stick around and not be a total douchebag," Sawyer adds.

"Yeah, I definitely didn't have this on my bingo card this year. He's always been there for me, even if it hasn't been in the conventional way," I say with a shrug. "I usually don't like to be bossed around because it always feels forced. With Cade, he was in control. Of the *entire* situation, my body included, and it was hot."

"Oh, we've all seen it. There's always been something between you two," Sawyer says with a smile before turning serious. "Have you tried to talk to him yet?"

Dirty Play

"No. I don't have anything to say right now. Besides, I'm pretty sure he said everything he needed to last night," I say as I look out the window, flashbacks of last night clouding my mind, and I just want to curl in a ball in my bed and hide from it all.

The only problem? Every time I close my eyes, I just see the pained look on Cade's face right before he broke me.

The broken boy staring back at me with so much sadness I couldn't breathe.

"So, what're you going to do?" Cassie finally asks.

"The same thing I always do. Keep moving along, throw myself into my job, and try to remember last night for what it was. A couple of orgasms."

"Do you think you guys will ever be okay?" Sawyer asks.

"I mean, eventually. But that all depends on him," I answer with a shrug. "It's him with the problem, not me. It was just me who got taken along for the ride."

Having a hangover two days in a row should be illegal, but I couldn't turn down the opportunity to sit in the sun with the girls for a couple of hours. Having some mimosas and getting some vitamin D made it all worth it. The girls ended up staying over for most of the day until Rex and Max came over to pick them up.

After making a tray of nachos, I ended up crashing

on my couch with a pint of brownie batter ice cream and *10 Things I Hate About You* playing on the TV.

I even left early this evening for work because I wanted to walk instead of take a cab—my feeble attempt to shake off my grumpiness with physical exertion. By the time I make it to the hospital, I have just enough time to grab a chai tea and sugar cookie from the cafeteria before my shift starts at eight.

Perfect.

"Coffee or sustenance?" Mariah asks, trying to hide her yawn as I get in line behind her.

"Aren't they the same thing? Caffeine is a must, but I'm also eye fucking that purple sugar cookie just sitting there, tempting me with its buttery perfect icing."

"My vice is their lemon bars—they melt in your mouth and are just perfect. But I don't think I'd turn down any of their desserts. They're all amazing."

The line moves pretty quickly. Right before it's my turn to order, Dr. Dickhead walks by with his food on a tray and a warm coffee in hand, but the warmth doesn't meet his eyes.

"You're needed over at the nurses' station. Room three needs to have a bunch of testing done tonight. She'll need to be prepped. So, whenever you decide you're done chitchatting like it's your job, please head over to your *actual* job," he says in his most condescending tone possible. "But by all means, take some extra time to get a snack first, everything else can wait."

Dirty Play

I notice Mariah looking down, obviously not as comfortable with confrontation as I am, but there's no chance I'm allowing him to talk to me like this and get away with it.

"Well, you see, I'd be more than happy to. As soon as I clock in. At my scheduled time. But until then, I'm going to enjoy my little snacky-snack," I tell him with the biggest, fakest smile I can muster up.

The doctor with Dickhead does his best to hide a smirk. It's well-known he can be a dick, but he's definitely not used to someone snapping back.

Out of the corner of my eye, I see Mariah watching us. Her eyes wide with shock but she's fighting back a laugh while Mr. Doctor here should probably get his blood pressure checked. He's so angry his cheeks are turning red. I can only imagine that much anger can't be good for your heart.

"Sorry, Ms. Murphy, I was under the impression you took your patients' health seriously and weren't worried about a couple of minutes, but now I understand," he says before turning to walk away, unable to admit he's wrong so trying to make me seem like a dick.

Fuck him.

"That man is literally the worst," Mariah sighs. "Can't wait for Dr. Mitchell to be back on nights soon, he's pretty to look at and nice."

Agreed. Dr. Dickhead is really starting to get on my nerves.

Lexi James

"Hello, Miss Kennedy, how are you tonight?" I ask as I walk into the hospital room. Kennedy sits on the bed while her mom paints her toenails neon green.

"Tired of being poked and prodded, but that's nothing new." She smiles, but I can see the exhaustion behind her attempt to be strong.

"I know, sweet girl. I'm sorry," I say as I check her vitals.

Looking over at Denise, I can see the worry on her face. Her husband, Josh, usually goes home during the week. They have two dogs, and his work is close to home, so it just makes more sense. He's always back here the moment he can be. I've gotten Denise to go home once or twice to get some rest, but it's a battle, and she always comes back at six the next morning to be here when Kennedy wakes up.

I get it. I really do. But sometimes, you just need a night in *your* bed with *your* person to recover, body and mind, while going through hard times. Most often, when people get stressed, they become overly emotional and altogether more fragile, especially when exhausted. It's like one wrong move, and we're ready to attack. She tries to be so strong for Kennedy all the time that sometimes she needs some time to feel broken.

"How are you, mama?" I ask Denise. "Have you had any food yet?"

Dirty Play

She looks up with a sweet smile. "Yeah, Josh left about an hour ago, and he brought us dinner," she says, putting away the nail polish before sitting back down on the edge of Kennedy's bed. "But I'm good. We're good. Hopefully these tests show her kidney levels are improving, but if not, we're just going to keep our fingers crossed we find that donor.

"I'm crossing my fingers and my toes," I say, grabbing her hand with a soft smile. I give her a quick squeeze before turning back to Kennedy. "You just never know when you'll find your match."

"That's what they keep telling me," Kennedy groans. "But damn. It's hard watching other people get theirs while there always seems to be something in the way of me getting mine."

"Language," Denise scolds as she rolls her eyes, but all you can see is the love for her daughter in those eyes.

"What? I can deal with kidney failure and miss most of my sophomore year of high school because I'm hooked up to all this sh—crap, but I can't swear?"

"I mean, it is just a word." Denise shrugs.

"I think of swear words as word seasoning. Not used toward others, but there to help spice up the sentence a little bit." I wink at Kennedy, who gives me one of her megawatt smiles.

She may only be fifteen, but she's been through a lot. She's been in and out of the hospital since she was thirteen, all starting with what they thought was a simple UTI. One turned into two, then three, then another one, until they discovered her frequent infections weren't because of infection—they were because her kidneys were failing.

Watching her battle this shit has been heartbreaking. She's losing so much time to be a kid, and to watch her miss all these milestones in real time has been devastating. Especially when she's been playing select soccer since she could walk and had college scouts interested in her. Now, she's on dialysis while we hope for a match. To say she's been nursing a broken heart these last few months would be the understatement of the century.

"Are you guys still re-watching *Gilmore Girls*?"

"Yes! We are only in season two, but it's getting so good," Kennedy squeals, her smile widening at the change of topic. "Jess just won a date with Rory in an auction, beating out Dean, and honestly, I wish I could save the look on Dean's face and make a t-shirt or something."

"But poor Dean just looked so sad," Denise adds as she starts to add another coat to Kennedy's toes.

"Well, he can cry a river, build a bridge, and get over it. We're Team Jess in this hospital room."

"I'm an OG Team Jess girl right here." I smile, grabbing all my stuff and closing out of the computer. "I'll be back around in a bit. Remember to press the button if you need anything."

Chapter 8

Cade

Lacing up my skates the morning of our last game of the season shouldn't feel so depressing, but it does. Not only is hockey my outlet—and now it's going to be less prevalent in my life for a while—but it's also Trevor's last game on the team before he retires, and that sucks.

It's the end of an era, and damn, it's sad.

When I first got drafted as a rookie to the New York Cyclones at twenty-one, Trevor was the first guy to really welcome me to the team. He made me feel like I was a part of something bigger, even if I didn't actually get a lot of playtime. He was also the first to believe in me when I did finally get on the ice. It was at the end of a game when our goalie got injured, only eleven games into the season, and it was up to me to take his place. Trevor had the entire team backing me up, believing in me, and supporting me that first game—and every one after that.

I was scared shitless, but you wouldn't have been able to tell because Trevor made me believe I was not only capable of doing this job but that I could be great at it. When we won the game 2-0 against Nashville, I blacked out the moment the buzzer went off.

Did I think we would win my first game out there? Hell no.

I felt like a baby deer on skates trying to walk out there on the ice—my pads felt like they were ten sizes too big. Add in the thought of going up against another team on live national television, and I was fucking terrified.

But he made me believe.

Did I think there was any possibility that we would not only win, but that I would get my first ever shutout?

Not in a million years.

Now, with his last game tonight, all I want to do is get him one last win. For everything he's done for the team and everything he's done for me.

Tossing my bag in my locker, I grab my phone off the bench to throw it in as well when a text pops up.

Kylie.

Fucking hell. Right as I go to throw it in without looking, a second text from her pops up, the words clear as day on my screen.

Dirty Play

> **KYLIE**
> I'm in town, let's get together.
> We need to talk about June.

Kylie has been bugging me since January to make plans to come home this summer. My brother Vince was able to get some time off of work and they want to throw an anniversary party for my parents. They're celebrating the big 4-0. I told them I couldn't make it because of work, but they quickly called me out on that bullshit. That's the downside to being a professional hockey player—they know it's the offseason and I'll have no problem making it work.

> Can't, sorry. I have a game.
>
> **KYLIE**
> I know, dipshit, I have your schedule.
> Can't miss the last game of the season! I already bought a ticket.

Son of a bitch.

> Well then, I guess I'll see you there.
>
> **KYLIE**
> You bet your ass you will.

My little sister is... well, a typical little sister. Huge pain in the ass, but a heart of gold. She's used to getting her way and isn't afraid to force the hand a bit if it helps her in the long run.

Slamming my locker shut, I walk out to the rink and link up with the rest of the guys. Harris and Miles are standing by the ice, watching as a couple of the guys race around, loosening up a bit, Trevor in the lead laughing like a fool. The good thing about tonight's game is we can enjoy it for what it is, the last game of the season, and Trevor definitely is. Playoffs have already been written off for us, so we're all out here just having fun, playing the game we love.

Did it suck not to make playoffs? Obviously. But at the end of the day, there are only so many teams that can make it, and it just wasn't our year.

"Hey," I grunt as I walk up to the guys.

"Late night?" Miles asks curiously, glancing at Harris like I'm walking out here in my underwear or something.

"No. Why?" I ask.

"We heard you and our little friend ended up spending some time together after Ellie's birthday party. Figured you met up for a round two, and that's why you're so tired," Miles jokes.

That would mean I hadn't fucked up that first night.

"You guys are the biggest gossips I've ever met," I grumble, grabbing water and taking a big gulp. "To answer your question, though, no, I'm not tired. I'm just annoyed."

Dirty Play

"Why?"

"My sister is in town."

"Wait, you have a sister?" Trevor asks as he skates up.

"Yup. Kylie, or Baby Williams as I call her," Harris pipes in for me.

Harris is the one guy—well, besides Rex—who knows the story of my family. Rex only knows because he caught me in a weak moment a couple of years back on the anniversary of Veronica's death. I ended up wasted and spilling the entire story to him. That was it, though, besides one other time, and we haven't mentioned it since. Harris, on the other hand, lived through it with me.

"Why do I feel like you have this entire secret life from us? Do you have a wife? Kids? Are you some super-secret spy sent to steal hockey secrets or discover the secret sauce in some restaurant?" Miles starts questioning me, shock evident on his face as he just stares at me, waiting for me to talk.

What should I say? I've done a good job of hiding my family because it's easier that way? Instead of constantly reminding myself of the pain I caused them, I chose to run, and the memory of it still hurts.

Every single time my sister reaches out, I wonder if I made the right decision. It's been eleven years since Veronica died and ten since I left. I went back a couple of times for Christmas, but after a while that stopped too. I haven't been home in at least five years, and sometimes I would give just about anything to get a big hug from my mama, but it always makes me feel guilty —like I'm undeserving of the comfort.

"Nope. Nothing like that. I guess I just don't really talk about my family."

"Is Kylie coming tonight?" Harris asks, sidetracking our conversation for me, obviously sensing my discomfort in entering this conversational territory.

"Yeah, she said she got a ticket.

"You're really letting her sit in the nosebleeds?"

"I mean... I guess I could give her one of my tickets. I didn't even think about it."

"Do that, and then make sure she's coming out with us after the game. I haven't seen Baby Williams in years."

"She's not a Williams anymore, remember? She's an Edwards now. I'm sure she doesn't want to hang out with us after the game. We aren't in high school anymore."

"Whatever, she'll always be Baby Williams to me. I'm texting her now."

By the time we finish our morning skate and I've changed, I send a quick text to my sister.

> Is it just you in New York, or is Brandon with you?

KYLIE
> Just me.

Dirty Play

Interesting. Kylie and her husband have been inseparable since they got together in high school. Back then, Brandon was one of my best friends. He, Harris, and I all grew up together, all living on the same block from the time we were born and all through high school. I should've known he'd end up with my sister, the way he was always checking in with her, asking me about her. Somehow, when I found out, it was still a shock.

I'm happy for her, though. He's a great guy, and she deserves someone to take care of her—deserves someone to protect her. Even though I'm her older brother, I'm no good at protecting anyone.

> K. I left you a ticket. Pick it up when you get here.

She may be an absolute pain in my ass, but Harris is right. My sister isn't sitting in the nosebleeds when I have a set of tickets that are never used. Well, unless Gwen wants to go to a game, but lately she hasn't been able to make it.

Not that I expect her here tonight, not after how I treated her the night of Ellie's birthday. I've picked up my phone no less than fifty times a day since that night, but every time I go to text her, I put my phone down, remembering she's better off without me. The sooner she realizes it, the better.

For her.

The thought of hurting her causes me physical pain, and knowing I intentionally hurt her makes it even worse. I wish I could tell her I regret fucking everything up. I wish I could tell her the night I spent with her was the best night I've had in a long time, all because I spent it with her.

But that's not me. I don't get the girl at the end of my story, and I realized that a long, long time ago.

"Good game," Kylie says, wrapping me up in a big hug as I walk out from the locker room, her face lighting up when she sees me.

Her excitement somehow makes me feel even worse—like I'm the world's worst brother.

"Thanks, Ky. Glad I could help Trevor get one last win before retirement. It was just a bonus to get another shutout. Although I think our win pales in comparison to Ellie's pregnancy announcement just now."

"Yeah, I wasn't surprised when they said they weren't coming out tonight." She smirks.

"I don't think anyone was," I tell her with a smirk. "How was the ticket? Did you have any trouble picking it up?"

We're both standing by the locker room doors while everyone else has started to move their celebration further out, slowly making their way to their families or out to the bar to celebrate. We've made it through post-game interviews and the team meeting at the end, so now we are free.

We have a couple odds and ends to finish up this week, but the hard part is done, and we get a much-needed break.

"Nope, it was easy. Your seats are amazing, though. I'm sure Brandon will be jealous when I tell him."

"Where is he? I thought you two didn't go anywhere without each other?"

"He's on a work trip. He works a lot," Kylie says, and I see the sadness in her eyes when she says it. I can't help but feel like I'm not protecting her yet again.

"Lame. Harris says you're coming out tonight?"

"Yeah... I mean, if that's okay. He texted me and asked, and I stupidly assumed Harris had checked with you, but of course he didn't because it's Harris and he's reckless," Kylie starts to ramble, and I just hold my hand up.

"Let's go, Kylie, it's okay. I mean, you are my sister and all."

"I am?" she deadpans before walking toward the doors.

THE BAR IS BUSY AS USUAL, ESPECIALLY AFTER A GAME, but we've tucked ourselves away in a corner to relax and celebrate. A few hours in, and that's what everyone is doing. Rex and Sawyer came out, along with Cassie and Max, and I can't help but feel disappointed Gwen decided to not come out tonight. I'm not surprised, though—I doubt she wants to be around me much. And who can blame her after everything that happened? It's just way more fun when she's here.

Kylie has proven she still fits into any group, no matter how long it's been or even if she's never met them before. She's out laughing with Cassie on the dance floor while Harris and Miles make fools of themselves doing dance moves that have no business being in this decade.

As much as it's been a little uncomfortable for me, it's been nice getting to see Kylie and catching up. In the car on the way to the bar she found her moment to talk, word vomiting the entire drive about how much everyone misses me, how Vince isn't the same, always angry now. How my parents are just sad a lot, always talking about how much they miss me.

It broke my heart when she told me how hard it's been for her since I left. Seeing the sadness in her eyes and how broken she looked—it hurt. I don't want to hurt her; I just don't know how to fix this.

She made me promise to consider going home for my parents' anniversary party, even if it is just a short trip. The brat even made me pinky promise, and it was at that moment I knew the chances of me going back to Ivy Falls were much higher than they had been in years.

Dirty Play

"I've given you time to figure your shit out. Now it's time to tell me what the hell happened to you two," Sawyer says as she slides into the spot next to me that's been empty for the last twenty minutes. "Because based on her side of the story, I want to punch you in the dick, but I'm willing to hear your side before I determine punishment."

"And whatever is it you'd like to talk about?" I ask, prolonging the torture this conversation could bring, knowing at the end of it, there's a good chance I'm getting dick punched. I also just feel like pushing her buttons. I knew eventually, one of Gwen's attack dogs would come for me, but truthfully, I thought it would be Cassie. Cassie is a bit scary, if I'm being honest, although it's all out of love. Sawyer, on the other hand, has a bit of a soft spot for me. Rex probably told her a bit of my life, so hopefully she'll take it easy on me.

"Cut the shit, Williams. What the fuck happened with you and Gwen?"

I sit back, grabbing my drink in one hand while I stare at her, "Based on your tone, you know exactly what happened. So, I think you're really trying to figure out *why* it happened, am I right?"

Her glare says enough, and anyone with a soul probably just felt it getting sucked away like a Dementor's kiss. Lucky for me, I don't have a soul.

Setting my drink back down, I fold my hands and pause, trying to figure out how to say this without making shit even worse.

"I don't have an answer for you, Sawyer. Truthfully, I wish I did. None of that night should have happened."

"Are you saying you used her?"

"No. I'm saying everything that happened that night shouldn't have happened."

"But it did, so what's the big deal?"

"Because my big brother has this martyr bullshit set in his mind. He believes everyone in the world is better off without him, including his family and anyone he might care about as more than a friend. Which from what I'm gathering, this Gwen chick might fit in that latter category."

Sawyer and I look to Kylie, who slides into the spot across from us and rests her chin on her fist as she watches us with interest. A little smirk tells me she's in the mood to start some shit.

"Based on the conversation I just walked into, it seems my big brother is continuing to push people away, even after he pushed his family away and left home."

And that's all it takes. The next thing I know, Sawyer has turned to my baby sister and spilled the entire story about Gwen and I—well, minus the parts no sister wants to hear about her brother. Yet she somehow makes sure to get the point across.

I hooked up with one of my best friends, told her it was a mistake, and then basically ghosted her.

I expect Sawyer and Kylie to team up on me, to

make me feel like complete and total shit for everything, but instead, it almost feels like there's a little more understanding.

It's still unnerving, though. I've been able to keep this shit away from everyone for six years, and Kylie meets them for *one night* and spills the beans, only for Sawyer to do the same, both enjoying swapping stories about me. I thought I'd be mad, maybe even upset at everyone knowing my business, but truthfully, I'm relieved.

Maybe if everyone knows my story, they'll understand why I am the way I am. Why I refuse to let anyone in. Why no woman has ever been to my home, and why anytime feelings start to crawl their way inside my heart I torch them until all that's left is dust. Maybe if they understand, they'll help me figure out how to redraw the line in the sand with Gwen.

"I'm certain he likes her; he's just protecting himself," Kylie says before taking a sip from her beer.

"From what?" Sawyer whispers like I can't hear, but before Kylie can answer, I squash it.

"Enough of your little gossip sesh. Where the hell is she tonight?" I ask Sawyer, who turns to look at me like she's seeing me for the first time. Like some puzzles were solved while new ones popped up.

"She'll be here soon. She isn't off until midnight, and then she's going to walk over, so she'll probably be here a little after then."

"She's going to walk here? From the hospital... by

herself?" I stammer, feeling my blood pressure rise at the thought of Gwen out in New York at midnight, all alone. "She can't do that."

"She walks home every night, Cade," Sawyer says.

I get up, slamming a wad of cash down on the table before turning to look at Kylie. "I'll be back. Let's not share all the family secrets on your first night, deal?"

She smiles, holding up her pinky, making me promise like always before I turn and walk out of the bar.

Running to the hospital after playing a brutal game of hockey is probably not my smartest choice, but thinking isn't exactly my strong suit when it comes to this woman.

Had I even slowed down for two seconds to think, I would've remembered my damn car was parked at the bar. But with only fifteen minutes left till midnight, I took off running.

Kylie laughed after our pinky promise and said something about how she knew one day someone would knock me on my ass, but I just kept going. Now, walking around the front of the hospital to the entrance, I wonder if she's right—is that what's happening right now, and I'm just too naïve to admit it?

Before I make it through the hospital's front doors, I see Gwen through the glass, sitting in the cafeteria

Dirty Play

laughing. Her smile is big and bright while she talks with another woman and a teenage girl, who is a spitting image of the woman I can only assume is her mom.

Gwen looks happy right now—like, truly happy, and I wish I could freeze this memory, and keep it close to remind myself what pure happiness looks like. To remind myself I felt happy when I saw her this happy —because this is as close to joy as I've felt off the ice in a long time. I lose track of time as I watch them laugh and talk until I realize it's now well after midnight and by the looks of it, she's going nowhere fast.

Pulling out my phone, I shoot her a quick text, refusing to leave until I know she's safe.

> Are you coming out tonight?

GWEN
Oh, now you want to talk to me?

> Just answer the question.

GWEN
No.

> Ok. I was just making sure you had a ride.

GWEN
Thanks, but in the future, you can waste your time worrying about someone else. I'm a big girl.

With that, she tosses her phone in her bag and

turns back to the girls. I can't help but feel like I just got dismissed, leaving me jealous they have her undivided attention.

But this is what I chose. This is what's best for her.

That doesn't mean I'm okay with her hating me.

Chapter 9

Gwen

> **MOM**
> Are you available for a phone call?
>
> > Yeah, I don't work till four tonight.

Seconds later my phone vibrates in my hand, my mom's picture popping up with a FaceTime call. Quickly answering it, I smile when her face shows up on my screen.

"Hi darling," my mom says sweetly into the phone. "How are you?"

"Hi mom, I'm doing well. Just been busy with work. How have you and dad been?" I ask as I finish putting the laundry away.

I don't mind working nights. It's just a downer when you have to spend your days sleeping and doing chores instead of being outside enjoying the nicer weather. Being the beginning of May, the weather is starting to get warmer and the days longer. The seasonal depression is slowly starting to leave my body. I feel like a plant seeing the sun for the first time in a decade, trying to soak up as much of the goodness as possible until it disappears again.

"We've been good. We just helped open the new teaching hospital down in Florida and spent a week or two on the beach after that before heading back to Connecticut."

My parents work at one of the leading teaching hospitals in the country, so occasionally they are put in charge of setting up a new hospital and helping to get everything running smoothly before they go back to their regular jobs in Connecticut.

My parents have always been workaholics, never having "normal" jobs—they've always been married to not only each other but also to their work, leaving very little time for me. These phone calls, while making me smile, also remind me just how clinical our relationship has become, and it fucking sucks. Like, dammit, I just want one day when my mom calls me and wants to hear the gossip or talk about a guy. Hell, even just to check in with me on how I'm doing, anything outside of the damn hospital.

"—but besides that, we haven't been doing much," she continues, snapping me out of my thoughts and back into our conversation. "We were actually thinking about stopping by one of these weeks to see you and the hospital."

Dirty Play

"Oh? Do you know when?" I ask, already annoyed it can't just be about me—it has to be about the hospital, too.

"We aren't sure. It depends on where your father wants to go and if he wants to visit any other hospitals. We'll let you know, though. I'm sure you'll be able to get the time off?"

"It shouldn't be a problem. Just let me know when you can."

"We will, darling. Now, I've gotta run. I have a meeting at five," my mom says, her typical short conversation well evident.

"Of course, talk to you later."

"Bye," she says before I hear the click of her disconnecting the call.

"Love you, too," I say to an empty line.

Why am I surprised? We've never been an overly lovey and affectionate family, but at this point, I don't think I'd know what to do if they gave me comfort, or hugged me, or even said I love you because it's been so few and far between my entire life.

The only benefit to being an only child to two workaholic parents is that you become very comfortable with being alone... a lot. I've sort of learned when you work in the medical field, it will always be a huge part of your life, which is why these past few years I've taken a huge step back from dating and had little to no personal life.

It didn't help that Dr. Dickhead told me if I were

spending my time dating in the first few years of becoming a nurse, it would look like I didn't care about my job. I know it's bullshit, but it was enough for him to get into my head. It also doesn't help that I turned him down at a bar before knowing who he was—I was out with a friend and wasn't interested. He was less than thrilled when I said no. A man with a hurt ego can really spew some bullshit, and he's definitely made his opinion of me known at work, which is why I haven't actually dated a man in four years.

No point in trying to start a relationship when I'm not going to have enough time to spend with them, and they'll end up leaving me anyway. At least this way, I don't have to get my heart broken.

Before finishing laundry, I spent a few minutes answering texts. To the surprise of no one, Sawyer and Cassie were in our group chat debating what the superior type of donut is. They were in a full-out battle over whether a glazed donut was better—Cassie—or if a chocolate donut with sprinkles was better—Sawyer.

> You're both wrong.

> Maple bar. I will accept no other answers.

I hover my finger over Cade's name, still not ready to talk to him but needing to know what he said when he texted me the other night. I can always just open it, read it, then close it... right? I don't have to respond, right? Giving in, I click his name, surprised when I see his message.

> **CADE**
> I fucked up, Tink. I already know.
> I hope you don't hate me forever.

I look down at my phone like it's in a foreign language. He didn't apologize. But, I mean, I guess he's trying. I want to forgive him, I do. And honestly, maybe I already have, I'm just not ready to admit it yet. I feel like as long as I don't admit I forgive him, I'm not admitting I let him hurt me.

> I don't. I just think you're a fucking asshole.

> **CADE**
> I agree.

Throwing my phone onto my bed, I turn my music on full blast while I finish laundry and do a deep clean of my apartment. Weekends are fun, but it's also the only time I have to catch up on life, and I only have four hours left until work, so it's time to get a move on.

MONDAYS ARE ALWAYS THE WORST DAY OF THE WEEK because it means Dr. D is here for the night shift again. It's a busy evening tonight on our floor, with three patients who recently had surgery and are almost ready to go home, while we have another patient recovering from a surgery yesterday. One of them had a brain tumor removed a little over a week ago, and they get to go home tomorrow with the good news that it was benign. The reports came back today, and it sounds like they got it all.

I have two patients right now—Kennedy and a boy named Benny. Benny had heart surgery, and while it was a rough start, he's nearly ready to go home and see his new baby sister that he's been so excited to meet. All the happy news makes this job so rewarding. The unfortunate part of healthcare is sometimes you do everything possible, and you still can't fight fate.

So, when I run into Denise and Josh and see tears in their eyes, my heart immediately hurts from their pain.

"Are you okay?" I ask as Josh hugs Denise into his side, her eyes rimmed red.

"It's just been a rough day, and things just don't seem to be getting better. She hates being here on dialysis, and when they talked to her about how she will probably stay here until she has a donor, she lost it. She didn't handle the news well and just broke down. She has never asked us to leave the room, but tonight, she demanded some alone time and started crying as I closed the door behind us."

"I'm so sorry, that's a lot to take in all at once, and I can only imagine how much that hurts to hear from your daughter. Kennedy loves you both so much. She just might need some time. We all process news differently, and it might take some time for her to grieve the path she thought she would be on. I'm sure it's difficult when it's your own kid, and you're struggling at the same time."

Josh nods, his jaw clenched as he fights his emotions. "She's just lost the joy she used to have, and I know it's because she's so tired of missing out on everything. She's constantly here fighting for her health. But she's stopped taking an interest in anything, and it's killing me to watch. She used to love sports—watching them, playing them, talking about them. I mean, soccer was her life. But now, it's like she just wants to watch TV and pretend nothing else exists, and it's hard not being able to help."

"Look, go take a walk, grab a coffee or something. I know it's getting late. Maybe grab her some ice cream. I have two more patients to check on, and then it's her turn. If she throws me out, we'll figure out a plan B, but maybe she really does just needs a minute to cool down."

"Thank you," Josh says as Denise starts to sob. They walk away with sad smiles, and I feel for them. They feel helpless, waiting for a match that may never come. Knowing everyone around them who's been tested has come back negative can be quite disheartening.

All I can do is hope somehow, somewhere, a perfect match shows up.

When I finally make it to Kennedy's room, she's turned on *Gilmore Girls* and is sitting up with a snack.

"Hey," I say as I walk in. "How are you?"

"Just peachy, but I'm sure you've already talked to my parents," Kennedy says, her typical sass gone, replaced by sadness, and I hate it.

"Yeah, but it's not them I want to hear it from. I want you to tell me what's going on."

She looks at me for a moment before grabbing the remote and pausing *Gilmore Girls*. Then she unloads. Every feeling, experience, and thing that has pissed her off comes out, and all of the emotions you would expect a fifteen-year-old girl to feel appear at once. She just wants to feel normal, be with her friends, play soccer, and kiss boys, but she can't because 'her stupid kidneys are trying to kill her.'

With perfect timing, her parents walk in, wrapping her in a hug while she collapses in their arms, sobbing, as they all grieve the life they thought she'd be living. I am praying and hoping it's not too far out of their reach.

An hour later, I'm ready to head down to the cafeteria for lunch, only this time I'm not going alone —I hope. I have a surprise. Slipping into Kennedy's room, I find her and her mom curled up in her bed, her dad has already headed out for the night, so they're just watching more *Gilmore Girls*, their nightly routine.

"So, what do you two say about going down to the cafeteria and having milkshakes with me? I need to have lunch, but nothing sounds good except a big chocolate peanut butter milkshake."

"Deal," Denise says, perking up and looking down at Kennedy, who is smiling at the thought of dessert. "I think we could all use a little cheering up today, and some fresh air out of this room might do us all some good."

"Meet me down there in fifteen minutes?"

"Awesome."

Quickly heading out of her room, I check in on Benny and his dad one last time, making sure they have what they need before letting them know where I'll be.

When I found out one of the coffee stands makes milkshakes, I was in heaven. Even if my hips continue to scream at my desire to order one every single day.

Not like I'm complaining, they're just more to hold onto... and if you have time to judge the weight on my hips, you're not fucking me good enough.

Scanning the cafeteria, I look for Kennedy and her mom, knowing they probably already beat me down here, but instead of spotting the two bubbly blondes, I see a set of brown eyes watching me from across the room.

My whole body freezes. Why is he here?

What is Cade doing at my hospital?

My heart starts to race as I just stare at him, my brain trying to make sense of why he would be here.

It isn't until he starts talking that I realize he's not alone.

Nope. Cade's standing with Denise and Kennedy. They are both beaming up at him while Denise FaceTimes with who I can only assume is Josh—one of the biggest hockey fans I know.

I want to stay here, not let these two worlds collide, but the moment he nods for me to come over, my feet start moving before my brain even realizes what's happening.

Chapter 10

Cade

After two hours of texting Sawyer and promising her all the desserts she could carry the next time we went to the store, she caved and told me Gwen would be at work tonight. I feel kind of stalkerish, but honestly, I haven't been able to sleep lately, wondering how many of these nights she's spent walking alone late at night while I was home warm and safe in bed.

It doesn't sit right with me, so today, I'm here to make sure she knows I'm walking her home. I was in such a rush to get here I forgot to throw a hat on, which is, unfortunately, the easiest way to limit the number of times I am recognized and stopped for autographs. This time, though, I don't mind at all. When a young girl and her mom stop me, their faces light up the moment they realize who I am.

Although the young girl, Kennedy, wastes no time telling me Miles is her favorite.

Apparently, I'm her dad's favorite player, so they end up FaceTiming him, and the look on his face matches the surprise on his daughter's. It takes me a moment of talking to these two to realize these are the girls Gwen was with the night I saw her. We spend a bit talking before Kennedy looks at me and says, "Why are you at the hospital this late at night, visiting hours are over."

Her mom looks appalled at her honesty, but I just laugh.

"I'm here looking for my friend. She works here, helping people."

"Oh, then I like your friend. Maybe she'll be able to get me a new kidney."

With her words, my stomach drops. The pit that's always sitting deep in my stomach worsening as every memory of my sister lying in that hospital bed comes flooding back.

"I-I'm sure she would love to be able to help you. She's one of the best people I know. I'm sorry you're going through that, it's a challenging fight, but you're strong. Always remember that, and even when you're not feeling that way, you're surrounded by people who care about you."

Looking around the cafeteria once more, I glance at the clock, hoping I didn't get her lunch break wrong.

Dirty Play

But then I see her, and our eyes lock, my whole body relaxing.

"Did you find your friend?" she asks, her eyes following mine. "Oh hey, it's Gwen. Do you think she has my milkshake? Maybe she'll be able to get you and your friend one, too!"

Gwen must be her nurse, and that's why I saw her with them that night. With a quick nod at Gwen, she starts to make her way over to us. Her body is confident, but I can see the uncertainty in her eyes, probably wondering what the fuck I'm doing here with her patient.

Tiny, little, invisible strings that all keep bringing me back to this woman.

"Hey ladies, Marsha started our milkshakes. She'll have them out shortly," Gwen says to Kennedy and her mom before turning to look at me with a less enthusiastic, more questioning smile. "Hey, Cade, what're you doing here?" she asks, her professional tone in full force.

"Actually, I'm here to talk to you," I say, not missing the way her eyes widen or the way Kennedy and her mom glance at each other with little smirks.

"Umm... okay," she says, looking over at Kennedy before coming back to me.

Just then, a woman who I can only assume is Marsha, walks over with their milkshakes, a big smile on her face as she chats with Kennedy and Denise while Gwen just stares at me, tugging her bottom lip between her teeth. And all I can think about is taking that lip between *my* teeth and drowning out her screams with my kiss.

Fucking hell, why can't I stop thinking about her like this?

"Would it be possible for us to get one more? My new friend, Cade Williams, is here, and I'm sure he'd love to try one of your milkshakes," Kennedy says.

"Of course, Mr. Williams, I'll be right out with that."

Gwen goes to speak, probably to cancel the order, but Marsha turns and disappears around the corner before she has the chance. "Excuse us for a moment," Gwen says sweetly before grabbing my arm and dragging me around the corner.

"Ow, you're hurting me," I whine. "Put your claws away."

"Don't be a wuss. You're used to pucks flying at your face at a hundred miles per hour, you can handle my little grip."

I look at her, eyebrows raised, unable to hide my little smirk at the obvious innuendo in her words. It's enough to have me wondering if she's thinking about that night too.

"I think we both know I can handle your grip, Tink."

We stare at each other for a moment before finally she snaps out of it. "What *do* you need to talk to me about that's so important it couldn't be a text."

Dirty Play

"First off, that would involve you actually responding to my texts, and lately that's been out of the question."

"Jeez, I wonder why I haven't really been in the mood to talk to you, Cade. Now cut the shit and talk. I need to get back to lunch."

"I don't like you walking home by yourself," I tell her, which only seems to piss her off more.

"I'm sorry you feel that way. I guess it's a good thing I'm not yours to worry about."

"You get off at midnight, in fucking New York City, Gwen. There's not a chance in hell I'm letting you walk home by yourself. You're an attractive young woman, and I don't want to watch you on the next episode of *20/20* from prison," I grumble.

The one time I texted her to ask what time she was off and if she'd wait for me, she all but told me to fuck off. I could've just showed up, but this damn hospital has at like forty-three hundred doors, and with my luck, I'd have been on the opposite end of the hospital when she left.

"I apologize that you have issues with my life choices, but I'm damn well not your problem to deal with," Gwen snaps, her eyes immediately narrowing as she gets more and more irritated with me.

"Gwen, I'm not fucking joking. People get robbed and kidnapped daily, and you're a five-foot-one female who weighs practically nothing."

"I'm not joking either, not all of us have disposable money we can spend how we please."

"What. Time. Are. You. Off?" I seethe, refusing to back down.

"Why are you even here?"

Her quick change catches me off guard, and honestly, I don't know how to answer her question.

"I'm not sure."

"Well, that's not good enough. Goodbye, Cade."

She turns to walk away, and I can't stand it. I can't stand her not listening to me, not knowing I care about her.

"You're all I can think about, and I can't fucking stand it," I blurt out. Her whole body freezes in place. "I can't stand that I always want you around me, even when I know the one thing we need is distance," I snap, more truth coming out than I expected, and by the look on her face when she turns around, I've surprised her as well.

She waits for a moment before a tiny smirk appears on her lips.

"Be here at midnight."

I smile, relieved she's not fighting me more.

"But you're leaving right now."

"What?"

"You're going to walk back over there with me and tell them you need to leave, something came up, and you need to go. Do you hear me? You. Need. To. Go," Gwen huffs.

Dirty Play

"Whatever you say, Tink," I smirk, letting her grab my arm and pull me back to the table where the girls are now enjoying their milkshakes. The one Kennedy ordered for me sits next to Gwen's.

When we get back to our spot, Gwen stops at the edge of the table, looking up at me expectantly, but when I see Kennedy smiling, I can't risk upsetting her by not taking her offer. After everything that girl is going through, the least I can do is sit and drink a milkshake with her, even if it unleashes Gwen's wrath on me.

"What flavor did we get?" I scoot past Gwen to sit right next to Kennedy, forcing Gwen to sit across from me, next to Denise.

"Chocolate peanut butter. It's my favorite," Kennedy says, her milkshake already half gone. "Are you going to sit down, Gwen? Your milkshake is melting."

Gwen shakes her head, snapping herself out of whatever daydream or voodoo spell she was trying to cast on me before finally taking the seat across from me.

You'd think spending an evening with a fifteen-year-old wouldn't be the highlight of my week as a twenty-eight-year-old professional hockey player, but damn, this girl is funny. She's got the right amount of dry humor mixed with immeasurable kindness, and I can't help but adore her already.

If I'm being honest, it's because she reminds me a

lot of my sister, Veronica. Yeah, of course, them both needing a kidney is definitely a similarity, but it's more than that.

Veronica was feisty, bossy, and took no shit. Most of the time she had the driest sense of humor, but the other ten percent was just pure silliness with the stupidest jokes I'd ever heard in my life, but I always ended up folding over in laughter. What I would give to experience that even just once more.

Hell, I'd give my left kidney if it meant I could hear one of those stupid jokes again.

By the time I've finished my milkshake, it's close to nine, and Gwen is standing up, ready to go back to work.

"Thanks for hanging out with us," Denise says as Kennedy and Gwen start tidying up. "This made her day... it was a rough one, and she was struggling to find joy."

She looks... worn out. Not in a bad way, but in the kind of way I remember my mom looking when my sister was sick. Beautiful as always, but a deep exhaustion that can only be seen in their eyes.

But this memory gives me an idea.

"Hey, no pressure at all if this doesn't work out. I understand hospitals have rules, but Miles happens to be one of my best friends, along with Trevor Adams and Harris Danielson. Maybe we could come visit sometime? We could bring Kennedy a signed jersey, cheer her up a bit?"

Dirty Play

Her eyes start to well up as she nods, covering her mouth as she mumbles yes. "Sorry. She would love that. We would love that. But if you come when my husband isn't here, he might actually perish. Could we..." she pauses, glancing over to Gwen and back to me. "Could we have Gwen coordinate with you?"

"Of course you can." Gwen looks at Denise before turning back to me. "I've gotta get back to work. Midnight. Don't be late, I won't wait."

With a salute and a smile, I turn around and walk out of the hospital feeling lighter than I have in weeks, with the memory of my sister fresh on my mind.

I make sure to be at the hospital fifteen minutes before midnight in case Gwen decides to test me and leave early or something. I know for a fact that she wouldn't hesitate to leave if I wasn't here the moment she was ready to go.

"Hi," she says as she walks right up to me. "Is my bodyguard ready to chaperone me home?"

"I wasn't late, was I? So, I'd say that answer is pretty obvious," I joke back, but she just glares before turning and starting to walk away.

"What's got you so grumpy, Tink?"

She turns to me, her eyes narrowed. "Where should I start? I have parents who don't seem to want to actually know the real me, a guy I hooked up with was a total prick and just up and left like it didn't fucking matter, and I have a patient who's going through a really rough time, so my apologies if I'm not all cheery and shooting rainbows out of my ass all the time."

I just stare, eyes wide, shocked she opened up so much. I was expecting her to yell at me, call me an asshole, or tell me she didn't want to be around me, which she basically did, but... there's so much more in that answer. So much truth, so much pain.

I want to know more.

"Do you want to talk about it?"

She stops, her head tilted as she assesses me. "Not really. With my luck, I'll end up laying it all out there and you'll disappear without a response," she huffs, her hands on her hips.

I stare back at her, and I'd be lying if I said I wasn't imagining my hands on her hips, grinding her against me as she rides my cock.

Definitely not what I should be thinking about right now, and based on her eyes narrowing, she's not amused by my staring.

"I'm not going to do that again, I promise," I tell her, surprising myself because I'm not one to make promises.

The look on her face when I left her—I'll never be able to get that out of my mind. That alone will make sure I never do something like that again, which means

Dirty Play

I need to keep my distance, make sure we keep our boundaries in place.

"Why am I supposed to believe you? I thought we were friends... friends don't treat each other the way you treated me," she says quietly. "You hurt me."

Her words feel like ten thousand little cuts, breaking me apart even further, but all I can think about is how much I've already hurt her.

Although I think walking away entirely would hurt her more.

"I'm sorry, Tink. I am. I can't explain it... I'm broken," I tell her, not sure how to explain I'm not good enough for her. That I hurt the people I care about.

"I don't know what to do with you," Gwen mumbles as we continue walking, the sound of the city all around us. This city never truly sleeps. Even in the middle of the night cars go by constantly, a lot of them honking their horns, and there are people everywhere, yet all I can hear is her.

"I don't know what to do with myself, either," I tell her the sad reality of my life.

Chapter 11

Gwen

Cade Motherfucking Williams is the only thing I can think about. When I saw him at the hospital last night talking with Kennedy and Denise, it stirred up all the feelings I have been trying to push down for weeks. His touch, his tongue, his cock... they've left an impression on me, and I don't know how to not compare everything to him. He's become the gold standard in my life, even if he is an absolute asshole. Even his stupid personality is somehow both infuriating and fucking endearing.

He's so capable of being sweet and caring, and he shows that more often than not. Even last night, he showed up for me when I told him I didn't want him to. He talked to me, actually asked me how I was, and looked concerned when I told him it was a rough night.

But that's not how it's been. Lately, the second he

opens his mouth, he fucks it all up. It's still hard to hate the man, though. Although I'm biased because I'm in a constant loop of thinking about his tongue on my clit, or his cock inside me, even though those are the last things I should want.

Definitely not his cock.

Shit. I'm going crazy.

It's my damn weekend—I'm supposed to be relaxing, cleaning my house, binging a smutty romance book, I don't know! Anything but lying around on a pile of laundry thinking about the six-foot-four goalie with golden brown eyes and all the dirty things I want to do with him.

He's the last person I expected to see last night. He has never been here before, so when I saw him with one of my patients, I was pissed. He was in my bubble, my space, and it felt like he was intruding.

But then I went over and heard them talking, saw the way he was interacting with Kennedy and her mom, and honestly, I was impressed. He did it with so much kindness—so much empathy—he was able to really connect with Kennedy, and it was so nice to see her with a genuine smile on her face. Denise told me all about how excited Kennedy was to meet him. Apparently, she loves watching hockey with her dad, so it was a nice bright spot in what had otherwise been a crappy day.

When Cade mentioned he could organize for some of the guys on the team to come to the hospital for a

Dirty Play

meet and greet, I knew it was something I wanted to set up as soon as possible. Kennedy needs something to look forward to, something exciting in her life, and what better than four professional hockey players visiting you and your parents?

Once I double-checked with her parents, I cleared it through all the right channels at the hospital and made sure everything was set up so there wouldn't be a problem.

But of course, since the request came in my name and not Cade's or the NY Cyclones, Dr. Dickhead had to be a huge pain in the ass.

That was until I kindly pointed out the names of the planned visitors and he shut right up. See, Dr. Dickhead is a huge fan of hockey, specifically the Cyclones, and he happens to be a season ticket holder. If we're being honest, he also has a bit of a hard-on for Cade. I've overheard him talking about games, and all he does is talk about Cade Williams and how he's the best goalie we've had in ages—how he walks on water and is basically the second coming of Christ. Or at least that's how Dr. D makes it sound.

I still haven't told him I'm friends with the guys, especially Cade. Figured I'd use that to my advantage when he really pisses me off or when I want to really piss him off. Either way.

"I can't do this shit anymore," I mumble, needing to get out of this apartment.

Rolling off my bed I grab my phone off the nightstand and open up my texts.

> Anyone up for a walk in Central Park?

ELLIE

We're at Trevor's parents for the day. Raincheck?

> Definitely!

CASSIE

When?

> Nowish? I can't lie on my laundry waiting for it to fold itself any longer.

SAWYER

I can be there in half an hour

CASSIE

See you then!

ELLIE

Have fun!

Changing out of my pajamas, which consist of the oversized t-shirt and panties I wore last night, I grab a pair of leggings and a sports bra and throw them on along with a thin sweatshirt and head out.

Walking through the park to our usual meeting spot, I immediately feel happier being outside. It's a nice day—people everywhere, some running through the park or walking their dogs, and everyone just seems happy.

I want to be too. I want to be happy more than I can

Dirty Play

put into words, but right now, everything sucks, and happiness seems so far out of my reach.

I'm irritated that my parents are always too busy to take an interest in me outside of my profession. I don't want them to take an interest in the Gwen who went to nursing school or the Gwen who works in PICU. I want them to like the daughter who loves yoga, reads trashy books, and binges reality TV. The daughter who loves any combination of chocolate and peanut butter and would eat cereal for dinner every night if it wasn't frowned upon.

My parents have no idea who I am, and that alone is enough to depress me. Throw in everything with Kennedy—her slow, steady decline in kidney function and the steps we're needing to take changing week to week at this point—and that's enough to keep me up at night worrying.

Then, of course, there's Cade. Which is why I called the girls. I honestly haven't even figured out how to feel about everything with him, and I need help. Right now, I just know it sucks, but I can't even pinpoint exactly what about it sucks so much. Is it because I want to hook up again? Because I regret it? Or is it because Cade is one of my best friends, someone who I've always felt connected to, and he fucked me and then left me, proving I'm really not worth anyone's time outside of just getting what you need.

"Gwen, over here!" Cassie shouts from the bench,

two iced coffees in hand, while Sawyer stands to the side on the phone, her emotional support iced coffee already in hand.

I wave and walk over, graciously accepting the coffee from Cass.

"Hey! Thanks for meeting me on such short notice."

"Not a problem," Cassie says. "Max is driving me crazy right now. Now that it's the offseason, he has so much extra time on his hands, and he is a human golden retriever. He needs constant attention and snuggles."

"That's because he's a pain in the ass, but you knew that before you started dating my brother, so it's your own damn fault," Sawyer says, planting her butt on the bench next to me. "How are you, though?"

"Me? I'm fine."

"Lies."

"I don't know, I guess. Everything is just kind of a mess, and I don't even know where to begin," I tell them truthfully.

"I have an idea. Let's walk to Stella's bakery, grab some desserts, and then I want to hear the whole story."

"Fine. But I want one of her cinnamon rolls for myself. And a Danish."

Dirty Play

ONCE I'VE GOTTEN MY PASTRIES, I TELL THEM ABOUT MY phone call with my parents and my annoyance and disappointment with them. As I'm finishing my Danish, I fill them in on the basics of the Kennedy and Cade meeting and how we're still hopeful we'll be able to find a match for her.

"That's a lot. You know how I feel about shitty parents; life has been so much better since I stopped giving mine too much airspace in my life," Sawyer says. "It's much easier said than done, but it made me a lot happier to put distance as well. There came a point when I realized I was mourning the reality of who I wanted my parents to be, not who was actually in my life. Once I realized that, I was able to grieve."

That's exactly what it is. I don't need to cut them out entirely, but I do think I need to have a conversation with them. Let them know how I feel. And if they aren't willing to make me a priority, then I'm not going to make them one. It sucks, and it'll hurt, but I can't just let them walk all over me anymore.

"I see what you're saying. But you're right—it's much easier said than done. I'll probably try to talk to them if they come visit, see what happens."

"So, what are you going to do about Cade?" Cassie asks quietly.

"And that, my friends, is the million-dollar question. Do I keep avoiding him? Do I go back to just being his friend and seeing him when we all go out? Or do I try to crack his shell and see if he might actually have feelings for me under there?"

"Option C, but with a little spice," Sawyer says with a smirk. "See, not only did I meet Cade's sister, Kylie, but she gave me some insider knowledge."

"What the fuck? Cade has a sister?" I ask as it becomes clear I don't really know anything about Cade's family. We never talk about our families, and it's weird to know I've fucked this man and don't know the first thing about how he grew up.

Not that you need to know that information about someone you fuck, but when it's one of your best friends, you just kind of assume you know.

"Yeah. It's a bit of a sad story. He has a brother and two sisters, but one of his sisters passed away about ten years ago when she was eighteen."

"Oh my god," I say. "Do you know what happened?"

"Kidney failure, she needed a transplant... and well, it never came. There's more to the story, but she said it was Cade's story to tell. I guess it fucked him up quite a bit, and he hasn't been home in a while. It's this big thing."

My mind starts moving at a mile a minute, processing everything she's saying as so many puzzle pieces start to fall into place. His inability to let anyone close? Check. His instant connection with Kennedy? Check. It breaks my heart knowing he went through all that pain and trauma as a teenager. If he hasn't been

Dirty Play

close with his family in years... Do they blame him for her death? Or is he pushing people away because he blames himself?

"You look like you're thinking. Are you okay?" Sawyer asks quietly. "I didn't say anything wrong, did I?"

"No, not at all. I guess I'm just starting to understand him a bit more—things are making a little more sense."

"Perfect. Because the rest of what Kylie told me has to do with you."

"With me?" I ask, looking at Cassie, who just shrugs.

"Yeah... did you ever watch the movie *Shrek*?"

"I mean, yeah? Who didn't?"

"You know how they talk about ogres being like onions? Having layers and whatever?"

"Umm... yeah? I'm not sure I'm following."

"Cade is like that," Sawyer says proudly.

"Cade is like an ogre?" I deadpan, watching her cheeks turn pink.

"No, no, no! He has layers like an onion. You just need to keep peeling them back until you figure him out."

"I'm so confused. I think that was one of the worst descriptions ever, although if you peel back all the bullshit, I can kind of see where you're coming from." Cassie laughs. "But that's just because I've seen *Shrek* a million times and actually know the quote. Basically, don't give up—keep poking the shit out of him, and eventually he'll crack."

"So, you want me to beat the man down until he surrenders and lets me keep fucking him?"

"Pretty much, yeah," Sawyer says. "Kylie says he's done this before—likes someone and then pushes them away. Based on the minimal conversations she witnessed about you, she definitely thinks you're not in the friend zone—at all."

"Well, I'm supposed to see him early next week. He and some of the guys on the Cyclones are coming to meet Kennedy and some of the other patients. I guess I'll see how he acts then. He's been hot and cold lately, and it's getting on my nerves. One moment, he's angry at me, and the next he's flirty. I can't keep up."

"Just hold on, young grasshopper, be patient, and let's see what happens."

Much easier said than done.

Chapter 12

Cade

> You guys are still up to meet at the hospital today, right?

MILES

> Do you think we'd actually let a kid down?

> I mean...

TREVOR

> Shut up. Of course, we'll be there. I've already picked them up.

When I told the guys about Kennedy and her parents, they were immediately willing to come help spread some cheer. The four of us are planning to meet at the hospital to link up with Gwen, who will navigate hospital politics for us. We are going to spend some time with Kennedy and her family, along with other patients in the hospital who are interested.

My phone vibrates, this time from Harris in a separate message.

> **HARRIS**
> I wouldn't miss today for anything, brother. Promise. I know I've been busy a lot lately, but I'll always be there for you.
>
> I'm not oblivious to why this means so much to you. Just know you can talk to me anytime.
>
> Thanks. See you at four.

Harris is the only one of the guys who truly knows, damn, well nearly everything. Growing up as neighbors, he grew up close to my entire family. He knew Veronica very well, and her death hit us all hard. He watched me push my entire family away and, to this day, never repair those relationships. He's tried to bring up the subject a time or two, but I squashed that years ago. My family is better off when I'm not around. They're better off without me.

It's not up for discussion.

But I'd be lying if I said I didn't wonder sometimes. The older I get and the more I learn, the more I'm starting to realize I didn't know a damn thing at eighteen years old. Although I acted like I knew everything and made a lot of grown-up decisions, I wasn't

Dirty Play

thinking about how many other people I was hurting in the process.

I may not take him up on the conversations, but knowing that he's there is enough to make me feel less alone.

WALKING INTO THE HOSPITAL WITH THE GUYS, OUR duffle bags are filled with all the signed swag we could fit. We are ready to make some people smile, starting with Miss Kennedy and her family.

Gwen has coordinated the whole thing for us, getting a gathering room where we can meet with them, which will give Kennedy time and space to talk to us and ask questions or whatever she needs to forget why she's still in the hospital.

Even if it's all I've been able to think about since I met her.

She's fighting the same damn thing my sister did.

The same fucking thing I was supposed to save my sister from.

But then I had to go and be a selfish asshole and get hurt, leaving a perfectly matched kidney stuck inside my body.

I can't keep myself from wondering if maybe, just maybe, I can help Kennedy now.

By the time we make it to the room, Gwen and Kennedy are waiting with her parents, who are sitting on the couch watching their daughter with proud smiles on their faces. Kennedy squeals the second she sees us, making us laugh. I'm sure you can hear it throughout the hospital.

The guys introduce themselves and tell a little bit about what they do for the team, which Kennedy quickly pointed out is highly unnecessary.

"So, do you guys do this often?" Kennedy asks.

"Do what?"

"Come and cheer up sick kids."

Denise gasps, but Kennedy starts laughing before anyone can think she's being serious.

"Sorry, my sense of humor is a little dark. I'm just used to saying what I feel... and right now, I'm a little bit over being the sick kid."

"Well then, how about we talk about what we can do when you get out of here? If your parents are interested?" Miles asks, waiting for her parents to nod before handing her a jersey. "Maybe something you could wear this to?"

When she opens it up, she easily puts her previous squeal to shame. Miles brought her a signed jersey, as well as pretty much any other gear he could find in her size. He wanted to give options to his number one fan. *His words, not mine.*

"We'll get you tickets—any game you want to come to, just let us know. Plus, once you get out of here, you can come down to the arena and we'll give you a tour anytime, all of you."

Dirty Play

They chat back and forth about hockey and her playing soccer, and I can't stay focused on their conversation because my eyes keep gravitating toward Gwen. She's not working this afternoon; her shift starts later tonight, but she still came to visit and enjoy this time with Kennedy.

And she looks fucking hot in jeans and a t-shirt, her dark, wavy hair framing her bright, green eyes that keep bouncing back to me.

It's good to know I have some effect on her, even if she's barely speaking to me.

The rest of the visit goes smoothly. We meet some of the other patients, bring some fun team gear to pass out to, and leave some at the nurses' station as a thank you.

It's not until we say goodbye that I realize I need to do something.

"Hey, I'll meet you guys out front," I tell the guys as they walk down the hall toward the exit. Turning around, I run back toward the office, thankfully catching Denise and Josh still outside, while Gwen and Kennedy make their way back to Kennedy's room.

"Hi, Cade," Josh says when he notices me. "Did you forget something?"

"No, well, I guess maybe," I say, stumbling over my words as I try to figure out how to ask this question. If it's even appropriate for me to ask this question. "Uh, my sister went through the same thing Kennedy is going through, and well... I was a match for her.

Unfortunately, I couldn't donate at that time, and she ended up passing. But that's not the point. I was, uh, wondering... I know you guys haven't found a match yet... I'd like to get tested, if that would be okay with you."

The moment the words are out of my mouth, tears well up in both their eyes— tears of both sadness and hope—and I know in this moment this is the right call for me.

"I—Are you sure?"

"Positive. I wish I could've done more to save my sister, but I couldn't. And if I can help save your daughter, I'd really like to."

Josh's hand immediately stretches out toward me, shaking my hand and pulling me into a hug. Obviously, this is just about getting the testing done. There's no guarantee or even a high chance of me being a match, but it's something. I think this is the spark of hope they needed to realize you just never know when you'll find that match.

"Thank you, seriously. For today—for making my little girl smile again. And hell, thank you for this," he says, choking on his words.

"I do have one favor, though. It's a little thing," I say, nervous because I hate secrets.

"Of course, anything."

"Can we keep this anonymous for now? I think by now you've realized that Gwen and I know each other outside of the hospital. She, uh, she doesn't know all the stuff I just told you, and I'm not exactly ready to get into all of it yet."

They exchange a glance, tiny smirks playing on their lips like they know an inside joke that I'm not a part of.

"Obviously, we will make sure to keep your name out of it. Although we'll have to let Sally know. She's the one who's been in charge of the testing."

"Actually, I'll just head to the front and go check in with her now. Might as well see how quickly we can get this started."

"What took you so long?" Trevor asks, leaning up against his truck.

To my surprise, Sally was at the desk when I went there, and she took me to get my blood drawn to start the process. I was in and out within ten minutes, so they haven't actually been waiting all that long.

"Got caught up talking with Josh and Denise. Sorry about that," I say, fidgeting with my watch, feeling a bit off for some reason. Out of the corner of my eye, I see Harris watching me, his eyes narrowed like he's assessing me. And dammit, I'm not ready to talk about what I just did. "Wanna go grab some lunch? I'm fucking starving."

"I can't. Ellie has to work tonight, so I've gotta grab Addy," Trevor pipes up.

"I'm in," Harris says.

"I'm Trevor's ride. Besides, I think I have a date," Miles adds, unlocking his car with a grin.

"You think?" Trevor asks.

He just shrugs and laughs.

"Whatever, meet me at Rocco's."

Getting in my car, I lean my head back before looking at my phone and a text from Gwen I've been avoiding since we got outside.

> **GWEN**
> Thank you for today. It really meant the world to Kennedy and her parents.

> Thank you for organizing it. They're a sweet family, glad we could bring them a little fun, even for a moment.

> **GWEN**
> You're a much sweeter man than you let the world see.

> Shh... don't tell everyone my secrets. That's just for you.

Why am I smiling? And why am I saying shit like this?

What the hell is happening, and why am I starting to have feelings again?

I thought I pushed this shit down years ago.

Dirty Play

WE MAKE IT THROUGH HALF A MEAL WITHOUT HARRIS harassing me, but as soon as our entrées are in front of us and I'm about to take my first bite of delicious steak, he pounces.

"Look, we can sit here and pretend that nothing happened between you and Gwen, but I'll be honest, I'm a nosy bitch and want to know. So, are you going to tell me what the fuck happened between you two, or am I going to need to make some phone calls or play twenty-one questions to get it out of you?"

I stop mid-bite, looking up at him with a glare, praying to whoever I can that he'll just drop this. Harris has known me long enough that he can get just about anything out of me.

"We've all heard the buzz that something happened between you two. I can either believe the gossip the girls mention—that you couldn't get it up and she left disappointed, or you can tell me your side of the story."

"The fuck you mean I couldn't get it up?! I doubt she was able to walk the next day without a constant reminder of what we'd done."

Harris just laughs as I fall directly into his trap. Fuck my life—that sneaky ass.

"So, now that we've covered that part, what happened next? I mean, to me, it sounds like everything went well... You two have been dancing around each other for years, the tension had to snap at some point, and I bet it was hot."

"Uh, we've barely talked since that night. We hooked up, it was incredible, and if she told you otherwise, I promise she's lying. But as soon as she walked out of her room, I panicked. I felt like everything hit me all at once, and I was immediately in too deep. I needed to get out of there as fast as I could, which means I was an asshole."

"So what? You just dipped out after fucking her? This is Gwen, you idiot, not some girl you picked up at a bar," Harris snaps, his voice full of disbelief and a little anger that I'm not used to hearing from him. "That's pretty cold, even for you."

I should be offended, but he's not wrong. I'm not exactly known as a warm and fuzzy guy, and he knows it. I've been the guy who's gone to a girl's house and then left after, but those were just one-night stands, expectations discussed up front. I wasn't just a dick for no reason. But this time, I was, and it sucks. I've never intentionally hurt Gwen. I've sort of kept her in the safe zone, but I fucked up.

"Well... no. Okay, kind of?" I grumble, tugging on my hair before reaching for my water. "Look, we went back to her place, hooked up, and then when she came out of the bathroom, I told her it was a mistake, kissed her on the cheek, and went home."

Before I realize what he's doing, Harris grabs a dinner roll and lobs it directly at my chest. Reaching for another one, he throws. It hits me in the face before bouncing onto my plate.

Dirty Play

"What the fuck, man?" I grumble, looking around to see if anyone else noticed, but they're all focused on their own meals.

"You're a fucking idiot," Harris says, grabbing his fork and knife and cutting into his rib eye, looking up at me with a mouthful of food—judgment clear as day. "And I've known you long enough to say that you know I love you like a brother but come on now."

"I know. I'm a fucking idiot, it's all I've been able to think about, but it wasn't without reason—we both fucking know it. And because of that, I just don't see how to fix it."

He points his fork at me like I'm a petulant child about to get scolded. "Cade, it's time you listen to someone for the first time in your life. Veronica would be absolutely furious if she knew this is how you were acting eleven years after her death. She died. *You did not*, so stop acting like a fucking martyr and actually enjoy your life."

"It's not that easy."

"No, it's not supposed to be either. Life isn't fucking easy, but we don't give up. We keep pushing through and fighting the battles we need to fight. I think it's time you stop running from everything and face it head-on, starting with Gwen. You have enough people around you who care about you and want to help you be happy. You just need to stop pushing them away. Gwen cares about you more than you fucking deserve, and you're an idiot to not see that."

Before I can say anything, our server brings another round of whiskey for us, and I politely ask her to keep them coming.

"Look, Har, I know she cares about me, and I know I care about her, too. That doesn't mean it's worth risking it when I know I'll just hurt her in the end. I'm broken, I'm fucked up, and we both know it. She deserves so much better than me. Besides, should we talk about our past? About running away from things that matter?"

"This is about you, not me. Stop trying to change the subject. Besides, that's not up to you to decide, Cade. She's a grown-ass woman who can make decisions on her own. Have you ever stopped to think that maybe it hurts her more that you won't give it a shot? That she cares about you and wants to show you, but you won't let her? Look, I don't expect this conversation to make miracles happen, I just want you to think about it. Gwen's miserable without you. Trust me, I know what that looks like. And your family, they haven't been the same since you left. They're absolutely destroyed without you. They lost Veronica—they didn't need to lose you, too."

His words sting, but it's not enough.

"They have Kylie and Vince. My parents are fine without me. As for Gwen—"

"You don't seriously believe that bullshit, right?" Harris asks, eyebrows raised as he stares at me like I'm a fucking idiot. "Kylie and Vince lost not one, but *two* siblings when Veronica died. The same with your parents, all because you ran. You left by choice, and I may not be a parent, but to me, that's an even harder blow to recover from."

I just stare, feeling like he ripped the rug out from beneath my feet. My entire world has been flipped upside down as I realize there might just be some truth to his statements. Fuck. Harris isn't supposed to be right, especially not about this.

I made the choice.

I thought that they would be happier, that they would thrive without me there to bring them down. I figured if I was here in New York, I could make them proud while not constantly reminding them how I couldn't save my sister.

Growing up, my parents sacrificed everything for me to follow my dreams—sometimes working two jobs to help pay for my gear or whatever traveling we were doing that month. The least I could do was make them proud by becoming the best goalie in the NHL.

"Look, I know this is fucking hard to hear, and I'm not exactly being the most sensitive in bringing this up, but you need to really think long and hard if these are choices that you're going to be proud of twenty years from now. Because if not, it's time you start fixing it."

"I—I don't know."

"Well, what about starting with Gwen?"

I sigh, leaning back and grab my glass, downing it as it's immediately replaced by another. I watch Harris sitting there, but all I can think about are the choices I've made since Veronica passed. I left—ran away—because I thought it was the best way to protect my family... from me.

But was that the right choice? Was it worse?

Was it even my choice to make?

Chapter 13

Gwen

"So, how did you manage to pull that off the other day? I mean, it's not every day that we see four hot as fuck NHL players hanging out with us at the hospital... well, unless one of them is in the hospital," Mariah says, leaning back in her chair, legs crossed as we enjoy a moment of downtime while we finish charting.

It's been the talk of the hospital, having the guys come and spend time with some patients and hand out Cyclones gear. It brought up the morale for a lot of people, parents excited to see their kid smile for the first time in a while.

The best part? The guys made sure that the patients who couldn't meet them, either due to their recovery or compromised immune systems, each got a signed jersey and FaceTime call.

It was the cutest thing I've seen in my life, even sweeter that it was all Cade's idea.

"Umm... it actually wasn't that difficult. They're kind of my friends."

"Excuse me? You're telling me that you are friends with those men, and you've never introduced me?" Mariah feigns horror.

"I didn't think about it. I guess I'm good at keeping my work and private life separate. The joy of having workaholic parents is that I've learned how to compartmentalize very well."

"But... have you seen them? I'm on Team Kennedy with this one, Miles is something else—he's both rugged and the boy next door, and damn, I wish I could teach him a thing or two," Mariah says, fanning herself while she daydreams about doing lord knows what with my friend.

At least she didn't say Cade.

"Yeah, don't get me wrong, they're all attractive AF. Trevor's dating my friend Ellie, but Miles and Harris are both single!"

"Weren't there four guys that came? I heard Dr. Demario mention that the goalie was here too—we both know how much he loves the goalie."

I blush at the mention of Cade, doing my best to school my face before turning to Mariah. "Yeah, that's Cade Williams. He was here, too."

"And is Mr. Williams single, too?" she asks, waggling her eyebrows excitedly, and I feel myself

Dirty Play

blush, immediately remembering our naked night together.

"Um, I guess he is," I say, still avoiding eye contact.

Turning to grab another file, I keep my head down in an attempt to look busy. I've worked with Mariah for a while. We are good enough friends that she can tell when I'm withholding things, and she can typically pull them right out of me. It also bodes well for her that if my mouth doesn't say it, my face surely will.

"Why'd you leave him out then?" she asks, smiling. "Is it the same reason you're avoiding eye contact with me?"

I look up slowly, willing my blush to stay down, not wanting to add any more fuel to the fire.

"I must've forgotten he was here."

"Really? Because Denise mentioned that there was a hockey player here the other night to see you... was it him?"

Fuck.

"Well, aren't you two just a couple of gossip girls," I say, still avoiding eye contact.

"Are you really not going to give me anything? Are you two dating? Are you fucking dating an NHL goalie and not telling me?" she whispers, her tone sharp, but she's smart enough to keep her voice down knowing that if I give her anything, it'll only be if no one else hears any of it.

"Umm... no, we are not dating. We've been good friends for a while, though."

"So, you're telling me that you and Cade are just friends?" Mariah says, the disbelief obvious in her tone.

"Yes. We are just friends."

"Then why will you still not look me in the eye?"

Finally caving, I look up at her, immediately noticing the twinkle in her eyes, and I feel caught, like I'm walking into her trap and she's about to hit me with more questions than I can fend off. Doing my best to avoid her inquisition, I give her the basics, knowing at least this way, maybe I could be in control of what I share.

"We had a bit of a drunken night a while back and ended up sleeping together, but nothing came of it. So, we're just friends."

"*You fucked Cade Williams*?" she shouts, much louder than necessary. But thankfully, when you work the night shift there are not as many people roaming around the halls, so we are in the clear this time.

"Keep it down, woman. I don't need the entire hospital knowing my business. Especially Dr. D— chances are he'd either hate me for fucking his dream hockey player or constantly bug me to meet him, and honestly, I'm not in the mood to have either conversation with him."

"How do you stay friends with someone that hot after you've seen him naked? He's got this dark, mysterious vibe to him. Whenever I've gone to a game he just seems like he has secrets. Secrets that make him that much hotter."

"It hasn't been easy if I'm being honest. That being said, it's not worth losing one of my best friends over, so if the only way Cade can be in my life is if I keep the naked time off the table, then that's what I'll do."

"There are other places you can fuck that aren't a table. You can fuck in a bed? A car? Against a wall? Hell, I'd fuck that man in a crowded room and let the world watch—he's that hot."

"Ugh, I know. And if you imagine him being a rock star in bed, times that by a bajillion. He made me see stars. I think I legitimately blacked out at one point, and it was the closest to meeting God that I've ever come in my entire life, and I was raised Catholic."

"Then what happened?"

"He doesn't date."

"That doesn't mean you can't still fuck each other, right? A little friends with benefits action never hurt anyone."

"Do you live under a rock? Everyone knows that someone always ends up hurt when people try to be friends with benefits, and I know it would be me so it's easier to avoid it altogether. This way, I still get to stare at the hot guy and keep him as my friend."

She stares but luckily keeps her mouth closed as another nurse walks past with Dr. D. I think I'm in luck and get to avoid talking to him until he stops and turns back toward Mariah and I, only this time he doesn't look mean—which actually might be more terrifying.

"I have some information that I'm waiting on for room six. When it comes in will you find me?" he says, skipping all pleasantries and getting straight to business.

Room six. That's Kennedy's room... is everything okay?

"Of course. Everything okay?"

"Yes, there's a possible donor, and as Kennedy's kidney function continues to drop, it's looking more and more likely that a donor is her best option. I'm really hoping to get the results in the next hour or two so I can still call the donor this evening and get something set up as soon as possible."

"Is the donor local?"

"I believe so, although we don't even have a real name. They told us it was a pseudonym because they want to remain anonymous, but they did leave a number with Sally so that we would be able to contact them."

It's not uncommon for donors to wish to remain anonymous, but usually, it's only with the public and the patient. Generally, hospital staff will know who the donor is, especially when they are a living donor who would need to come in and have surgery to remove their kidney.

But, different strokes for different folks, I guess.

Dirty Play

"I'll find you as soon as it comes in, fingers crossed we get a match."

"Yes, Miss Kennedy is definitely due for some good news."

With that, he nods at Mariah and walks away. Some may perceive it as rude, but that's only when he's opening his mouth.

I can't help but get my hopes up that this might finally be the moment we've been waiting for. Kennedy has been on this list for over a year, and we've only ever had one positive match, but that fell through during the removal process—the organ wasn't viable.

It was heartbreaking. It felt like someone was holding a treat just out of reach—we could see it but never quite reach it.

"Well, that's good news," Mariah says, standing up and getting ready to do the next round of checks with our kiddos. "I'll be back, I need to go grab some juice for room three and then do a round, but don't think you're getting out of this conversation so easily. You need some fun in your life, and what better way to have some fun than with a hot as fuck goalie... who just so happens to be walking up to us right now?" Her eyes widen, and her mouth drops. Instantly I'm confused until I hear a deep voice coming from behind me.

"Hey, Tink," his gravelly voice rumbles, instantly turning me on, especially when he uses that nickname.

I turn and smile, not missing Mariah's eyes

widening as she also notices the nickname. Dammit, I can only imagine this is going to rile her up again.

"What's up? I'm not off until midnight, remember?"

He just smiles and passes me a cup. The smell of vanilla chai instantly hits my nostrils and I'm salivating. Looking up, he's still smiling as he introduces himself to Mariah, who looks starstruck.

"What's this for?" I ask when he turns back to me.

"Was just in the area and had to drop something off to someone who was bummed they missed out on us the other day. Gotta make sure everyone's reppin' the right NY team," Cade says, leaning up against the counter, watching me stare at the tea like a fool. "Before you even ask, yes, there's one extra pump of vanilla and an espresso shot because we all know you like it dirty."

Mariah giggles, and I immediately flush, the innuendo in his words evident. Now that she knows we've fucked, I can only imagine what she's thinking. Hell, if it's anything near what I'm imagining, I'm not sure I can look her in the eye.

But it's Cade's facial expression that's most surprising as he stands there with a little smirk, watching me squirm. And he looks happy—like he's enjoying this. I'm not used to his flirtatious side anymore, especially not after he called everything a big mistake, but apparently, my body didn't get the memo. His little smirk is turning me the fuck on.

Even weirder than that, though? He remembered

my exact drink, something we'd only gotten together twice, and that was over a year ago. That little moment is enough to fan the coals a bit, adding a little heat to the fire I'm so desperately trying to extinguish.

"You remembered my drink?"

"I did," he smiles, pushing himself off the counter to stand up, glancing down at his watch. "I'm going to drop off this jersey and then go workout, I'll see you back here at midnight."

"Bye, Cade." I wave, little butterflies taking flight in my stomach. I know I can only tread lightly in this situation, praying I don't drown.

But I'm heading straight for the deep end, just hoping I survive.

Chapter 14

Cade

I don't know why I'm so nervous. I mean, yes, these results will impact everything. At least they will short term. If it's positive, I'll have to recover from a major surgery during my time off—the time I'm usually resting, but also working on my strength to be ready for the next season.

But outside of that, none of this really affects me long term... except for living with one less kidney. But even as I think this, it all feels like a lie. This whole situation is impacting my life already. Gwen is struggling as she watches someone she cares about get sicker, unable to help them. I know how that feels all too well, remembering the day I stood next to Veronica's hospital bed, finally recovered from my accident, and was told she was no longer strong enough for the transplant.

My whole world stopped at that moment, and until

recently, it's remained that way, leaving me stuck and alone. But if I can help Kennedy, help her get back to being a teenage girl and doing what she loves, it will all be worth it. All of it. The weight lifted off of Gwen will be an added bonus.

I've only picked up Gwen from work a handful of times, but it seems like she's slowly starting to hate me a little less. I've been trying to be friendly, show her that I care, without showing her how much I care. She doesn't need to know how much I've thought of her, or that it's her name on my lips when I come in the shower.

Every. Single. Night.

But she does need to know that I was wrong that night. It wasn't a mistake, and I don't regret it. Even if I'm too afraid to let it happen again.

So, I started tonight by bringing her chai tea. I wanted her to know that not only do I listen to her and remember her favorite things, but that I care about her, even if I really suck at letting myself.

It was hard, though, seeing her, knowing I was coming down here to meet with Sally, yet not knowing how to tell her what I was doing. Would she be mad that I was getting involved with her work life? Mad that I didn't tell her right away? Knowing someone you care about is having surgery can be scary, so it feels much easier just not to tell her until it's over with.

Sally walks over to the waiting area I'm sitting in, giving me a polite hello, and we're walking back to her

Dirty Play

office. I was here earlier this week to get the testing done, but it's scarier today, surreal, because it feels like I've been in this exact place before. Every step I take feels like some combination of seventeen-year-old Cade mixed with twenty-eight-year-old Cade, and I can't escape the irony.

I have been here before, though, maybe not in this exact hospital or this exact room. But I've done this whole process before, sat in the chair across from someone as they told me the results. And this time I swear, if it comes back positive, I will make sure I'm able to go through with it.

"Have a seat, Mr. Williams. Thank you for coming in to meet me tonight."

"Of course, thank you for being so willing to meet in the evening," I say, remembering the shock on her face when I asked to meet at eleven p.m. I used the excuse that it would help keep me anonymous, which she was immediately fine with... but if I am already coming to the hospital, I might as well make it close to the time Gwen gets off.

"Not a problem. We always want to help people out, especially when they're participating in such a wonderful thing," Sally says, putting her glasses on before opening a folder that I can only assume contains the results. "Now, have you spoken with your family about your decision? A friend?"

"No, ma'am," I tell her truthfully. "But I have talked to a friend who said they could bring me to the hospital and take me home. I can also stay at their place for a while."

I won't. But she doesn't need to know that. Don't need to burden them any more than I already am.

Her face falls as she leans forward, her elbows on her desk as she watches me. "Mr. Williams, this is a serious surgery and a serious life choice you are making. Are you sure you want to make these decisions without talking to your family?"

"Yes, ma'am, I'm comfortable with my decision."

She sighs, accepting defeat and passing me the folder. My eyes scan the document, looking for the results, and my heart stops as she says the words aloud.

"You're a match, Mr. Williams."

Waiting outside the hospital for Gwen has been brutal this time, although when I left Sally's office at 11:30, I made sure to walk around the block a couple of times. I called Rex because I was a little stressed after I met with Sally, like the nerves and the excitement over the results filled my body with adrenaline. I couldn't pull it together and needed to vent. Knowing that Kylie pretty much spilled the beans about our sister, although she was nice enough to leave my part out, I knew he'd understand why I was a bit torn up about Kennedy.

He let me vent, but, of course, it led to questions

Dirty Play

about what the hell I've been doing at the hospital so often. He didn't like my answer that it was a good route for a run, especially since it's midnight.

He's not an idiot. He knows I'm struggling with my feelings for Gwen, but he's a good friend, so he doesn't push the subject.

I'll eventually tell him more about what's going on, but I need to figure it out myself first. I'm struggling to wrap my brain around it, though, like how I've been a perfect match for not one person but two in my lifetime—at only twenty-eight years old. I'll stop by his place later this week and tell him about the surgery.

When I was leaving Sally's office, she asked me to think about my choice before I let anyone know. She said I would at least need to be picked up from the hospital after surgery, so having someone aware of what was going on was important. I tried to tell her that I would talk to a friend. But she just used that as an opening to bring up Gwen, told me she's seen me leave with her a couple of times and that she would probably be the most helpful person to know about it.

I lied and said I would think about it. The thought of telling Gwen is enough to give me hives, but I should tell her, especially since the surgery is scheduled for the day after tomorrow. Kennedy has had a couple of rough weeks, so they want to schedule her ASAP. It's hard to believe it's already almost June, but thankfully I'll have enough time to heal before the season begins —otherwise Coach will kick my ass.

Watching Gwen walk out of the hospital, tucked into a big jacket, a million bags on her—I want to laugh. She looks ridiculous, like the Stay Puft Marshmallow Man, but pocket-sized.

"Hey," she says as she walks over to me, as I sit on my usual bench waiting.

Standing up, I grab her bags, lifting them over my shoulder with ease.

"Cade, you don't need to carry my stuff. I've got it."

"Gwen, you're over a foot shorter than me. These bags go down past your knees, and all I can imagine is you tripping and falling."

She looks up at me, her head barely meeting me at waist level, the height difference clear.

"It's not my fault you're pocket-sized," I say with a smile as she starts to walk.

"I prefer to call myself fun-sized," she says proudly.

"Well, you're not wrong there. You're definitely fun." I smirk, again unable to stop myself from making little flirty comments—unable to accept the line I drew in the sand.

I'm sure I'm confusing the fuck out of Gwen, but that just means she's along for the same ride as me. My brain is in a constant state of confusion, usually at my own doing.

She turns her face away from mine, but I don't miss the little smile. She looks so beautiful when she smiles. Out of everything she wears, that smile looks the best on her.

Dirty Play

"So, how was your shift?" I ask as we make our way across the street.

"It was actually really good. We had a couple of patients get discharged, it's nice to see the kiddos get to go home. It's always emotional, especially because parents come in so flustered, not knowing how to help their child, and while they're in the hospital, we pretty much help with everything. A lot of parents end up feeling overwhelmed, even scared, at the thought of going home and needing to manage it all by themselves."

"I can only imagine how terrifying that would be. I'm not a huge fan of hospitals and even I can see how they might prefer to be here than home."

"Why don't you like hospitals? I mean, you've been in one quite a bit these last couple weeks. I would've never thought you hated them."

How do I answer this question without mentioning my family? Without mentioning just how identical this situation is to the one ten years ago?

"Just a lot of... history in hospitals, all they do is make me think of people who are sick or dying."

"There are also a lot of good things that happen at hospitals—broken bones get fixed, people get saved, babies are born."

"Well, in my experience, not everyone can be saved."

"Would it change your mind if I tell you that we found a match for Kennedy?" Gwen asks with a huge smile on her face. "Kennedy made me promise that I would tell you the next time I saw you. She said something about how you said I would be able to help her get a kidney and that it's finally coming true. She even went as far as to say you were a good luck charm, but I set her straight."

She gives me a little wink, joking around with me, and it's one of the first moments that I wonder if maybe I didn't completely fuck things up with her. I want to tell her. I want to say fuck it all and tell her that it's me, I'm the match, that I'm excited, yet somehow... a little scared.

But that would involve me telling her about Veronica, about *why* I'm so scared to fuck this up. Because if Kennedy turns out to be another person I can't save, I'm not sure I'll be able to live with myself. But I can't tell her all that—it's too private, too much, and I can't bear to see the look on her face when she realizes that it's all my fault my sister died. That my selfishness killed Veronica.

I made the decision to go snowboarding even though I knew I had surgery the next week. I'd been snowboarding since I was five, so I felt confident I was ready. Until another snowboarder hit a patch of ice and came barreling into me. I got a concussion and ended up needing surgery for a broken arm. With all the trauma to my body, they made us postpone the transplant. By the time my body was ready, hers no longer was.

Dirty Play

"It does, a bit. A girl like that deserves all the good news she can get."

We spend the rest of the walk talking about random things, which include me scolding her for going to this café alone at midnight, just because she loves their French toast. By the time we are outside her apartment, it feels like the ice has been broken, that we're slowly making our way back to our usual friendship.

But the moment I go to hand her one of her bags and our hands touch, the heat from before swallows me up, and I'm right back to craving the feel of her skin on mine. It doesn't help that I remember what it feels like when she's naked, writhing beneath me as her nails scrape down my back.

No, that memory doesn't help at all.

When she looks up at me, her eyes are dark, the typical bright green now hazy with desire. Before I realize what I'm doing, I'm leaning down, my face slowly angling to meet hers. And just before I kiss her, a drunk couple comes out of her building screaming, "Baby got back!" at the top of their lungs, and the moment is gone.

Taking a step back, I force distance between us, knowing that if we cross that line, there will be no going back. It's hard enough having her once and keeping myself away, if I taste her a second time, there will be no hope for either of us to get out unscathed.

If she's uncomfortable, she doesn't let it show as

she takes a step back, reaching for the rest of her bags. "Good night, Cade, I'm sure I'll see you tomorrow, same time."

And with that, she walks inside, leaving me in desperate need of a cold shower.

Chapter 15

Gwen

> S.O.S.
>
> He's dickmatizing me again.

SAWYER

Good. That just means he's coming to his senses.

CASSIE

I sense that he'll be coming in you veryyyyy soon.

> Fuck off, you two are no help.

CASSIE

kissy face

SAWYER

<3 you

Today's a big day at work and I'm exhausted because I've barely slept. I was up until four in the morning because of Cade and his teasing, and I'd already switched to the day shift to be at the hospital for Kennedy's surgery. I couldn't turn him down, though. It's so much easier when he acts like a dick, but when he's a little flirty, not to mention the way he looked when I swear he was thinking about kissing me... yeah, I'm done for.

But that's not what I should be thinking about today. Today is about Kennedy. I received a message that we'll be discussing the plan with her family tonight, and the transplant should take place within the next few days. It feels surreal—like this isn't actually going to happen. But I can't think like that, it's going to happen, some wonderful person got tested and they're giving Kennedy the gift of life.

I only wish I knew who it was so I could shake their hand.

When I told Cade about her transplant last night, I saw a moment of sadness on his face, and it took everything in me not to tell him that Sawyer told me about Veronica. It's not my story to share, and I definitely don't want him to feel like I've violated his privacy, but I wish he knew he could talk to me about this. That I would be there for him.

I guess at this moment, I need to let my actions show him. Maybe then he'd believe it.

Dirty Play

Grabbing my phone, I take a deep breath before I pull up his name and send a quick text before I chicken out.

> Hi. Want to meet me for lunch?

CADE
Is everything okay?

I wait, hoping he'll answer my question, but when no little dots appear, I know that's his answer. I start responding but before I can press send I get another response.

CADE
Sorry, yes I would like that.

Is everything okay, though? I guess I'm just surprised you're asking for more time with me when I thought you already hated me walking you home.

> I guess I like it a lot more than I let on.

Now to take a shower and pull myself together.

TODAY IS THE KIND OF DAY YOU DREAM ABOUT WHEN working in the PICU. Another patient was able to leave earlier than expected, and we got the official go-ahead to put Kennedy and her donor's surgery on the schedule. Two days from now, Kennedy will be the proud recipient of a brand-new-to-her kidney.

The best part of the day has been that even though Dr. Dickhead is working tonight, he's actually been pleasant. He can be a huge asshole, but he truly does care about these kids. Hearing the news about Kennedy, and realizing she's getting what she needs, has put him in a good mood today.

By the time I'm walking into the cafeteria for lunch, I'm smiling. I'm kind of excited to see Cade—hopeful things will eventually get back to normal, which is why I'm also planning on telling him that I signed up for a dating app. It's not that I'm necessarily looking to date someone. It's just that some male company is nice from time to time. After my one night with Cade, I haven't been able to stop thinking about him and his perfect dick, even if the night ended horribly.

This time, if I hook up with someone, I want it be damn clear it's a one-night stand, and I will be the one making the escape.

I find him already at a table, and he surprisingly already has food for us.

"Hey," I say with a smile, pulling up the chair across from him and sitting down. "What's all this?"

"I was walking past the deli, so I grabbed us club sandwiches. This one is yours, no tomatoes, extra pickles, and a side of honey mustard," Cade says as he passes me a bag, almost looking... shy?

The more time I've spent with Cade lately, the

more I've learned about him. He's way more attentive than I ever realized, remembering little things about me—like what my tea order is and my favorite sandwich made exactly the way I like it. I'd be lying if I said that didn't make me really fucking happy, and if I was a little more naïve, I might think this meant he actually liked me.

"Pretty sure this was exactly what I needed tonight. Thank you, Cade. We've been running around getting everything scheduled for the transplant surgery in two days, and I've barely taken a minute for a snack or water." I smile, unwrapping my sandwich as Cade does the same.

"That's gotta be exciting. I'm sure Kennedy is thrilled."

"She is, but she's also nervous. I can't believe we were able to find a donor—a local donor at that. It's made the whole process so much smoother, and it's helped us move everything along faster to minimize complications with her health."

He looks down, staring at his sandwich and I almost worry I've said too much—maybe I've sent him down memory lane, remembering the struggles his sister went through. But just moments later he's grabbing his sandwich and taking a bite.

We sit in comfortable silence for a few minutes while we eat our sandwiches—our table a little pocket of peace in the hustle and bustle all around us.

"Do you have any plans during the offseason?" I ask, trying to poke him into talking a little more.

"As of now? No. Just taking care of my health and making sure I'm keeping my strength up. I might be taking a trip home for a couple days. I guess it's my parents' fortieth anniversary or something, so my sister is making it a big deal."

I lean back, watching him as he tells me more about this party his sister is throwing for their parents. This is the most I've heard him talk about his family in the years I've known him. I almost don't want to respond or interject from fear that he might stop talking.

His family lives in a tiny little town called Ivy Falls, about six hours northwest of New York, and apparently, he hasn't been back home in at least five years. My parents drive me crazy, but I still go home at least every other Christmas. The pain in his eyes tells me there's a lot more to this story than I realize, but I'm smart enough to know that if I try to push him too far, too fast, he'll run, and I'll never learn more.

Maybe Sawyer is right, I need to treat Cade like an ogre.

"How about you, Tink?" he asks, watching me intently. "Do you have any plans? Taking any vacations?"

"I don't have plans to take any vacations later this year. I may use some vacation days here and there, but I haven't taken a big chunk of time off, well... ever.

Dirty Play

Sawyer keeps bugging me, telling me that if I don't take a vacation, I'll burn out, so who knows? Maybe later this year, I'll take a couple weeks off and go relax somewhere quiet."

"So, nothing exciting planned?"

"Nope, the most exciting thing I've got planned is that I am thinking about getting back out in the dating world—I re-downloaded a dating app. Recent... experiences have made me realize just how much I've missed spending time with a man."

Grabbing my drink, I guzzle a bit, washing down my sandwich and the nerves of finally admitting this to Cade. When my eyes meet his, his jaw is clenched, his eyes dark as he watches me with an almost murderous look, and I've either really pissed him off or made him jealous as fuck.

Guess only time will tell...

The walk back to my place is much quieter than lunch. It almost feels like I'm spending time with an entirely different person. The joking, the laughter, the easy conversation we had just hours ago are all gone, and now I'm lucky if I get more than a few words out of him.

When we make it to my building, he stops out front, and I realize something.

I don't want him to leave. The look in his eyes, the

pain I've noticed, even if he doesn't want to talk to me about it... he doesn't have to leave.

"I know it's late, and I'm sure you have other things you would rather do... but, uh... would you want to come up and watch a movie?" I ask, struggling to maintain eye contact, the fear of rejection strong.

But after a moment, when I'm expecting him to turn me down, he smiles, just barely, and gives a little shrug.

"Lead the way, Tink," Cade says, his arm outstretched, waiting for me.

Oh fuck. I did *not* expect him to take me up on my offer.

What the hell do I do now?

Chapter 16

Cade

I tried to say no. I really did. I actually stood there for a moment, wondering how I could turn down her invitation without undoing all of the progress we've made these last few days. But when I racked my brain for any excuse to walk away, I realized I didn't have a good reason.

Not. A. Single. Damn. One.

All because I didn't *want* to turn her down.

Even the fact that I'm hiding a big secret from her isn't enough for me to put distance between us. It's hard to hear her talk about Kennedy finally getting her surgery without telling her I'm the donor. She may be excited for Kennedy, but she's still nervous because it's a major surgery on someone she cares about. I also know Gwen cares about me, and I don't want to worry her any more than she already is.

I just want to spend time with her, with other

people or alone—it doesn't matter to me as long as I'm with this girl.

So here we are, sitting on her couch watching *The Proposal*, popcorn in hand, as I try to convince myself not to reach over and touch her. She's sitting too close for me not to think about touching her, even if that is against the rules, which is how we got into this mess in the first place. The only problem is I'm not the best at following rules, even if they are my own.

She's sitting there, doing her best to keep her eyes on the TV, but I've noticed her looking in my direction a couple of times when she's trying to be sneaky, thinking I'm not paying attention.

At least I'm not the only one stealing glances.

It's hard not to—I'm in awe of this girl. She makes me feel things I'm not used to, and it's more than just attraction. When I'm with her, I feel peace. My brain is able to relax and settle down. When I close my eyes, I don't see the racing thoughts—the things I should've done differently—or overthink all of the things I screwed up, and it's quiet.

Whenever she's around, I feel happy—happier than I have in years—and she makes me feel like I'm worthy of these good feelings, even if they feel so foreign that it's almost a little scary.

In the last eleven years, I can count on one hand the number of times I've felt happy.

Three. Three times.

Dirty Play

1. The day I signed with the NY Cyclones.
2. The day I moved away from Ivy Falls.
3. The day I kissed Gwen.

But just because she brings me peace doesn't mean I bring her the same, so I need to keep reminding myself that although we've crossed a line, we can go back to just being friends. Right?

We would probably be able to if I wasn't constantly thinking about the way her lips felt on mine or the way she tasted, like spiced cherries and vanilla, and how her tight little cunt suffocated my cock while I was buried deep inside of her while she screamed my name. Yeah, all of that makes it really fucking difficult to want to just be her friend. Throw in her mention of how she downloaded a dating app, and I haven't been able to stop thinking about claiming her since I walked away from lunch earlier this evening.

The idea that some other man would get to kiss her, taste her, fuck her?

Yeah, no.

Fuck. That.

It makes me damn near feral just thinking about it, which is why my hands practically burn from not touching her as I sit on this couch.

"I'm going to change really quick," Gwen says, standing up. "Need anything?"

Yeah, you.

"No, I'm good with just the snacks for now," I

mumble, shoving my mouth full of popcorn before I let my inside thoughts become outside thoughts and tell her to get on her knees. With a shrug, she walks to her bedroom, tempting me in the worst way possible.

You're no good for her, Cade. Just. Let. Her. Go.

I pause the movie and scroll on my phone for a minute, waiting for her to come back, knowing I need to distract myself from following her into her bedroom. Thankfully the group chat has been blowing up, everyone giving Harris a hard time for skipping out on the last couple of guys' nights. They typically just consist of beer and food, usually at the bar so we can hang out in the offseason, but we still count on everyone showing up because, honestly, we're a needy bunch.

Catching up on that was enough to distract me for a while but not long enough to miss her walk out of her room in just an oversized hoodie and tiny spandex shorts, leaving absolutely nothing to the imagination.

"You paused the movie?" she asks casually, grabbing a blanket and sitting down, this time even closer to me, snuggling in like this is an everyday occurrence. She's not actually touching me, but somehow fits perfectly beneath my arm outstretched on the couch. Yeah, she's being a damn tease on purpose, and her little smirk confirms it.

The lord is testing me today.

"I did," I grumble as she throws the blanket over both of us and grabs her phone, thankfully giving me a moment to adjust my dick in my sweats. "I think the Betty White part is next, and I figured you didn't want to miss it."

"Thanks, it's my favorite part of the movie and if I had missed Betty White singing 'Get Low,' I probably would've cried," she says, her eyes on her phone as she plays around, distracted by whatever she's looking at.

It isn't until she scoots closer that I can see what she's doing, and I'm immediately furious.

She's swiping on that damn dating app, messaging back and forth with a couple of guys like she's not sitting here next to me, a man who she's well aware can make her come.

Multiple times.

"What're you doing?" I growl as I watch her.

"Oh, just finishing a few conversations from lunch. Mariah was helping me swipe, and I was just checking to see if I matched with anyone else," she says, looking up from her phone, just staring at me with her big doe eyes like she's trying to gauge my reaction. Probably trying to figure out how far she can take this, but the truth is I don't even know what the limit is anymore, and she's making it really fucking difficult for me to figure out right now.

When I do nothing but stare at her, she smiles wider, and in a quick move she's turned her body, her head now using my lap as a pillow.

"Wanna help?" She smirks, her legs now on the

couch while she shows me her phone with all the dating profiles and messages she's received already.

My jaw clenches, her close proximity doing nothing to help my stiffening cock, the mention of other men talking to her pushing me. I hate the thought of someone else getting to touch her. It pisses me off.

No, that's an understatement.

It infuriates me. It makes me wish we had a hockey game coming up, and I could drop gloves—throw a few haymakers at the first person to piss me off. I always give Harris a hard time for being so chirpy on the ice because he spends enough time in the sin bin as it is, but right now I get it. Every time she giggles at a profile or smiles while responding to a message, I feel my blood boil.

She's fucking teasing me, pushing my buttons, and I can feel myself cracking even if I know this was her plan. I could see the wheels turning in her eyes as she assessed me—like she could taste my indecision and see that my walls were faltering. Instead of helping me hold them up, she's holding a grenade and tempting me, just waiting to detonate everything around us, bringing them down completely.

And I want to let her.

But I know that if I have her a second time, I'll be done for. There will be no letting her go.

"What do you think of this one?" she asks, showing

Dirty Play

me her phone with a shirtless man whose bio is almost as cringy as his picture.

"I think you should block him and delete the app."

She looks up, her dark hair falling down, but she just smiles as she looks at me through her lashes. "And how would that help me get laid, Mr. Williams?" she purrs, her voice raspy, and I feel another crack forming in my resolve.

When did she become so brash? When did she get so outgoing, going after what she wants? And why is that making her so much more irresistible?

Brushing her hair from her face, I stare down, willing myself to stand up and walk away, to be the bigger man and not give into this dangerous game we're playing. But the second she goes to look back at her phone, I snatch it from her hand and throw it to the other couch across the room.

"What the—" she starts, but I'm already lifting her by her hips, placing her in my lap as her hands grip my shoulders to steady herself, her eyes already wild.

"Delete. The. Fucking. App," I growl, my fingers flexing against her, holding her in place.

She watches me, well, more specifically, my mouth, her tongue gliding out to lick her lips, and my cock twitches.

"Give me a reason to," she counters, her eyes back on my own, her lips just out of reach of my own as we've been slowly inching closer and closer.

I can smell the cherry of her ChapStick mixing

with the spice from her chai, bringing me back to that night, and I want to taste her. No, we're past wanting—I *need* to taste her.

"I... I won't be strong enough to walk away from you twice, Tink," I mutter, dropping my forehead to hers.

"Then don't walk away this time. Just kiss me, make me yours."

Her plea is the last straw; my walls shatter as my lips crash down on hers. There's nothing delicate or soft about this kiss, no technique, no finesse, just pure hunger coming out to play.

This is years of me holding myself back from taking her, weeks of knowing the way her body feels wrapped around my own, and still trying to keep her at arm's length. This is me taking something I've known was always meant to be mine, even if I'll never feel good enough to be hers.

My hands move from her hips, grabbing her ass in these tight little shorts, grinding her against my cock as my tongue fucks her mouth like it's her pussy. Her hands grip my hair, her soft moans melting on my tongue, the sweetest, most delicious sounds, and I just want to give her more.

My hand slides along the band and down the front of her shorts until my fingers brush against her, expecting more fabric but only finding bare skin.

She's not wearing any panties. *Fuck me.*

Before I realize what she's doing, she's pulling back

from our kiss and leaning back to rest on her heels with a devilish look on her face. She licks her lips again before sliding down to the floor, resting between my legs.

"Fuuuuuuck," I groan when she sits up and reaches for my joggers.

"Off," she demands, and I have no fight left in me, so I lift my hips, helping her slide them down—briefs and all—leaving my cock bobbing, precum glistening on the tip as she stares down at my cock like it's the best thing she's seen in her life.

This vision of her on her knees, looking up at me with a hunger that matches my own almost has me coming in my pants.

"Are you going to suck my cock or just stare at it, Tink?" I goad, knowing she's never been able to back down from a challenge. "Or are you just scared you won't be able to take it all?"

Her eyes sparkle as she leans forward, sticking her tongue out and swirling it around the head of my cock, licking up the precum with a little moan like I'm her favorite dessert.

My hips rock up on instinct. The desire to be all the way inside her mouth is too much to push down. I expect her to stop, to want to put me in my place, but instead of pulling back, she opens her mouth wider, taking me in further. Slipping past her plump, wet lips, I slide as far as I can, her hands gripping my thighs. Her tongue swirls around as I slide back out. Eyes darkening as I watch her, I grip her hair in one hand as I slide back in, further this time.

Her eyes widen, but when I go to pull back, she follows me, opening even more to take me to the back of her throat, only stopping when she gags.

"Oh, fuck," I groan, doing my best to think about state capitals, primary colors, and every politician I can come up with to stop myself from spilling down her throat this quickly. Gripping her throat, I force her eyes on me, my cock still in her mouth as she holds me there, deep inside. "If you keep going, Tink, I'm going to come down this pretty throat of yours."

When she pulls back, a proud look on her face, I want to kiss her, fuck her right here, but she swats my hand away when I try to grab her.

"Fuck my face, Cade," Gwen smirks, her hand pumping my cock slowly, at a pace that's only meant to drive me wild. "Then I'll fuck you."

She pumps my cock once more, lazily, before sliding me all the way in her mouth. All the way back until she gags again, only this time she doesn't fight it. She doesn't stop—she just breathes and slowly pushes until I'm sheathed completely inside of her.

Then she waits.

It takes me a moment to realize what she's playing at... she's not joking at all. She really wants me to fuck her mouth.

I look down, eyebrows raised as I use both hands to grip her hair, holding her in place a little tighter this

Dirty Play

time. "Tap my leg twice if you want me to stop, do you understand?"

She nods.

"Unless you do that... I'm not stopping until I'm pouring down this hot throat of yours."

Pulling back, she releases me with a pop, her eyes twinkling as she stares up at me.

"Are you just going to stare at me or are you going to fuck my throat?" she teases, and that's the last straw. I grip her hair and shove my cock back down her throat, pistoning my hips as I use her mouth, her tongue, fucking her face with no regard for what I think she's feeling. Trusting Gwen enough to know what she can handle. If this is what she wants, this is what she'll get.

It doesn't take long until I'm close again, my thrusts sloppy as her lips constrict, making it even tighter, even more fucking irresistible.

"Touch yourself. I want you good and ready for my cock because I'm not going to take it easy on you," I grunt, practically speaking caveman, every word harder to get out than the last. But like a good girl, she listens, slipping her shorts down and showing me her pretty pussy as she slips her fingers between her legs. All the while, my thrusts get faster and wilder, getting me closer and closer to the edge.

Fuck. I don't want this to end. I want to keep going, keep thrusting my cock in and out of her mouth until we're both spent and boneless.

But when she starts rubbing her clit, her soft moans vibrating around my cock, I'm done for. With my grip on her hair, I pull her off my cock until I'm sliding out of her mouth with a pop, drool hanging from her lips.

She actually looks offended for a moment before her eyes shift to watch me pump my cock, my pace slow but steady. Enough to keep my orgasm there, but not enough to finish.

"Open your mouth, Tink, let me paint that pretty tongue white."

Her eyes haze over, her mouth falls open, tongue out like she's ready and waiting.

It doesn't take much, a few rough pumps and my orgasm hits like a freight train, starting at the base of my spine and shooting out like fireworks. My whole body starts tingling, every touch almost too much, but I continue pumping my cock until I'm unloading everything on her pretty tongue and lips, barely missing her sweatshirt.

Fucking hell, I thought she looked perfect earlier, but this is from another world. I wish I could take a mental picture of this moment, Gwen on her knees, covered in my cum, looking up at me like I hung the moon, while her fingers rub circles on her clit.

Grabbing her hand from my leg, I help her up, sliding her shorts down before lifting her back onto my lap. Her tongue glides out, licking my cum from her lips as she slides her two fingers, the ones she had just been fucking, between my lips. The taste of her now coats my tongue, her eyes twinkling as I lick her fingers clean.

"Delicious," I grumble, slamming her lips into mine, the taste of her release mixing with mine, the combination enough to make me want more. My cock starts hardening between us, and I'm ready to take her again. Pulling back, her eyes widen when she feels me at her center.

"Already?" she moans as I rock my hips up, hitting her now bare clit, making her eyes roll back just slightly.

"For you? Always."

Grabbing a condom, I tear it open and roll it on, all while she watches me with intrigue. Lifting her up, I angle my cock at her entrance and pull her down in one quick motion, filling her to the brim in one motion.

"Cade," she groans, her voice raspy as she stills, adjusting to the sudden intrusion. "You're so fucking big."

"I told you to get ready for my cock, Tink," I growl. "Now fuck me like you've dreamed about, show me exactly how you want me."

Her eyes darken as her hips roll, each motion bringing me in deep, rubbing against her clit while she tries to find her rhythm. I bring my thumb down, gathering wetness before sliding it against her clit, the pressure just enough to drive her wild.

"You feel so good," she groans, leaning forward to kiss me.

Our tongues tangle and teeth clash as I move to grip both her hips, lifting her and slamming her back down, matching her pace as we both race to the finish line. A faint flush on her cheeks tells me she's getting close. Her movements turn frantic as she chases her release, and when she squeezes my cock, I know it's here.

"Come for me, Tink," I growl, pulling back from her lips. "Scream my name and let every one of your neighbors know exactly who you belong to."

With my words acting like a match to gasoline, she combusts, dragging me over the edge with her. By the time she's done, she collapses on me, her head on my shoulder, her breathing heavy. Instead of feeling the urge to lift her off me and leave, I want to stay.

Chapter 17

Gwen

Ever since Cade and I spent the night together, I've been in the best mood—of course, it helps that I had the day off. Today is no different, even if it is also stressful, with Kennedy's surgery happening. I figured we would watch a movie, hang out a bit, and then he would go home. I didn't expect him to spend the next four hours worshiping my body in every position he could think of.

Cowgirl, reverse cowgirl, pretzel dip, lotus... the list goes on, each one more impressive than the last. When we finally went to bed at nearly five in the morning, I fell asleep expecting him to be gone again when I woke up. Imagine my surprise when I roused to find his naked body still wrapped around my own, spooning me.

I had to practically peel his arms off me to get up to use the bathroom, and somehow, he slept through the entire thing. Once he was finally awake, which took a little coaxing from me, we spent the day eating, watching movies, and becoming more familiar with each other's bodies.

It was the first time we've hung out, just the two of us, that hasn't felt forced. We talked about life some, although not too deeply. And we spent most of the time watching *Harry Potter*— while still naked—so it's not surprising we have absolutely nothing figured out. I have no idea where we stand, and it's a little unnerving. Where I'm used to living in a world of black and white, we are surrounded by a sea of gray.

When he was leaving this morning, having spent two nights at my place, he acknowledged that we were in the unknown. He voiced the one thing I needed to hear, though, when he told me that he cared about me enough not to run and wanted to give us time to figure out what this was between us. When he admitted it might not be easy for him and asked for some patience, I knew I would wait it out with him.

I mean, only time will tell how this all plays out. Are we friends who are having fun, messing around until we get this out of our systems? Or have we always been something more and just avoided acknowledging it until it became too much?

So far, this is enough for me. I don't need him to be

Dirty Play

my boyfriend this second. Hell, I'm not even sure I want a boyfriend. How can I work, spend time with friends, *and* have a boyfriend? I barely have enough time outside of work as it is. I just need him to be my Cade—the added orgasms are just a bonus.

I'm walking over to check in with Kennedy one last time before her surgery. They have already started to prep the donor, getting them ready to go, and I can't wipe the smile off my face at the realization that this is all finally happening.

Denise and Josh went up with Kennedy to start helping her get prepped, but not one of them looked nervous. That's not usually the reality with one of these surgeries, but I think they've all struggled with this illness for long enough that even a major surgery feels like a relief because it's a step in the right direction—hopefully, a fresh start.

When I head down the hall toward her room, Dr. Dickhead is walking toward me with a nurse, probably on their way to get ready.

"What are you doing?" he asks, his snippy tone mixed with confusion.

"Oh, I was just checking in with Kennedy one last time," I reply with a smile, not letting his attitude bother me today.

"No."

I turn to look at him, confusion evident on my face, but it's Karla, the nurse standing next to him who speaks up first.

"We've been trying to reach you for a while. A man named Cade has been trying to get a hold of you for the last hour."

"Oh, he can wait until after this. I'll give him a call once her surgery has started," I tell them, turning to look back toward Kennedy's room. I'm sure Cade is just calling to wish me luck. He knows today is a big day.

"No, sweetie, he actually can't," she says, her smile soft. "Why don't you just go talk to him? He's in room 442."

Room 442?

Why would Cade be in room 442?

That's the room the donor is in.

"You must be mistaken," I tell them. "That's the room the donor is in."

Dr. D turns to look at me, an incredulous look on his face. "Cade Williams is the donor," he says in a snarky tone before turning on his heel and walking down the hall toward the operating room.

My heart stops.

This can't be true.

Cade can't be the donor... could he?

Without another thought, I turn and sprint down the hall. I ignore every single rule about running in the hallways. I don't wait for the elevator. I go straight for the stairs, not stopping until I make it to the room. I open the door, expecting to see some random person lying in the bed getting prepped. I'm shocked when I see a pair of warm brown eyes staring back at me, filled to the rim with fear.

"You came," he says quietly, his voice hoarse, breaking my heart.

I walk over to Cade with tears in my eyes, falling to my knees as I grab his hand in mine. I have questions. So many questions. Like, why the fuck is he here? What is he doing donating a kidney? But most importantly, I want to know why the fuck he didn't tell me, especially when we just spent the night together?

"Wh-what are you doing here?"

"By the looks of it, I'm about to have surgery," he says softly, squeezing my hand in his.

"But why?" I ask, ignoring the nurses around us as they get ready to move him to the OR.

"I don't know." He shrugs. "I guess I met a sweet little girl and her mom one night, and she let it slip that she needed a new kidney. I mean, why should I have two perfectly good kidneys while she needs one just to survive? When I found out I was a perfect match, it was a no-brainer."

I just gape at him. He sounds confident, like this is an everyday occurrence, getting ready to be put under for surgery. But he's definitely not confident, I can see it clear as day. I can see it all, the fear in his eyes, the slight tremble in his touch. I can feel it all. Dammit, all

I want is for him to know he's going to be fine—but that it's okay to be scared.

I may be annoyed that he didn't tell me before today—pissed off, even—and I definitely need to know why. But he called for me. He wanted me here with him before he went in, and this vulnerability from him means more than anything else—he's letting me see that he's scared.

I'm scared, too.

"Mr. Williams, we're just about ready to take you back," one of the nurses says with a smile.

I shake my head. "Just give us one moment," I tell her, looking back up at Cade.

"Why didn't you tell me? Who brought you?" I ask, my words hoarse as I watch him squirm, not wanting to make him feel bad but needing to know why he hid this from me. How he could spend basically the last two days with me and not tell me that the surgery I've been so excited about is one that involves him, too.

"You were already so stressed out about Kennedy. I didn't want to give you someone else to worry about. I know how much Kennedy and her family need you, I don't want to add anything else to your plate," he says softly, his eyes drifting away like he can't quite look at me. "I wanted to be strong for you. Besides, Rex already sort of knew. I convinced him to bring me in."

"I worry about a lot of people, Cade. I worry about my patients, my friends, all of them. What makes you think I wouldn't worry about you, too?"

Dirty Play

"I know you would—I just don't think I deserve it."

My heart breaks even further, knowing that this big, sweet teddy bear of a man doesn't think he's deserving of someone to care about him. What has he gone through that makes him think he's not worthy of love? Not worthy of people's time and energy?

I want to be mad at him. I want to yell and let him know how I feel, but when I look at him all I can see is a man baring his heart to me, even if it is a bit of an unconventional situation. What kind of friend would I be if I got mad or, even worse, walked away?

No, now I need to show him that I'm here and that nothing he does or has done will make him unworthy of me being right here with him.

"What changed?" I ask, urging him on, knowing we are seconds away from them kicking me out and bringing him up to surgery.

"I just wanted to fix something I broke, and helping Kennedy seems like a good place to start. But when I got here, and they started telling me what they were going to do... I freaked out. All I could think about was that I wanted to talk to you one more time, that I needed to see your face just once more... that it might help me believe it would be okay," he tells me, the nervousness apparent in his voice.

"It will be, Cade, and lucky for you, now I'll be waiting. I'll go let Rex know I'm here and give him updates if he'd like," I tell him. Standing up, I lean forward, surprising us both when I lay a soft, chaste kiss on his lips. "I'll see you when you wake up, Grumps."

With that, I watch as they wheel him out, leaving me with the next four hours to stress eat and try to stay focused on work.

Keeping my mouth shut about Cade being in the hospital was more difficult than I expected, especially with our group of friends. It's nice to have Rex, but it's not the same as if I had Sawyer or Cassie. The day of his surgery was easy enough because I was at work and ran around until it was done, then spent the rest of the day making sure both he and Kennedy were okay.

After that, it became more challenging because I had so many questions about his plan once he was released. I couldn't just invite myself over to his house and force him to let me take care of him. I've heard the guys talk about Cade, how even they've barely been to his house, and that he's for sure never brought a woman there.

Ever.

I wanted to call them, text Harris, and let him know what was going on, but Cade made me promise not to. He didn't care that I was just trying to help, that his friends cared about him and deserved to know, especially when he needed some support. He still said no,

Dirty Play

that they had their own stuff going on, and it was bad enough he had to bug Rex with it.

At least I know he wasn't originally planning on going into that surgery with no one knowing what was happening.

I spent more time with Cade after surgery, checking in with him on my breaks, sneaking in afterward to snuggle him, making sure he knew he wasn't alone. I also made sure to pass along updates about Kennedy. Denise wanted to make sure he knew how she was doing—that she was still recovering but that her body seemed to be accepting the transplant so far.

But now it's the day he's getting discharged, and I need to know what his plan is. Walking into his room —on my day off, mind you—I smile when I see him sitting up. These last couple of days were a bit rough with the pain management—in other words, he thought he was too badass to need pain medication and would be able to tough it out.

Spoiler alert: he was not that badass and proceeded to press the nurse call button at least forty-seven times between two and three in the morning, getting both of us in trouble because I was still visiting him.

We ended up having to play catch up with his meds to try and get ahead of the pain, and it made for a rough go there for a while.

"Hey, you. Are you ready to bust out of here?" I ask, sitting on the side of his bed as he gives me a smile.

"Been ready," he grumbles, his hand grabbing for my leg to give it a quick squeeze.

Things have seemed normal between us these last few days, and it's been nice. Although I think part of it is that he's been in a hospital bed recovering so there's really been no time for anything past a few stolen kisses and *lots* of snuggles.

That's not to say that he hasn't been flirty and suggestive every once in a while, making me blush more than once, which Mariah has gotten a kick out of. Plus, he's been a lot touchier these past few days, grabbing my hand or kissing my cheek, pretty much anything he could do to have a physical connection with me. I would even catch him tracing circles on my bare skin—the feeling of his fingertips running against the inside of my wrist had me shivering, his touch hot against my skin, yet I felt goosebumps everywhere.

But that's how it's been this last week since surgery. Now, we're about to leave, and I have no idea what's about to happen. Is he going to run for the hills, regretting everything between us? Or will he stand beside me like he said, promising to wade through this mess to see what we could be?

I haven't missed the way he's been looking at me; the tiny glances he sneaks my way while I'm talking to his doctors. Or the way his eyes light up when I laugh at something he's said. He's confusing as hell, but I'm starting to wonder if maybe Sawyer was onto something. Although maybe it's not Cade who's like an ogre... perhaps it's our relationship that has layers. We have this vision of what everything is between us, but it's possible we can't see the whole picture.

Maybe we just need to peel it back until we can see what's been hiding inside.

"Well, I heard they were getting everything signed off for you to leave, so hopefully, it'll be in the next hour," I tell him, playing with the blanket on his bed. "Have you figured out what your plan is? I have the next three days off, but after that, what are you going to do?"

"I actually wanted to talk to you about that. It's kind of a crazy idea, so I know there's a chance it won't work, but... uh... is there any chance you might be able to take a little time off?"

"What do you mean, take a little time off?" I ask, expectantly, not sure where this conversation is going and what this has to do with his recovery. "I already have the next three days off to make sure you're settled."

"How about two weeks?" he asks, his eyes scrunched like he can avoid my reaction.

My jaw drops. "Two weeks? What for?"

Before he can answer, the discharge nurse walks in with his paperwork, and I swear I hear Cade sigh in relief.

"You're finally free," she says with a smile before turning to me. "Will you be driving him, Gwen?"

"Yes, Clara, I will. I can't let this fool try to drive

himself because, believe me, he'd try," I say with a smile, but I hope he can hear the truth in my words. I know damn well he's stupid enough to do it himself.

Probably some bullshit excuse of not wanting to inconvenience anyone.

Which is why I'm not telling him that I'm taking him to my place, not his.

This way, he can't argue.

Chapter 18

Gwen

After we got to my apartment and got everything brought upstairs, I convinced Cade to have a movie day on the couch with me. I grabbed every blanket and pillow in my apartment and pushed both couches together to make a big bed. It looks like heaven.

Cade kept trying to help, but after I threatened to call Harris and tell him about the surgery myself, he finally listened and got comfortable while I set everything up.

Little did I know that his version of comfort leaves him in a pair of gray sweats slung low on his hips and a backwards hat—nothing else. And damn, he looks good. The bandage on his left side is enough to force me to keep my distance, though.

An hour later, we have snacks on the coffee table,

the next Harry Potter on the TV, and we're both snuggled into the couch. Not actually snuggling together... but right next to each other, and at the moment, it's enough. I can tell that Cade's in pain, but he's been trying to rely less on pain medication. I try to explain to him that he's done more moving around today than he has in a while, so he's going to be in more pain, but he just growls something about being strong enough to handle it before stealing the bowl of popcorn for himself.

Whatever, tough guy.

"Uh, so remember earlier, at the hospital, when I asked if you could take some time off?" Cade asks nervously.

"Yeah?"

"Do you also remember how I mentioned that my sister Kylie was planning something for my parents' fortieth anniversary?"

"Yeah?" I say, still confused how any of this involves me.

"That party just so happens to be planned for next Saturday."

"Are you fucking kidding me, Cade? Why the hell would you have a major surgery before you're supposed to be traveling home? How, exactly, were you planning to drive there? That's at least a seven-hour drive!" I yell, moving to stand up, but his hand grabs mine, stopping me, and pulling me back against the

Dirty Play

couch. "What does any of this have to do with me, Cade?"

His mouth opens and closes a few times before he finally talks. "The surgery couldn't wait; we both know that. I think we're both aware of the concerns they had for Kennedy if she'd gone much longer without a transplant. The sooner she had the surgery, the better her chances for a full recovery," Cade says.

I'm guessing there's more to his story, this isn't just about the last two weeks, but I'm sure he'll tell me on his own time. And I know he's not wrong—she needed the surgery, badly. Just the day before the surgery, we had a bit of a scare—luckily, they were able to stabilize her enough to have the surgery. I can't imagine what it would be like to have a perfect match, surgery scheduled, and not be able to go through with it because your body isn't strong enough.

That would be brutal, so I'm thankful for Cade for putting aside his own personal plans to help her. But that leads me back to this situation. What does this have to do with me?

"That still doesn't explain why I would need to take two weeks off?"

"So, you can go with me," he says matter-of-factly. Like he didn't just spring a two-week trip back to his hometown—six hours away. A trip where I'd meet his parents for their fortieth anniversary, sprung on me so casually you'd think he was asking what I wanted for lunch.

"You want me to do what?!" I ask, my voice starting to rise again, but his look stops me.

"I need you, Gwen. I can't go back there alone," he says, a sad look crossing his face before he shakes it off.

"But—" I start, but he cuts me off.

"Look... like I've said, I haven't been back home in years. For a lot of reasons, but mainly because a lot of shit happened, and well, I'm not entirely sure my parents want to see me as much as Kylie thinks they do. But on the off chance that she's right, I feel like I do need to be there. My parents sacrificed so much for me when I was growing up to make sure I could be my best at hockey. I feel like this is the least I could do."

"But why me? Why not bring Rex? Or Harris... isn't he from there?" I ask, not understanding why I'm the best person for this adventure when there are people he's known longer who don't have to take time off to go with.

"They're not you."

It's like his whole demeanor is one big contradiction. His eyes are soft, jaw clenched. But he continues on. "This is a big celebration for them. They have been married for forty years and have three grown-ass children, and if it means a lot to them, I should try to be there to celebrate. There are already enough people who won't be able to make it—I don't want to be one more."

I stare at him, unsure what to say. The only thing I

do know is that now I have to figure out how to convince Dr. Dickhead to give me two weeks off to take care of this grump. In his hometown. All the while trying to figure out what the heck we are doing.

Shit.

"Fine. But we're taking your car, and since I have to drive I get to pick the music. And we're stopping to get snacks... but like, road trip snacks, not that healthy shit you try to pass off as a snack. These are non-negotiable," I finally say, not missing the way his face lights up. "I'm sure I'll come up with more stipulations—those will be non-negotiable as well."

"Thanks, Tink," Cade says before his hand slips behind my head, turning me toward him. "I owe you one." He leans in, pressing his lips to mine in a slow, languid kiss that has my toes curling, but then, as quickly as it began, he's pulling back.

With a quick smile, he wraps his arm around me and pulls me in, pressing play on the next movie. We spend the next couple of hours watching the third and fourth *Harry Potter* movies—ordering pizza in the middle, which we've already devoured. Now that I've made sure Cade's had all of his medication, I'm going to be surprised if he stays up much longer.

To the surprise of no one, Cade falls asleep within minutes of starting the next movie, his head resting against my shoulder while he snores softly. He looks so peaceful—so happy, and I love getting to see him like this. It's such a contrast to his usual grumpy demeanor, never feeling worthy of those close to him, ignoring all of us who try to show him just how deserving he is.

Forcing myself to stop staring for a minute, I grab my phone and shoot a text out to the girls.

Me: I might need another girls' night soon.

Cassie: How about later this week?

Me: I'll be in Ivy Falls then.

Sawyer: Ivy Falls? Isn't that where Harris and Cade are from?

Cassie: GWEN. WHY ARE YOU GOING THERE?

Me: Cade sort of asked me to.

Ellie: We're gunna need a little more than that.

Me: He's still recovering from surgery so he figured it would be easiest to have help while he traveled home.

Sawyer: SURGERY? What the hell is happening? Why am I just finding out about all of this now?

Me: Come over in the morning? I'll explain everything.

Cassie: You better be ready to play 672 questions because I need all the details.

Setting my phone down, I look back over at Cade, who is still sleeping peacefully. I definitely don't mind that he's resting because it means I can finally get an up close and personal look at his tattoos. I've been dying to do this since I saw them the first night we hooked up. I've seen his full sleeves up close before—a combination of different shapes and hockey designs, a deep black against his skin, they're beautiful. But I've never gotten a good look at his chest piece. The shapes spill out from his left arm over to that side of his chest, where there are trees—evergreen trees, six of them. Two big trees, three small trees, and one last tree off to the side, all by itself.

It reminds me of those family bumper stickers. It's beautiful, even if I don't understand it.

Unable to help myself, I take the Sharpie I've been coloring with and start drawing on his skin, in the blank space on his arms between his other tattoos. I start slowly, pressing lightly as I draw a small circle to start a flower, stopping to see if he wakes up.

Thankfully, his breathing remains steady, his soft snores continuing, letting me know I can keep going. After that, I start to draw more at a time, slowly filling the space on his forearm with little flowers. It's the only thing I can think to draw that doesn't look like a four-year-old who tried to draw with their eyes closed.

Thirty minutes later I've drawn tiny little flowers throughout most of the blank spaces on his arm while watching *Harry Potter and the Order of the Phoenix*. I'm instantly reminded that Dolores Umbridge is one of my least favorite characters in these movies—only behind Bellatrix, of course.

When I grab my phone and shine the light on his arm, I can't help the giggle that escapes when I look at my handiwork. The stark contrast between his dark, detailed designs and my thin-lined flowers looks silly, yet somehow it works perfectly, almost like they were meant to be there.

A piece of me loves the fact that I marked him, that somehow, maybe, I can make him mine.

But that thought scares me as much as it excites me. I've spent years single. Years dating only my job, spending my free time thinking about work and never going out on dates. With the help of Dr. Dickhead, I got it in my head that I couldn't be good at my job *and* be a good girlfriend.

But what if I can do both?

I mean... I have been spending more and more time with Cade these last couple of weeks and I've had no complaints about slacking off at work. I've still spent the same amount of time at work. In fact, I even picked up a couple of shifts this week.

It helped that Cade was in another wing of the hospital and I could sneak off to go see him on my breaks if I was already there—but that's beside the point.

I haven't felt the stress that I expected to feel if I tried to spend time with someone I liked while trying to remain devoted to my job. Cade and I are not dating, we're not anything except two people who enjoy each other's company, both dressed and naked. But the time we've spent together is similar to what I'd spend with someone if I were dating them.

So... maybe I can actually have both? Maybe this thing between Cade and I really can be something more. Not just something we're passing through, but maybe a destination.

Cade is definitely someone I can imagine being my destination, someone I can enjoy life with.

He's quickly becoming more to me, and I'm afraid I'm too far in to try to stop it.

Chapter 19

Cade

I finally convinced Gwen to come with me on this trip. Even after she agreed, I still had to promise that one day she'd hear more about my family. We faced a little hurdle when her initial request for leave got denied, but when she mentioned that the doc was a huge fan of mine, I used it to my advantage and asked him myself. All I had to do was tell him I needed help with travel for my parents... Oh, and I slipped in a pair of tickets for the first home game next season.

Oh well, it's worth it.

I had her drop me off at my place so I could get everything packed while she went back to her place to hang out with the girls for a bit before we left for Ivy Falls.

"What the hell do you mean you donated a kidney?" Harris barks into the phone.

"I don't know how else to say that... it's self-explanatory," I retort, grabbing my duffle bag from the closet.

"Start from the beginning. I need to hear the whole story before I decide if I'm calling my mom."

"Fuck off, Harris, you wouldn't."

"Wanna bet, fucker?"

"No. No, I actually don't," I tell him, grabbing my toiletries and tossing them into my bag.

"Good. And actually, hold on story time, I'll be there in five," he says, disconnecting the call.

God dammit.

While I wait, I start throwing clothes into the duffle bag. Well... setting them in gently, not moving too much, and making sure not to lift anything over ten pounds—and whatever other bullshit Gwen said before she left. I've still got a few more hours before we head out. I've timed it so that way we arrive before it gets too late but not too early that we'll have to face the whole inquisition tonight.

I walk around, putting everything away until I hear a knock on my door less than ten minutes later. I guess it's time to face Harris.

Shit, I thought I had more time, he must've been closer than I thought.

I let him in and immediately see the concern on his face as he quickly checks over me from head to toe.

"Aww, Harry, were you worried about me?" I joke, and the concern is replaced by anger.

Dirty Play

"Fucking hell, Cade, you can't just drop this shit on me. You had surgery? What the fuck? That kind of thing is planned in advance. *Especially when it's something like donating a damn organ*," Harris snaps.

Eyebrows raised, I just stare down at him. "You done yet?"

"If you hadn't just donated a kidney, I'd punch you in it," Harris seethes, barreling past me into my apartment, heading straight for the living room.

Shutting the door, I follow him, taking my spot on the couch while he takes a seat across from me, elbows resting on his knees, fingers intertwined like he's holding himself back from that kidney punch.

His concern and the fact that he's so angry at me for not talking to him—I'm feeling some things over it. For one, like I'm a pretty big asshole for not telling my friends about this, especially him. I can only imagine what's going to happen when I actually see my family and they find out.

Between my mom and Ky, future me might be fucked because they don't mess around. Just like Gwen, which is part of the reason I like having her around so much.

The other feeling, though, is that I'm cared for. This fucked up situation is making me realize that these wonderful people—my best friends—that I keep at arm's length, really care about me. They think I'm worthy of their time... so why the fuck can't I believe it's possible?

"We calm now?" I grin, intentionally poking the bear on purpose while also trying to give him some time to be pissed at me if he needs it. It's what I love about Harris—he doesn't hold grudges—he just needs a little time to fume and call you a dick, and then he's back to being happy.

"Yes... but I won't be if you don't tell me how the hell this happened so quickly. We're barely a month out of the season and you've had a major surgery, and apparently, you're shacking up with our friend, and you haven't thought to really tell any of us? What the fuck, Cade? How about we start with that?"

Okay, maybe he's a little more pissed off than usual.

So, I listen to his words and give him what he wants. The story—starting at the beginning, from the first night I spent with Gwen. He knew most of it, but since it's how I ended up meeting Kennedy, I figured it would be helpful for him to see the whole picture. And this way I'm also telling him about Gwen and the mess I'm making. The big clusterfuck of a mess that's become my life. By the time I'm done explaining it all, and I mean all of it, he's staring at me with wide eyes. I guess that's probably the most personal information I've willingly shared in... well, about eleven years.

"Oh... fuck," Harris finally says, running his hand through his hair. "I mean... I get it. Like, I get why you did it. I bet it kind of feels like that part of your life came full circle a bit."

I shrug. I had that thought once or twice, and I'd be

Dirty Play

lying if I said it didn't take a tiny bit of weight off my shoulders. Knowing that I was still able to help someone made me feel like a little less of a failure.

Doesn't mean I haven't spent every single day since *that* day wishing Veronica was here.

"I want to be pissed at you, and I am, but not because you had this surgery. I know you'll be good to go. I'm just pissed you didn't tell me before. Actually, I'm pissed you didn't tell anyone. I can only imagine how that felt for Gwen, getting the news just minutes before you went to the OR. If I were her, I'd have offed you myself. Then you would've had two kidneys to donate."

"It was definitely touch and go for a bit… especially because she doesn't know about Veronica."

"You've gotta stop this, Cade," Harris begins, shoulders slumped like he's given up. "You need to stop keeping all of us just out of reach. We all care about you—more than you realize. You're so dense. You've made yourself believe that you can't be loved—that you aren't worthy, even though some of us have spent years trying to prove to you that you are. It's exhausting. But what's really tiring is seeing one of the best people I've ever known—the most selfless and loving person—cock block his own happiness."

"I—I should have told—" I start, but Harris goes on.

"I'm not done yet," he grumbles. "It's time for me to lecture you some more, this time on Gwen and your family. You made the choice to start something with Gwen. Something we've all known should happen, but you were too oblivious to notice. And now that you've started it, it's up to you to figure your shit out so you don't fuck it up. You both deserve to give this a shot, especially because it's something you've danced around for at least two years."

I sigh, knowing he's right. The more time I spend with Gwen, the more I realize just how much I shoved down. I never allowed myself to think about how deep my feelings for her went—something I'm now trying to uncover, and I know it's worth it.

"I know. I'm not going to sit here and say I'll be great at it or that I'm not going to fuck it all up... but I do know that she's the only person who's made me feel alive since Veronica died. When she died, she took a piece of me—the piece that made me feel alive. I became a shell, destined to go through life but never truly live. But Gwen—"

"Made you feel like you could breathe for the first time? Like you've never truly known what life was supposed to feel like until you met her?" Harris adds, his face solemn, and I know he's thinking about *her* as he says this—the one we're not allowed to talk about. The same one I know he snuck off with at Mama Lockwood's charity event last year.

But he's not wrong.

"Exactly," I say.

"Then do me a favor, brother. Don't fuck this up."

Dirty Play

"I'll do my best not to."

"That's all anyone can ask," he says, a little smirk on his face now. "As for your family, I could sit here and lecture you all day, but we all know the second you get home, Kylie is going to let you have it. She's nice enough to not lecture you from afar. But face to face... you're fucked."

I groan because he's right... I don't feel dread this time.

I'm almost looking forward to seeing them.

After Harris leaves, I use the last of my time before Gwen gets here to run to the corner store down the street. She mentioned stopping to get snacks, but I figure it might be a nice surprise to have some ready for her.

Besides, I know exactly what she'd get, so I might as well get it for her. If she knew I was going out alone and walking this far, she'd probably kill me, so I'm trying to make it a quick trip.

I'm not quite as quick as usual, but I still make it to the store in record time. Grabbing a basket, I head to the snack aisle and get to work. I start by grabbing her favorites, Flamin' Hot Lime Cheetos, Extra Toasty Cheez-Its, and *all* the candy—especially the sour kind, including extra Sour Punch Blue Raspberry Straws because they're her kryptonite. Once the basket is filled with drinks and snacks, I head over to the register to pay right as I receive a text from Gwen that she's on her way.

Shit, time to see just how quickly I can make it home.

Chapter 20

Gwen

"So let me get this straight. We've gone from a one-night stand, friends with benefits situation, where he bailed in the middle of the night, to long walks and secret hookups that you damn well should have told us about. And now you're going home with him to meet mom and dad?" Sawyer asks as she sits on my bed, her eyes wide as she attempts to summarize the entire story I just told them.

"Let's not forget the kidney donation," Ellie adds with a smirk that tells me she's loving this. Trevor and Ellie haven't been together for that long, but she fits into our group like a missing piece. Luckily, she's stuck with us forever, though, since they're having a baby later this year.

Sawyer, Cassie, and Ellie all came over this morning after our text convo last night. I'm pretty sure that the second I mentioned I was going to Ivy Falls with Cade, they set their alarms and made sure to show up with their questions locked and loaded—and snacks at the ready, because Cassie gets me.

"I mean... yeah. After that first night, we didn't see each other again for quite a while. But then Sawyer's big ass mouth told Cade I would be walking home when I got off at midnight, and then he became, like intent on making sure that I was always safe, so he started walking me home."

"That's actually pretty fucking cute." Cassie smirks. "I mean, it's obvious that man is crazy about you. We've all known that for quite some time, but the fact that he's so protective is hot. He's like your guard dog."

"It really is, though. It makes it even hotter that he's so much taller than you, helps with the guard dog vibe," Ellie says, giggling. "Like a big pit bull."

"No, pit bulls are cute and cuddly and will pretty much treat most strangers like their long-lost friend. They want to snuggle anytime, anyplace, and with anyone." Cassie laughs. "That man is like a Rottweiler or a German Shepherd. You'd have to be dumb as fuck to walk up and try to hurt someone they care about, and once they love you, they're loyal for life."

"See, that's a much better comparison than an onion, Sawyer." I smirk, which earns me a bag of chips to the face. Lucky for me, I'm hungry.

Cade behaving like a Rottweiler is a comparison that I can see. They're basically big ass teddy bears with scary looking eyebrows. They seem a lot more vicious than they really are... unless you fuck with them.

"But what does this mean?" Sawyer interjects. "Like... all of this has happened, you two have crossed these lines, physically, but has anything changed between you guys outside of that? Aside from the obvious—*he invited you back home with him.*"

"I know... I'm honestly still shocked that he invited me. We've talked—well, sort of—but it's enough, for now. Whatever this is, we want to continue doing it and see what happens. But we haven't labeled it. I know that sounds dumb as fuck, but I don't want to push him. I'm basically treating him like a scared animal. No sudden movements, no loud voices, and definitely no asking Cade to be my damn boyfriend."

"That doesn't sound dumb at all. It actually kind of makes sense," Sawyer says. "You can tell that man is closed off, has been since before we've known him. So I guess at this point, progress is progress if you're making your way through those walls. Do whatever works for you both. Just be sure you're getting what you need from him too, and I don't just mean in the bedroom."

"I have zero complaints in that department. As for the two of us? I mean, only time will tell, but things seem different this time."

Walking into Cade's apartment with a suitcase and bags, I can't help but notice the doorman's shocked expression when I tell him I am heading up to meet Cade. It looks like he's seen a ghost, enough so that it almost makes me laugh out loud. I guess everyone wasn't lying when they said he never brings women over.

Internally, I'm kicking my feet and giggling that I get to be the one he brings home—both to his apartment and to his mama's, but I refuse to let that show as I raise my hand to knock on his door. Before my hand connects, the door swings open like he's been waiting for me.

He looks hot as fuck in his usual gray sweatpants that fit just right and a fitted black tee with the Cyclones logo that shows off every muscle. He's basically a walking sex ad, and I'm not sure I know how to behave right now.

That backwards hat does it for me every time. I've never once shied away from letting him see my approval, and that was before we got together. Now that we've seen each other naked, my cheeks flush, and I'm almost embarrassed at how badly I want him right now.

"Hey, Tink," Cade says, bag slung over his shoulder, with a smile on his face that tells me he just watched me check him out.

"As much as I love that you're happy to see me, get that damn bag off your shoulder before you strain yourself. We don't need you hurting yourself further."

His smile widens as he drops his bag and pulls me into a hug. I'm not used to this type of affection from Cade. We've never really hugged before. We kind of just went from not touching to fucking, not a whole lot of stuff in between.

"Hug me back, dammit," he grumbles, noticing my arms still t-rexed to the side. I oblige, wrapping my arms around him. It's surprising—his arms wrapped around me and his chin on my head, feel a lot like home.

"Good girl," he mutters, and I want to melt into a puddle at his feet. But then I remember he's still recovering from surgery that was not even two weeks ago, and I hold myself back.

"What's this for?" I ask, my voice quiet. I'm doing my best not to show him just how badly he's affecting me. He's trying, sneaking in a few kisses here and there, but I stop him anytime he tries anything more. The man is insatiable, and I already know he'll end up popping his stitches if I let him get naked with me.

Not to mention, I'm still a little hurt about him not telling me he was having a damn major surgery. Was I just going to find out the next time I saw him? I mean, the man has barely missed a single night of walking me home, and if I didn't find out, what was he planning to do in the days he spent in the hospital?

"I've missed touching you," he says, surprising the

shit out of me with his honesty, but I bury my face in his chest to hide my smile. "Plus, I really need to apologize."

"For what, exactly?" I say, pulling back just enough to look at him, his arms still wrapped around me, now resting on my ass.

"For not telling you about the surgery, I know I fucked that up. I definitely shouldn't have let you find out about all of that while you were at work. You deserve better than that," Cade rasps out, his voice cracking, and I can tell this isn't easy for him. But he doesn't run, and for that I'm thankful.

"You're right. I deserve better," I tell him, his eyes widening at my bluntness. But I lean up and give him a chaste kiss on his lips before looking him square in the eye. "And next time, you'll do better. Now, let's get loaded up and on the road. I need snacks pronto."

Cade turns, grabs another bag, and looks at me sheepishly. "I think I've got us covered," he utters, sounding quieter than normal. "But if I forgot anything, we can stop. At this point, we're going to be there by ten, so we've got plenty of time."

I peek in the bag that's filled with every snack I can imagine, but the Flamin' Hot Lime Cheetos and Sour Punch Blue Raspberry Straws stick out, proving that this man really hasn't missed a single thing.

How did I miss just how attentive he is?

Unable to stop myself, I pull him in for a hug as

Dirty Play

gently as I can. "You're really just a constant surprise, Mr. Williams."

With Morgan Wallen playing through the speakers, we finally make our way off the freeway toward the town of Ivy Falls.

I'm absolutely dead tired, especially since I didn't want to stop more than once, which was for dinner in the middle of nowhere, not exactly my idea of excitement.

"So, are you going to tell me anything about your family, or are you just going to make me walk in blind?" I break the silence, needing to talk to wake up a bit.

Long drives at night aren't exactly my favorite, but Cade's been doing a pretty good job of keeping me company and playing DJ, taking every single one of my requests. But now I need some info.

"What do you want to know?" he grumbles, adjusting himself in his seat to better face me, his back against the door.

"Why don't we start with who I'm going to be meeting," I say, my eyes on the road, trying to see where I'm going. The further we drive, the fewer street lights there are, making it damn near impossible to see.

"Well, we'll be staying at my parents' house, so there's my mom, Shelly—she'll be the one to welcome you with open arms and a smile on her face. She's a good one. I feel like you'll get along with her great."

"She sounds lovely. I'm excited to meet her."

"Then there's my dad, Carson. He's quiet and more reserved than my mom but once you crack him, he's funny. Really funny. It's more of a dry humor that can often come off as rude, but damn, it's funny."

"Well, at least now I know where you get that from." I look over at him and wink, and he just grins and shrugs. "Is there anyone else?"

"My brother, Vince, and sister, Kylie, live in town, so I'm sure you'll meet them tomorrow. They're both younger than me. Kylie is twenty-seven, and Vince is twenty-five. Don't be surprised if Kylie pulls you to the side for 'girl talk.' She can talk to *anyone*. You'll find that out right away. She might come on strong, but she means well."

Cade is already standing up for people he hasn't spent time with in years. People he's pushed away but is still putting first. It's in moments like this that he shows me the little parts of him that I've always longed to know. The parts that show me just how good of a man he really is.

"Well, that doesn't seem that intimidating. I mean, I'm still not a fan of meeting new people, let alone four new people in one day, but we'll figure it out."

"Yeah, just ignore my brother, though. From what I hear, he's broody and grumpy all the time."

"Again, sounds like someone I know," I joke,

Dirty Play

earning me a glare. "What? Are you worried I'm going to flirt with him, too?"

His hand quickly moves from his lap to mine, squeezing my thigh, high enough that I can almost feel his fingers against my pussy.

"No, I'm not afraid of you flirting with him because you won't. You're mine, Tink. Even if we haven't figured out what that means yet, you're mine."

"But—"

"I don't share, Tink," Cade growls, cutting me off.

His grip tightens on my thigh and I squeeze my legs together, my clit throbbing, just craving his touch. It's been too long since I've touched him, and damn, I miss him. It's hard forcing myself to wait, but I couldn't live with it if I hurt him.

I just smile, trying to hide my blush, and continue driving. Deep down I'm kicking my feet and squealing after hearing him call me his.

"I can't see anything, Cade. There are no freaking streetlights out here," I groan, only fifteen minutes later. I'm ready to fall asleep just about anywhere. My body doesn't do well when I switch between night and day shifts, and I usually need a good night to crash to get back to normal.

"No shit, Gwen, we're in the middle of nowhere," Cade responds, obviously getting tired as well. It's been a busy day for him, and whether or not he'll admit it, he's still recovering and needs to take it slow.

When we pulled off the highway about thirty

minutes ago, I thought we'd be there in minutes. I didn't realize that we still had almost an hour left to drive, all of which is on this tiny little road that has no lights. I'm worried about driving us off a cliff.

I doubt there is even a cliff around, but I'm convinced that if there were one, I'd head straight for it.

"Take a left here," he says the moment a street sign pops up. Thankfully, the reflection from his headlights is just enough to make the turn smooth. We learned the hard way that if I don't turn slow enough, it's a bit rough for him.

"I don't know how you get around out here. I'd always be lost."

"I grew up out here, and trust me, I spent many nights as a teenager driving these roads," Cade says nonchalantly like he didn't just send my mind into overdrive.

The thought of him driving these roads with a girl makes me grumpy. I don't like the thought of them driving these roads at night, alone, looking for a quiet place to fool around. Yeah, I don't like that thought at all.

It makes me angry and, dare I say... jealous?

That's not an emotion I'm used to.

"Damn, woman, if you think any louder, the whole town will hear." Cade chuckles, his eyes darkening as he watches me, a little hint of a smirk playing on his mouth, and I wonder if he actually knows what I was just thinking about.

"I—I don't know what you're talking about," I grumble as a blush rises on my cheeks. Now I hate these dark ass roads just a teeny bit less.

"When we were growing up, Vince and I used to fuck around on these back roads. We both had 4Runners, so we would always drive around like a bunch of idiots," Cade explains. "Before you even ask, yes, we would have girls with us."

At his words, my stomach turns. Hearing him say the words somehow makes it that much worse.

"The only girls Vince and I ever brought back here were our sisters."

"It wouldn't have mattered anyway. It's not like I'm jealous or anything," I state, keeping my eyes forward as we pull up to a big gate that is thankfully open.

It hits me all of a sudden that he just said sisters. As in plural. This is the first time since I've known Cade—especially since I've known about Kylie—that he's mentioned Veronica, even if indirectly.

"Whatever you say, Tink." Cade laughs a low, happy laugh that makes me smile. Even knowing he doesn't believe my lies doesn't matter because seeing this man happy has me forgetting what we were even talking about. "This is my parents' driveway, follow it right up here and park on the right."

As we make it around the corner, I see his parents' home. I was expecting a small ranch house, but this place is stunning. The whole house is white with black trim and has a porch that wraps around the entire thing. I'm in love with it.

"This is beautiful, Cade," I say as we park.

"It really is," Cade says as I turn the car off.

Reaching across the center console, I grab his hand, giving it a quick squeeze, reminding him he's not alone.

"You ready?" I ask.

"As ready as I'll ever be," he says before opening his door.

Chapter 21

Cade

Walking up to my parents' house after not being here for years feels weird. I feel like I shouldn't be here, like there's a reason I've been gone so long. But Gwen grabs my hand as we climb the steps toward the door.

It isn't until I reach for the door that she lets go, which I understand, but I still miss her touch. The door immediately swings open, my mom standing on the other side, her smile so wide you'd think she just won the lottery.

"My boy," she says, stepping out and wrapping me in a hug. The kind of hug that only moms can give, the kind that makes you feel safe and loved. "I'm so happy you're here. I've missed you so much."

I feel something crack inside of me. I've missed these hugs.

Stepping back, smile still in place, her hands

squeeze my arms while she looks me up and down like she can't believe I'm here.

Me either, Mom.

"And who's this young lady with you?" she says with a smile, turning to look at Gwen and immediately pulling her into a hug, just as expected.

"Thanks for coming with Cade," she says, pulling us both inside. "Both rooms down at the end are set up for you. I'm sure you're tired, so make yourselves comfortable."

"Thanks, mom," I say, yawning now that I'm thinking about how tired I really am.

"Hey, son," a low voice says from behind me.

I turn around and see my dad. He looks good—looks strong—and the smile on his face makes me think he's happy, which makes me happy.

"Hey, Dad," I say, stepping closer and pulling him into a hug. He's not a hugger like my mom, so it's quick, but it's my first hug from him in years, which hurts.

"It's good to see you. Thanks for driving all this way."

"Of course, I didn't want to miss this one," I tell him truthfully.

"I'm glad," he says with a smile. "Now get some sleep and show this young lady where she can lie down. It can't be easy driving with you for that long... I know how you get," he teases.

Dirty Play

THE FIRST THING I NOTICE WHEN I WAKE UP IS THAT I have something hard pressing against me, specifically against my cock. But then the memories of last night come rushing back, and I remember how I crept in here at one in the morning because I couldn't sleep.

Between the pain from sitting in the car for so long and forgetting to keep up with my meds again, I just couldn't get comfortable. And the anxiety about being back in this house after so long, I just didn't really want to be alone. Thankfully, I was in my old room, and Gwen was in Vince's. A Jack and Jill bathroom in the middle made sneaking over easy.

Not that I needed to *sneak* over to see Gwen—we're grown-ass adults—but damn, I'd at least like to say hello to everyone before they find me in her bed. Even if all we did was sleep.

Gwen wiggles a bit and then freezes, finding my arm draped over her because, apparently, I didn't move at all and stayed spooning her all through the night.

"What're you doing in here, Cade?" she whispers like anyone might hear us here. Vince and I had rooms on the opposite side of the house from the rest of the family. We loved it, and it worked for my mom because she didn't have to smell the stinky boys and their stinky sports equipment all the time—her words, not mine.

"I'm sleeping," I grumble, nuzzling her hair as I pull her in close. I'm sore, and my body definitely hurts, but that won't stop me from cuddling her.

"Yes, thank you for stating the obvious, Mr. Williams. But why are you in my bed when you have a perfectly good one next door?"

"Well, technically, it's my brother's bed."

"*Caaaade*," Gwen whines, "what are your parents going to think of me if they see you in here? They've barely even met me, and for all they know, I'm just here to help you out. Which, if we're being technical, is the reason I'm here."

"You're grumpy in the morning."

"Yes, I need my caffeine, and I'm definitely not going out there until I look presentable," she grumbles, and I know that's her little hint that she needs to get up and get ready unless I want to deal with Grumpy Gwen all day.

"Fine," I agree, pulling my arm back. I move to let her get up, but she surprises me when she flips over and kisses me instead. Not a quick peck either. Her hands find my face and her mouth opens in a slow, languid kiss. This is definitely my type of good morning kiss, only, I'm not ready for it to end.

With my hand in her hair, I pull her in for one more as I get an idea. "Do you trust me?"

She pauses for only a moment before nodding.

"Then get naked."

I watch her as she casually slides off her tank top, showing me her tits. My marks have already disappeared, which just gives me the urge to leave more. She starts untying her shorts, watching me as she bites her lip—that little smirk is my undoing.

I stand and move to the chair at the end of the bed, sitting down to face Gwen, her sexy body almost fully unwrapped now, and I feel like she's a present I'm not allowed to touch.

It's torture.

And it gets even worse when she slides her shorts down, revealing she's bare underneath. My hand slides into my briefs, gripping myself tightly as I watch her scoot up on the bed, leaning back on her elbows to watch me, her excitement palpable.

I know she won't let me touch her, but that doesn't mean I can't still be in control of her orgasms. Her eyes fall to my lap, my hand stroking my dick, and I watch as she clenches her thighs, hiding the one thing I want to see right now.

"Like what you see?" I growl.

"I do."

The side of my lip curls up—her boldness is such a turn on. Lifting my hips, I slide my briefs all the way down and lean back in the chair.

"Is that better?"

"It'd be better if I were sitting on it," Gwen whispers, her eyes never leaving my dick, "but you're not cleared, remember? Not a chance in hell I'm injuring you because we fucked before you were ready. Not sure your doctor would ever let me live that down." She watches intently as I fist myself, sliding my hand up and down as beads of precum start forming.

"What do you have planned for me that I might get injured? It sounds kinky." I grin and watch her blush immediately, the flush taking over her cheeks and spreading down to her breasts—she's so fucking pretty. She looks up at me and smiles, opening her legs, finally showing me exactly what I want. "I may not be cleared to fuck you, but they said nothing about me jerking off. I mean, how do you think I've survived not fucking you this long? But right now... it's not about me. I'm going to make good on a promise and make you come without even touching you."

She quirks an eyebrow at me, obvious disbelief on her face, but there's a glint in her eyes. My girl likes this.

"All you have to do is follow my directions. Can you do that for me?"

Her cheeks pinken, and for a moment, I think she's going to walk away, but she nods and says, "Okay."

"Circle your nipples. I want you to gently tease them with your fingers. But nothing more, Tink."

Her eyes widen, but her fingers start moving up her body, gliding over her stomach until they're cupping her breasts. Her fingers start tracing wide circles around her nipples, teasing herself, and as I start slowly stroking my cock again. The little minx smirks, her eyes locked onto my hand.

"I want you to play with yourself, tease yourself,

Dirty Play

pinch your nipples. Whatever you want, don't hold back. With your other hand, I want you to touch yourself. Lightly circle your clit like you'd imagine my tongue would," I growl, gripping my cock hard. I need to stop stroking or this'll be over before I've even had my fun. It's just so fucking hot seeing her like this.

"Why did you stop?" she whispers. "I want to watch."

"Watch what?" I growl, slowly moving my fist up and down my length again.

"I want to watch you touch yourself. I want to watch you come... while you make me come."

Her words spur me on, my cock hardening even further as I continue to stroke myself. "Like this, Tink? Is this what you want?"

Her eyes darken, and her fingers continue to make small circles against her clit that has her squirming already.

"I need more, Cade. Please."

"What do you want? Do you want to show me what you do when you're thinking about my cock?"

Her nod is frantic, her eyes wild, yet she still waits for direction like the good girl I know she is.

"So obedient when you want to be," I say, my voice hoarse, the tingling sensations already starting at the base of my spine telling me my orgasm is close. Not yet, though. I want to watch her come first. "I want to watch you finger yourself. I want to see what you do when no one's watching. When you're imagining my cock inside of you."

Slowly, she glides her other hand down her body, her pace tortuously slow, but my eyes are locked on, watching everything. When she passes her clit, she slides through her wetness to coat herself and looks over at me, legs spread, and smirks.

I may be in control right now, but we both know who has all the power.

"Like this?" she whispers as she slides two fingers inside herself, eyes fluttering at the intrusion. I can't help myself; I move closer. I want to see her up close and personal. Walking to the end of the bed, I watch her, her eyes glossy as she starts working herself faster and faster, one hand circling her clit and the other fingering herself, now with three fingers. Her soft moans are getting louder, more unguarded the closer she gets.

"Just like that, Tink. You're doing so well," I growl, my fist pumping faster, unable to keep pace. I watch her touch herself, wishing it were my cock as her eyes flutter closed, her body trembling from the start of her orgasm.

"Fuck, I'm—" she starts.

"Eyes open. I want to watch you when you come," I growl and her eyes snap open. "Come for me."

She watches me as she falls apart, and I lean forward, my free hand covering her mouth to muffle

Dirty Play

her screams, her entire body shaking as her orgasm crashes through her.

She looks so fucking perfect.

The sight is enough to bring me to the edge, my fist sliding faster, rougher, bringing me closer and closer. Her freshly fucked look is all I need—three rough strokes later and I'm spilling hot cum all over her stomach.

Her eyes are dark, daring, and I want to push her, climb over her fully, and take her. Instead, I just laugh as I stand up.

"What the fuck just happened?" I ask as I look down at her, her body painted in my cum, her cheeks flush from an orgasm I directed, and her perfect smile wide like she's the happiest person in the world. She looks happy.

She also looks like she's mine.

"Hold on," I say, running to the bathroom and grabbing a wet towel. After cleaning her up, I toss it into the laundry to deal with later.

"Fuck, Tink," I groan, pulling her into me. "Have I told you that you're perfect?"

She looks up at me, stares into my eyes, and smiles. "Not today, but you can do it now."

I lean down and kiss her, my tongue languidly sliding against hers. "You're absolutely perfect."

"You're not too bad yourself," she teases.

"I'd say so. I just made you come with only my words—I'd say I'm pretty fucking awesome."

She blushes, rolling over to get up, but she stops when she's sitting at the edge of the bed, looking back at me.

"Where'd that nickname come from? Why Tink? She's a tiny blonde fairy, and well... I'm quite the opposite of that."

She's not wrong in that aspect, but it's less about what Tink looks like and more about her attitude.

"When I was growing up, my sister, Veronica, was the oldest, so she used to always pick what movie we would watch—she loved Disney movies, specifically anything with a fairy or magic. Her favorites were *Peter Pan* and *Cinderella*, so we watched those both at least one hundred times each," I say, remembering one of the times we watched *Cinderella*, and she sat next to me quoting it line for line like it was her job.

Staring at the ceiling, I think about how to explain this.

"This might not make sense, but Veronica used to give me a hard time. She said I would need someone fierce to put me in my place—someone who could hold their own. One night, when we were teenagers, we were watching *Peter Pan*, and she mentioned Tink would be able to keep me in check and force me not to be so naughty all the time. We all got a good laugh out of it, but the more I thought about it, the more I watched the movie, the more I realized that Tink did have the kind of fierceness that I admired. Flashforward to meeting you. I immediately knew you were

Dirty Play

bold and feisty, and I liked it even when I fought it, so the nickname Tink just sort of happened. It's just funny that we ended up here, doing whatever this is, and you really might be the only woman who can put me in my place."

"How can you be such an asshole sometimes but then you can turn around and be so damn cute and genuine? It's infuriating," she says, but her blush and megawatt smile tell the true story.

"It's a gift and a curse. Now, go on and get ready before my mom gets impatient and comes to find us."

She comes in for a quick kiss, before she stands up, her long t-shirt just the right length to show off her perfect legs and incredible ass, both of which I want to sink my teeth into. Walking toward the bathroom, she smirks. "I'm going to shower. Why don't you head out there, and I'll meet you once I'm ready?"

"Yeah, but you might wanna let me sneak through the bathroom first. Unless you want them all to see me slip out of your room?" Her eyes widen immediately, and I start to laugh as she all but shoves me through the door, locking it behind me.

Chapter 22

Cade

After just a few minutes of indecision, I drag myself out to the kitchen. My parents are sitting at the table, each with a cup of coffee in hand and their usual reading materials. My mom's a reader. Any book she sees, she'll probably read it. My dad, on the other hand, loves reading the paper, always starting his morning with his coffee and the crosswords.

At least, that's how it was when I lived here.

I feel their eyes on me, staring as I walk in. It's my mom who cracks first, standing and running over to me with a smile that both makes me happy and crushes my soul because all I can see is the pain Kylie has been telling me about—the pain I didn't believe existed until I saw it first-hand.

"I was starting to wonder if I dreamed seeing you

last night," my mom says, still hugging me, only letting go when my dad comes over for a hug.

"Hello, son," he says warmly, but it doesn't quite meet his eyes like he's holding back, and it hurts. It makes me wonder if I should've stayed home.

Everyone in my family has the same look in their eyes when they see me, the same look that tells me how much they hold back. It's that look that I've been running from for years, the look that tells me I've disappointed them.

"Hey, dad," I say before grabbing a cup of coffee and starting Gwen's drink.

"It's good to see you. It's been way too long," my mom says as I sit down across from them.

"It has been too long, I—" I start, but she cuts me off.

"No, no. We aren't going to do any of that right now. Right now, I'm just happy you're here. Now, tell me about how you're doing. I feel like I've missed so much."

Now would be the best time to tell them I've had surgery—break the ice before Gwen comes out. But like most times, I chicken out right as the front door opens, and like a tornado, Kylie and Vince come blaring into the house, both scanning their surroundings, obviously looking for me. I see the surprise on each of their faces when they find me actually sitting at the table with our parents.

They probably thought you'd bail, again.

Dirty Play

Kylie runs over and gives me a quick hug before sitting next to me, while Vince passes by, giving my shoulder a squeeze before sitting next to mom. All of them notice as I wince in pain, my side more tender today than yesterday. That damn drive really did me in.

"You good?" my dad asks, a concerned look on his face.

"Uh... yeah. About that, it's kind of part of the reason I'm here... I probably, no—definitely, should've told you guys about this but, uh—I had surgery almost two weeks ago."

Just as expected, they all start talking at once, all trying to be heard, and each of them making sure I know how pissed they are. Which I deserve. After a minute or two of them complaining, the concern and questions start. Their desire to want to understand will always impress me.

"What do you mean you had surgery?" Kylie asks incredulously. "Isn't that something you'd want to tell people about? What kind of surgery?"

Gwen chooses that moment to make her way into the kitchen, thankfully giving me a moment to gather my thoughts as my family all turn to stare at her, curiosity on my parents' faces while Kylie and Vince just look confused. I grab her drink and set it down next to me, her surprised smile the best part of my day so far.

Well...second best.

"Hi, sweetie," my mom says as she stands up and

wraps Gwen in a hug. I probably should've warned Gwen that my family is very huggy... but she's handling it well, only starfishing for a second or two before hugging my mom back. "It's nice to see you in the daytime, I hope you slept okay."

"I did," Gwen says. Her cheeks redden, probably remembering how we woke up this morning, my cock hard, rubbing up against her ass. Yeah... I wouldn't mind waking up like that again.

Which is weird, considering I never like sleeping with people.

Unless it's Gwen, you like sleeping with her.

"Thank you so much for coming to help Cade... even though it seems we are just now finding out why it's needed," Kylie says, turning back to glare at me, and it feels like tiny little needles poking me.

"Well, if it's any consolation, I work at the hospital where he had the surgery—specifically with the recipient—and he still waited minutes before the scheduled time to let me know."

And there she is, ladies and gentlemen, the Gwen I know and adore is out and ready to play. Her first victim: me.

"Cade Williams, I raised you better than that," my mother scolds as she leads Gwen to a seat. "You really didn't tell anyone about this? Harris, maybe?"

"Nope, and don't worry, he already yelled at me enough for all of y'all."

Dirty Play

"It's about time someone told you how it is," Vince murmurs.

"Hold up a second," my dad says, his eyebrows scrunched when he looks at me. "Did she say recipient?"

"Yes, sir," I say, feeling the air change in the room like it's harder to take a deep breath.

"Recipient... for what?" he asks, and I watch as they exchange knowing glances, understanding finally crossing each of their faces. They know after everything that happened, there's only one reason I would ever go through this... another perfect match.

"Kidney transplant," I mumble, Gwen's hand gripping my thigh like she knows I need to be grounded. It's hard having this conversation without Gwen knowing everything, and thankfully, my family hasn't figured out that she's not just my nurse so they won't go into detail unless I initiate it.

"For who?" my dad says, still looking confused.

"A fifteen-year-old girl I met at the hospital. Her name is Kennedy."

"How is she doing?" my mother asks, tears in her eyes, memories thick in the air.

"She's doing well," Gwen jumps in. "She still has a way to go because she's been fighting this for a while, but she's making progress every day."

Gwen fills my parents in on how it all went, letting them know about my recovery, but I'm lost in my siblings' gaze, both of them staring at me, obviously hurt they didn't hear about this.

For the third time since the surgery, I feel an overwhelming sense of guilt for not telling someone.

It doesn't take long this morning for everyone to disperse, the usual work of the day taking over. Vince and I get up to help my dad, which Gwen thinks is a great idea. Although she gives me strict instructions that I'm basically not to do anything, just watch and supervise. If she finds out I lift anything and hurt myself, she's bound to kick my ass. Both my dad and Vince get a kick out of her attitude. And before I can say anything, Kylie and my mom make their way out to the porch with a pitcher of tea, Gwen in tow, their favorite way to spend a day.

The thought shouldn't make me so happy, but it does.

By the time we make it out to the field where they're working on fixing the fence, I find a seat on a tractor and just watch them. It's not like I can do anything. If I even pick up a fence post, I'm sure Gwen will find me.

Besides, the longer it takes me to recover, the longer I spend not inside her, and dammit, that's the only place I truly want to be right now.

"Vince, will you grab that shovel over there so we

can start digging a new hole? We're gonna need to bury this pole a little deeper. Maybe that'll help."

He grabs it and gets to work while I help my dad measure everything, feeling pretty damn useless since the only thing they are letting me do is hold a tape measure. "Have you thought about securing this pole with the other one for extra support?" I ask.

"Do you even know how to fix a fence anymore, Cade?" Vince grumbles, out of breath from digging, tone is annoyed.

"Vince," my father warns.

"No, Dad. I'm not going to baby him. He hasn't really been here in eleven years and he's going to show up today and tell us what to do?"

"I'm not—" I start, but he's not finished.

"He left us, he left the ranch, he left the house, he left our family, and now he's back and wants to tell us what to do? Fuck that."

I want to get defensive, tell him he's wrong, and that's not what I'm trying to do. I'm honestly just trying to talk, not shut myself in like I always have, but I'm clearly fighting an uphill battle. I know it isn't going to be easy, and fuck, I just have to grin and bear it because I know deep down I made this mess. Now it's my turn to fix it.

"Now isn't the time, Vince," my dad says.

"You're right," I say, knowing it's not worth a fight, and it's just best to concede. "I did leave, I did run, and we can sit here and talk about it, but do we really need to do that while fixing a fence?"

"No, we don't, Cade, let's just keep avoiding it. Why don't you sit there and look pretty and let us work? I'm really not in the mood to listen to you spew your martyr bullshit at eleven in the morning."

My mouth gapes. This is the first time that Vince has spoken to me like this. Being three years apart meant that we became really close growing up, especially once he got into sports. It gave us something to bond over.

It's not even that he's yelling at me, it's the pain in his voice—it's knowing that I've hurt him. I've hurt my entire family when I was only trying to protect them.

I fucked up.

Chapter 23

Gwen

Sitting on the porch with Cade's mom Shelly and Kylie was not something I ever thought I'd be doing... today or any other day if we're being honest. I was really nervous at first when Cade agreed to go help his dad. The thought of being alone with two women who are extremely important to Cade... well, it's scarier than walking across a glass bridge and I have a fear of heights.

Flash-forward three hours, and I'm pleasantly surprised that I'm actually having a lot of fun. It helps that these two are absolutely hilarious and seem to be in a competition to see who can share the most secrets about Cade, even though I keep insisting we are just friends. It doesn't surprise me at all that Cade and his brother got caught streaking through town when they were in high school or that he got in more fights than they could count because boys kept being rude to Kylie and Veronica.

They even tell me a little bit about Veronica, not going too in-depth, just enough that I can tell she was a special girl. The way they describe her, she was strong-willed, took no shit, and was really loyal to the people she loved. Although it seems like she also knew how to piss her brother off and chose to do it as much as possible, probably because she was the only one who could put him in check.

"The boys should be heading back soon. Carson doesn't like to work too late, so he's always back by three. Plus, I bet Cade is just itching to get back," Shelly says as she looks down at her phone to check the time.

"There's no doubting that. He didn't let you out of his sight the entire time we were talking, even when Dad and Vince tried to get him to go talk on the patio. I'm sure he's out there acting like a lost puppy dog," Kylie adds, and I'm already blushing.

"No, no, you guys have this all wrong. That's not what this is. I'm a nurse at the hospital in the PICU, and he ended up being a donor for one of my patients. Since we're friends outside of all that—I'm best friends with his friend's girlfriend—he asked if I'd come with him to make sure he's okay... Plus, he needed a driver."

"You either think I was just born yesterday, which I can guarantee *I was not*, or you're delusional." Shelly laughs, and I'm not sure what to do.

Dirty Play

Does she know about Cade and I? Fuck.

"I, we, uh... I don't know," I tell them, sighing, not sure what to say.

"Well, if it makes this conversation any easier, when I hung out with Sawyer we got nice and liquored up, so I happen to know a thing or two about you and my big brother," Kylie says with a sly grin that tells me she has enough details to know just how close the two of us have gotten.

Son of a bitch. My face reddens immediately, and I can feel both their eyes on me. I want to disappear. I'm equally in shock that she knows about this and that she'd say something about it in front of their mom, but she just laughs. I'm not good at hiding things, and I'm even worse at brushing them off when people ask me point-blank. I want nothing more than to stop hiding this thing with Cade.

Whatever it is.

"Look, moms always know. We have a sixth sense about these things. Besides, anyone paying attention can see the way he looks at you. I saw it last night, and I was with you two for ten minutes. Which reminds me, I need to thank you."

"You need to... what? Why?" I ask, looking at Kylie like she might help me understand, but she just shrugs.

"Yes, you brought my boy home. I think... no... *I know* that if it weren't for you, he wouldn't be here."

Shelly says it so matter-of-factly that it's hard for

me to not just take her word for it, but I really didn't do anything. I start fidgeting with my sweatshirt, trying to figure out what to say.

"Mrs. Williams, I really didn't do anything. This was all his idea. He just brought me along for the ride," I tell her, uncomfortable with the undeserved praise.

"Sweetie, it's been almost eleven years since he's walked into this house with a smile on his face. It wasn't until last night, when he walked in with you, that I saw a glimpse of my boy. He's been so isolated, doing his best to stay away and push everyone away in the process. But your energy reminds me of someone I love, and people like you don't take no for an answer, so I'm not surprised you're breaking him down a bit. I think having someone like you in his life has pushed him to want more."

"What do you mean, more?" I ask, not sure what I have to do with any of this.

"Look, I don't know how much you know which makes this a bit challenging. But given it's my son, I can guess that it's the bare minimum, at most," Shelly starts, and I just nod, knowing there's so much to this story, and I just have the top layer of it. "When Veronica died, a part of Cade died too. They were the best of friends since they were babies, only fifteen months apart."

Kylie reaches over and grabs her mom's hand. It's never to talk about losing someone, especially someone you loved so much.

Dirty Play

"After she died, he left. At first, he just checked out mentally, but as soon as he could, he went away to college and played hockey. He was off and running, never looking back. Don't get me wrong, his dad and I always dreamed of him making it to the NHL... I guess we just figured he would still visit us every once in a while." Shelly's eyes well up, but she looks at me and smiles. "This is the first time he's come home in over five years, and the first time he's stayed in this house in ten. *You* are the only change. The only reason I can think of that could've brought my boy home, so thank you."

She stands up and wraps me in another hug—two in one day—and I can already tell I like it. These hugs make me feel content like I have people that care about me. More than just my girls.

I officially adore these people.

"Oh hell, are we walking into a sappy love fest?" Cade asks as the guys all walk up the stairs onto the porch.

Stepping back, we both just laugh.

"Something like that," I say as I grab my phone. "I'm actually going to run to my room to call the hospital. I want to check and see how Kennedy is doing."

Kennedy ended up needing to stay in the hospital for a bit longer—her body just needed a little more time to get stronger. I've been getting updates, but only when Mariah is working, and today is her day off.

"Let me know how she is," Cade says seriously,

reaching for my cup of tea and taking a big gulp. Watching the way his Adam's apple bobs as he swallows shouldn't be so hot, but I don't think there's a thing he does that I don't find attractive.

I nearly die when I notice everyone around us is watching me ogle Cade. Well, time to run away.

"I'll be back in a bit," I say, turning to walk away.

"After that, you and Cade should take a walk. Let him show you around a bit. It might be nice to get out and stretch your legs," Shelly says with a smirk that makes me think she's up to something.

Cade looks over at her before shrugging back at me.

"If you're up for it we can go when you're done with your call."

"Okay, I'll be back down in ten," I say as I scurry off, needing a minute away from him to regain control.

All of their eyes on me made me realize just how often I look at Cade.

CADE'S CHILDHOOD HOME HAS GOT TO BE THE MOST beautiful place I've ever been. Not only is the home absolutely perfect, but their property is amazing. Cade showed me the barn, where they have their little goats, and then we ended up at a pond with lots of cute duckies.

"Where do you think the mom is?" I ask as I get a

Dirty Play

little closer to where the ducks are playing in the water.

"I don't know, but do you really wanna fuck with mama duck? They aren't very nice."

"They are too," I say, glaring. "Geese are the assholes."

"How do you know this?"

"I read animal facts every morning. It keeps my brain engaged and learning new things—and I happen to love learning about cute little animals."

"Because you aren't busy enough as it is," Cade says before sitting down, while I continue to search for more ducks. "Tell me another."

"Another what?" I ask as I walk over and sit down in the grass next to him, dropping my head to his shoulder.

"An animal fact."

I lean back on my elbows, look up at him, and think. I could tell him about hummingbirds flying backward... or how polar bear skin is black. Hmm...

"Otters hold hands while they're sleeping so they don't get separated."

"Really?" he asks, eyebrow cocked like he doesn't believe me.

"Yup. Google it."

"Nah, I believe you. That's just kind of... adorable," he says with a shrug. "Another one."

"I've got a good one. Did you know that crocodiles can't stick out their tongues?"

We spend the next couple of hours telling stories—his mostly about playing hockey as a kid, with one or two about all of his siblings mixed in. It's the most I've heard him talk about his family and definitely the most personal information he's been willing to give me.

I'm more thankful than I realized I would be that another layer of this man is peeling back. Maybe it's because he's home that he's opening up.

"I actually really enjoy it here," I tell him with a sigh.

"Me, too, Tink. Me too."

It's not just being here that I enjoy—it's being here *with him.*

When we make it back to the house it's after five, and I can smell something delicious as we walk through the front door. I hear laughter in the kitchen, and Cade grabs my hand and pulls me in for a hug. With a kiss on the top of my head—something I didn't realize I loved so much—he holds me for a moment.

"Thank you for coming out here with me," he says. "I'm not sure I could've faced this without you."

I look up, stretching my neck back to see him. Everything his mom said earlier comes rushing back—how I changed him, how I brought him back home—and I start to wonder... am I helping Cade? Am I

Dirty Play

helping him work through his past and realize that he has a million people around him who care about him?

If I am, I just hope he realizes I'm one of them.

"Anytime, Mr. Grumps," I say, leaning up to press a quick kiss on the corner of his mouth, just enough to make him want more but still chaste enough to almost be a cheek kiss. Pulling back, I head toward the kitchen, ready to help however I can.

When we walk in, they don't notice us right away. Both his parents are in the kitchen pulling lasagna and bread out of the oven while Kylie makes a salad. It smells absolutely delicious, and my stomach starts growling, reminding me I probably should've eaten more this morning.

"Perfect timing, you two. Dinner is ready to go on the table, and Vince will be here in five," Shelly says as she carries the lasagna over. "The table is set and everything is ready, so why don't you have a seat."

Feeling rather lazy but not willing to argue, I sit down, thankful when Cade takes the seat next to me.

"Did you guys have a good time?" Carson asks as he brings the bread over and sits down. Kylie and Shelly each bring a few things over and sit down, too.

"We did, you have a beautiful property. I'm sure I could spend days exploring it and still never be done."

"You're not wrong. Did you guys go over to the pond?" Shelly asks.

"Yeah, that's actually where we spent most of our time. She found little ducks in the water, and we ended up watching them play for two hours until the mom came around," Cade interjects, still annoyed that we got chased out of the area by a mama duck who, apparently, wasn't very nice.

I hear laughter as Vince walks in. "You and those damn birds," he says as he walks over and gives everyone a quick squeeze before taking the seat next to Cade.

"Well, now that everyone's here, let's eat," Shelly says.

It isn't long until we have all finished our meals and are sitting back to listen to more stories. More memories, I love the picture they are painting of Cade—someone loveable, strong, and passionate. His hand moves under the table to grip my thigh, and I feel grounded knowing he's right there, even if no one else can see.

Everything is going great until someone mentions Veronica again. This time, Vince mentions the surgery and how this was the second time Cade was supposed to have kidney surgery. I feel the temperature drop in the room, his grip on my thigh tightening just enough that I can tell how uncomfortable he is.

Cade looks toward Vince. "Drop that topic, please," he says. I can't see his face, but his voice sounds desperate.

I watch Vince as he just stares at Cade, his eyes narrowing, fingers tapping on the table like he's assessing the situation.

Dirty Play

"No," he says, and I feel everyone hold their breath. "You can't run from everything for the rest of your life, Cade. It's time to man up and handle the past. It fucking sucks, trust me, we all lived through it while you ran. So don't sit here and act all high and mighty like we can't talk about something that we all fucking lived through."

"Vince," Shelly says, desperation in her voice, and I can tell she just wants to keep the peace. She's got all her babies under the same roof, and she just wants to hold on to it.

"No, mom. I'm done walking on eggshells around Cade. I'm done pretending that when Veronica died, he didn't die too. He left us. He left us because he was too much of a pussy to deal with everything, which meant he left us to mourn the both of them, and I'm fucking tired of it," Vince says, his voice breaking.

I feel like this is the last place I want to be right now, the tension in the room skyrocketing as everyone watches Vince and Cade in a stare off, neither of them saying anything. I think Vince is hoping that this will make Cade talk, but it's probably shutting him down further.

"I said no," Cade seethes, his hand shaking against my thigh. I want to hold him, make him feel better, but I can't.

Vince surprises us all when he stands up, slamming his chair back as he looks directly at Cade. "The day you decide to fucking man up and be my big brother again is the day I'll sit at this table with you," he says, voice thick with emotion as he turns and walks out the door.

Cade sits there for a moment before standing up and storming out in the opposite direction of his brother, the back door slamming behind him. The rest of us are left in silence.

Fuck.

No one says anything—we don't move, just wait. Kylie must notice my sadness because she moves to sit next to me and wraps her arm around me.

"Look, it'll be fine. They'll both cool off and maybe this will be the push they need to actually sit down and talk about everything," Kylie says, sensing my obvious discomfort with what just happened. "Why don't we all go out tomorrow or the next day. It'll be fun and maybe it'll help them chill the eff out."

"They're both hotheaded," Shelly says with a smile.

"Yup, just like their mother," Carson says with a wink as he starts to carry dishes to the kitchen.

Shelly just laughs, swatting him with her towel as he walks by, a big ass grin on her face. "That's who you fell in love with, Mr. Williams. Don't start talking trash about it now."

I stare at these two like I'm watching a movie. They are the exact depiction of what being in love should look like. They have what I've dreamed I would find ever since I was a girl. Not only that, but they seem downright happy together as a family. Hell, they really didn't even blink when Cade and I showed up, hugging him after years away. And they welcomed me with open arms—it's a feeling I'm not quite used to.

It's also a feeling I'm scared to get comfortable with... What if this doesn't work out? What if whatever this is between us fizzles out, or he gets bored? What if he doesn't feel the same way about me?

What do I even feel for Cade? Do I like him? Do I like-like him? Do I...

I don't finish that thought because I'm not sure I'd know what to do with the answer. Admitting just how strong my feelings for Cade are is something I'm not quite ready to navigate.

Not yet, at least.

Chapter 24

Gwen

When Kylie invited us out tonight, I wanted to say no. The thought of being out with everyone sounded overwhelming because I'm still not quite sure how to act around Cade. Especially after he and Vince had their blow up. So far, nothing has come of it, but they haven't really talked all that much.

Even with the tension, it's been a fun time. The bars out here aren't wild and crazy like the ones back home, just enough excitement to make for an interesting night. We start at a tiny bar in town, where Kylie and I hit the dance floor while her husband, Cade, and Vince sit at a table and glower. Brandon was less than thrilled when Kylie wanted to dance, so I figured what the hell, I'd do it. Based on the looks she's been getting from her husband, he's really regretting his decision.

"My brother hasn't taken his eyes off you the entire

night." Kylie practically has to shout over the music to be heard.

She's not wrong. Anytime I've turned around, his eyes have been on me. Even now, he's staring, jaw clenched, fisting his drink so tightly I'm surprised the glass hasn't shattered. He's trying so damn hard to hold back; he has been since we got here. It's not like he's being mean... I can just feel the distance between us. He's still been sneaking into my room every night since we got here, but it feels like we've taken a step back. I'm trying to convince myself to be patient. I've waited what feels like an eternity, but I can wait a little longer—I can give him some time to figure this shit out with his family.

That being said... I wouldn't be me if I didn't fuck with him.

"Well, my apologies for TMI, but staring doesn't make me orgasm," I tell her. "My books do, though." With a wink, I scan the floor, looking for the nearest single guy, specifically one Cade can see.

"Gag me, and not in a good way. I'm just glad to see that Cade has found someone like you, someone who can deal with his condition."

"His condition?" I ask, confused as fuck now.

"Yeah, apparently, someone lodged a stick up his ass about ten years ago and no one's been able to remove it. Symptoms include grumpiness, permanent scowl, unique ability to keep everyone at arm's length,

Dirty Play

and my favorite, the aura of pure dickishness that surrounds the man at all times."

I can't help the very unladylike laugh I let out at the imagery, but she's nailed it right on the head. It probably doesn't help that Kylie and I keep sneaking off to take shots, much to the guys' dismay, so everything is much funnier than usual. To be fair, we've invited the boys to join, but they're being party poopers.

Cade seems to be feeling much better today, at least physically. He seems like he's starting to feel more like himself. He let me look at the incisions, and everything looks great, which is a relief.

"I mean, I know he's all of those things, but when I look at your brother, those are the last things I notice."

"That's what makes you so good for him. He needs someone who can look past the act and see through to who he really is. You may not realize it, but you've changed him—he's more like the brother I used to know."

"Well... if he's acting more like the brother you used to know, then tell me, how does he do with jealousy?" I ask her, scanning the dance floor again.

"Well, by the look of his white knuckles, he's about two seconds away from an ER trip, so my guess is it won't take much... why? What are you plotting?" Kylie asks, eyes twinkling with excitement as she follows my gaze.

"I'm just thinking about doing a little more dancing... If it makes him jealous, maybe he'll tell me—or show me—how he feels. I don't expect him to caveman carry me out of the bar—he did have surgery two weeks ago... but I need something."

"Well, you have two options, three if you really wanna be fucked up. Option one is Marcus over there, next to the lady in red. He's harmless, I promise, but he has no rhythm, so he basically holds onto your hips to follow your lead the entire time. It's a bit weird but whatever. Option two is Thomas. He knew my brother back in high school—they were pretty good friends—it'd definitely annoy Cade to see him dancing with you."

"That was only two options."

Her eyes widen. "So, we're going for really fucked up? I knew I liked you."

"I mean, I'd at least like to hear about it. I like making informed decisions," I tell her with an evil grin.

She smirks before turning in the direction of the DJ, nodding toward a really fucking attractive man with sandy blonde hair, although he does nothing to my body.

"That's Derek. Him and my brother have been enemies for a long, *long* time, and well... let's just say that I wouldn't mind if Cade—or Vince, for that matter—punched him in the face."

"Not Brandon?"

"Pretty sure Brandon wouldn't notice if I got naked and danced with him myself," she says, her eyes sad for

Dirty Play

only a moment before she turns back to Derek. "Just go up and ask him to dance, the man won't say no."

"Game on, but if we have to bail Cade out, I'm blaming you."

With a smirk, I walk toward Derek. Thankfully, he's already looking in my direction, smiling as approach.

"Wanna dance?" I ask quietly.

He nods in response and I turn, my back to his front. He moves his hands to my hips, surprisingly in a safe zone. He's not too touchy, and while his standoffishness is not what I expected it definitely helps my situation—I'm cringing that I have someone's hands on me, someone who isn't Cade.

We don't even make it one full song before Cade is in front of me, grabbing my hips and pulling me toward him.

"Sorry, Miller, this one's mine," Cade growls, his arm holding me possessively like he's afraid Derek will pounce. Fortunately, he just smirks as he nods toward Cade before turning back to the bar.

Uneventful in all the right ways.

But when I turn to face Cade, he grabs me by the hand and pulls me to the other side of the dance floor. The side that's furthest away from everyone. Turning me away from him, he grabs my hips and pulls me back until my ass is pressed against his cock, his very hard cock.

Fuck me.

"What're you playing at tonight, Tink?" he growls,

his teeth scraping down my neck as his hands slide lower.

I can barely form thoughts or words, let alone sentences, when he has just a hand on me, and right now his entire body is pressed to mine. All I want to do is scream for him to take me right here.

I turn my head to the side, bringing my mouth to his ear to talk over the music. "There are no games tonight," I purr, the way his grip on my hip tightens to nearly the point of pain has me whimpering. I'm not an idiot. I know he wants me. But that doesn't do me any good if he won't admit it. "I was just dancing and made a new friend, that's all."

"Your new friend was fucking touching you," he rumbles, voice gritty with anger. "Miller's a prick, and if he touches you again, I'll chop his hands off."

Why is it so hot when a man threatens another man for you?

I don't want him to actually do it, obviously, but it's so romantic when he threatens violence for me.

"I mean, I *wish* someone was touching me. I couldn't exactly bring my vibrator to your parents' house, that would've been in poor taste," I whisper, my patience for this stupid little dance already over.

"You think I don't want you? Haven't I made this clear to you? You're the one who won't let me inside you right now when you're the only thing I want," he growls in my ear, teeth nipping my lobe. He sighs, body collapsing around mine, his hands on my hips while he holds me still. "Do I need to prove to you just how badly I want to touch you?"

I should move, but I can't. I'm frozen, unable to do anything.

"I told you I'm not going to run, that I want to figure this out. It's time you start believing me."

Thrusting his hips forward, he presses his hard cock into my ass, his thumb playing with the button of my pants. But I don't want to give in this easily. I want to make him suffer. Suffer the same way I have.

"Move your hand, Cade."

"Okay," Cade says, sliding his hand down past the band of my pants and into my panties. He doesn't hesitate, his fingers immediately finding my clit, which is already swollen and throbbing from watching him watch me. I'm sure if he touched me just right, I'd combust in seconds.

"What are you doing?"

"You told me to move my hand, am I doing it wrong?" he asks, his fingers still working their way inside me, his thumb pressing firmly against my clit.

"Yes, I mean no. Fuck, I don't know, Cade, we're in a freaking crowded bar and you're doing this?"

"Would you prefer me to stop?"

"No... but fuck."

"We can do that later. But right now? Right now, I'm going to finger fuck you in this crowded bar. Just try to keep your moans down. Don't want the entire town to know what you sound like when I make you come."

His fingers start to move in and out at a pace that's driving me wild. His thumb keeps a firm hold on my clit while his mouth presses kisses down my neck, and I think I'm having an out-of-body experience. The thought that we could get caught at any time, that someone could walk up to us while Cade's hand is deep inside my cunt, makes this so much hotter—I'm already about to come.

"I'm so cl-close, please don't stop."

And he doesn't. He continues, his mouth attacking my own, smothering my scream as I fall apart against him, riding his fingers on the dance floor.

As I stand there, he slowly slides his fingers out, slipping them into his mouth with a throaty moan that has no business being that hot.

"What the fuck are we doing?" I ask, startling him with my out of the blue question.

"Not running."

"Should we stop until we figure this out? Before things get too messy?"

"No."

"Why not?" I whine.

"Because I know I don't want that," he says. His eyes are glassy, the normally vibrant color muted as he battles with indecision. I wish I could help him and make this easier, but I can't. I know this is hard for him, but sometimes knowing the things you don't want can be enough.

Dirty Play

"But you don't want this. You don't want a relationship."

"I—I've never wanted this, you're right about that. But you're wrong if you think I don't want you—if you think I don't want whatever this thing between us is. I want all of you, Gwen, even the parts that drive me crazy. Those are actually my favorite things about you. The way you blow up my phone until I respond, but only because you're making sure I've taken my medicine or seeing if I need anything, it makes me feel wanted. Like I matter. Between that and the random penguin facts you sent me every day I was in the hospital, I'm downright cheerful every time I see your name, even if I hate my damn phone. I can't explain it, but every time I try to walk away from you, every time I try not to text you the second I wake up, I feel sick to my stomach. Do you know what the only thing that takes away that feeling is?"

"What?" I whisper, not sure if I actually want to know.

"You," Cade growls, his hands pulling at his long hair, gripping it in frustration. His words stop me in my tracks, my brain trying to make sense of what he's saying. The urge to both run from and to Cade is overwhelming.

"You've made it clear that you—"

"I know damn well what I've said, Gwen. I've always been good at walking away, fighting any sort of feelings for anyone, knowing I'm no good for them. But

I'm not good at walking away once feelings have taken up residence in my heart, and you've made your own fucking home inside my heart, and now, I'm not letting you go. I'm no good at relationships but with you... you make me feel like I can try. Like I want to try."

Pulling me in, he stares down at me, his big brown eyes filled with so many different things, indecision still among them. But I also see another emotion... one I'm not quite ready to put into words. Something that feels pretty freaking wonderful coming from him.

"I'm going to fuck up a lot of things, that much I can promise. I'm going to be an asshole even when I don't mean to be. I'm going to say and do all the wrong things, but I want to try. I want to try to make you as happy as I am when we're together, I want to try to be worthy of your... attention," he says, and I feel like I could cry. Or like Ashton Kutcher is going to jump out at any second and tell me I'm *Punk'd*. But then he really knocks the air from my lungs.

"Will you try... with me? Will you be mine?"

"I always have been, Cade. I've just been waiting for you to realize it."

Chapter 25

Cade

"How are you all able to drive out here this easily? Like is this a part of the Williams family DNA?" Gwen asks, breaking the silence as we head back to my parents' house.

After I found her on the dance floor, we all had a couple of drinks while catching up a bit. The drinks helped me deal with Kylie and Vince's constant staring in our direction, which only got worse once Brandon left. Apparently, he had a work emergency.

My siblings weren't very good at being sneaky, either that or they weren't even trying to hide it. When I noticed them looking our way, I glared back, trying to force their eyes off us, but they just smirked like the little shits they are.

Something has shifted between Gwen and me since my surgery... truthfully, since the night we spent together before it. Since then, we have been navigating this new normal, trying to figure out what we're doing. As long as we're doing it together, I'm happy. My whole family has noticed, my mom even mentioned that I seem more like myself than I have in a long time. She didn't outright say it's because of Gwen, but the constant smiles at my girl, especially when we're together, are enough for me to hear her unspoken words loud and clear.

They like her.

"I mean, we loved it out here, so we came a lot," Vince says, lowering the music down as he turns down my parents' street. "It helps when your sisters are little daredevils and always want to go off-roading at night. Man, Veronica used to egg us on so badly, tease us until we went out driving with her."

I feel Gwen tense at the mention of Veronica and I'm silently kicking myself that I still haven't told her the full story. I really need to. She deserves to know that part of my life. She deserves to know what life choices led me to where I am now

"We were young and dumb, but we had a lot of fun," Kylie adds with a laugh.

"I feel like I'd need my high beams on at all times. The streets are barely marked and the signs that are there... well, they suck. I'd constantly be lost," Gwen huffs.

"Nah, you'd eventually figure it out," I say, pulling

Dirty Play

her toward me in the backseat. I don't miss Vince watching us in the rear-view mirror, but I can't bring myself to care.

Why am I nervous to have my family see me with Gwen? To see me happy?

What if your happiness upsets them? What if they get mad at you for being happy when you're not deserving of it?

Shaking my head, I try not to think about it, knowing that Vince is definitely already pissed. We've been avoiding each other since dinner the other night when he decided to explode and unload a few of the things I wish I'd been able to tell Gwen. I'm thankful he drew the line at telling her about the surgery. I haven't told Gwen that I was a match or about the snowboarding trip and my accident.

I need to tell her... I know I do. Vince made it pretty damn clear that I've been selfish, and I believe him. At this point, I think I'm just so scared of fucking everything up and hurting Gwen. And that she'll realize I'm not worth her time.

Vince and Kylie drop us off at my parents' house and we sneak inside, tiptoeing our way through the dark, doing our best not to wake anyone up, which is easier said than done when you're a bit tipsy.

Walking down the hallway toward our rooms, I don't even ask, just open my door and tug her inside with me.

"What're you doing?" she gasps as I push her

against the door. I press my hips against hers, loving her soft moan when my cock rubs against her.

Fuck, I want her. I want to sink so deep inside of her I lose myself.

Lightly gripping her neck with my left hand, I push her hair out of her face with my right. Gripping her throat tighter, I pull her in until my mouth is at her ear.

"Taking what's mine," I growl. Stepping back, I flick the button of her jeans. "Now, strip."

She stares at me for a moment, her mouth gaping open, the shock evident across her face, and I want to laugh... except I'm not joking. She must realize it because she doesn't say anything—just takes a moment to assess before stepping around me to undress. I lean back against the door, watching her every move until she's down to her bra and panties. She unclasps her bra, dropping it to the floor, and slowly slides down her panties, watching me with a devilish smirk the entire time. Standing up straight, completely bare, she looks at me confidently. She has the kind of beauty that I can't comprehend.

"Now what? We both know I won't fuck you until you've been cleared. Definitely don't want to have to explain to my boss that I'm the reason your recovery went to shit."

"No one said anything about fucking, Tink. Now, get on the bed," I growl as I lie down, my head on the pillow, and just watch her.

She listens—walks to the end of the bed, climbs

Dirty Play

on, and sits down. She's really being a brat tonight, taking everything I say literally, down to the word. The mischievous look in her eyes tells me she's doing this on purpose.

"Now what?" she asks, almost daring me. "Besides you taking your shirt off? At least then I would have some skin to look at while I'm completely naked."

With one hand I grip my shirt and gently lift it over my head, avoiding my left side and tossing the shirt on the ground. Her eyes watch me, landing first on my tattoo-covered chest and then snaking down my arms. I love watching the way she looks at me. I know she loves my tattoos—I can tell by the way she's biting her lip while staring at them.

"Crawl to me, Tink," I tell her, a sly grin on my face. I want her at my mercy, falling on my every word. But her eyes are fixed on my arms, on the new ink that's just starting to heal.

I watch her stare for a moment before she's on her hands and knees, slowly crawling over to me and into my lap. When she stops, her bare pussy resting right on top of my cock, I nearly say fuck her rules and take her right here, but her hands distract me. Her fingers immediately trace the new design.

Her design.

"Cade..." she whispers, her voice trailing off. "Wh-when did you get this?"

I look down, watching her stare at it in awe, and I'm almost nervous that she's going to hate it. I got this tattoo the second day we were here. I was tired of trying to avoid washing it all off every time I showered. Benji, a friend and the only tattoo artist I've ever gone to, was luckily able to squeeze me in first thing in the morning, so I was able to do it while Kylie and Gwen went flower shopping for the party on Saturday.

It took some convincing once he knew I was recovering from surgery, but thankfully, I wasn't taking pain meds anymore and told him I was healing well, so he agreed. It helped that I sent him a picture of my arm with the flowers Gwen had drawn and told him my idea. He put two and two together and realized that these tattoos were sentimental, and the large, tattooed man is one of the biggest saps I've ever met.

"After we got here. I snuck off while you and Ky were busy one morning," I tell her with a shrug, never taking my eyes off her.

"But how... didn't it come off? I did that the first night home from the hospital."

The first night we were home Gwen and I spent the evening together because she refused to let me recover alone. There wasn't much to do so we ended up lying on the couch and watching another *Harry Potter* movie. I fell asleep, which seems to be a theme for me lately, but when I woke up an hour later, she was snuggled up with a new movie on, and I had a brand new tattoo. Thin little flowers covered any blank spots on my sleeve, such a sharp contrast to the thick lines and bold

Dirty Play

colors I already have, but somehow they were so complimentary.

"I know. I just knew that I wanted to get it added permanently, so I made sure it didn't fade," I tell her.

She looks so cute like this, her dark hair has fallen in her face, her naked body still straddling me while she inspects my new tattoos.

"But why? You've told me that all your tattoos have meaning, every one of them, and now you do this?" she says, obviously confused.

But I don't know why she's confused, the answer is pretty obvious.

"Because it's from you. That's meaningful enough," I tell her, not needing any more of an explanation. "Now, come here."

But this time, she doesn't. Her hands trace the flowers, barely touching me but still enough to set my body on fire. I hate that she's making me fight to get her where I can kiss her and touch her, but she's being a pain in the ass and making me spell out exactly what I want from her.

And what do I want right now?

I want her to sit on my face.

"Tink, look at me," I grumble, my voice raspy. "Come up here and ride my face. Let me taste you while I make you come."

Her eyes widen, shifting to look down at my mouth, as she licks her lips. Darting my tongue out, I slide it along my bottom lip, already thinking about her sweet taste. It doesn't take more than a few seconds before she's moving, sliding up my body until she's hovering over my mouth, her hands on the headboard.

I wait, expecting her to lower down, but she doesn't. She's hesitating.

"Sit, Tink. Smother me with this beautiful cunt," I say, gripping her hips and waiting until she drops all the way down.

Her movements are tentative at first, hips rocking gently as I slide my tongue through her center, flattening it when I get to her clit.

"Fuck, Cade, right there," she moans, her movements picking up, the pressure increasing as she starts to find her rhythm.

I can feel her wetness dripping down, coating my tongue as I swirl it around her clit. Her sweetness has me rock-hard and ready. Reaching down, I palm myself through my pants, willing the pressure down. I want her. I want her so badly it's taking everything in me to not fuck her right here. My hands grip her, holding her in place as my nails dig into her thighs, anything I can do to stop myself from fucking her.

Pulling back for just a moment, I look up at her. Her eyes are wild, the dark green filled with the fire of her desire—she looks perfect.

"I wish you could see yourself like this, see how perfect you look. Your tits bouncing with every thrust, your eyes blazing. And this cunt, perfect and pink for me to taste and touch. This is my heaven."

Dirty Play

She tastes so fucking good, my cock filling as I lap at her wetness. My fingers move to find her clit. Coating them in her wetness, I rub firm circles as I slip two fingers from my other hand deep inside her. The mixed sensation has her screaming as her hands fall to my hair, pulling tightly as she starts to move her hips wildly.

"Yes, Cade. Don't stop," she whimpers, and I can tell from her movements she's getting close. She's almost frantic as she chases her release.

Sliding my fingers in and out, matching her pace, I flick my wrist, turning just enough that every time she rolls her hips, my fingers hit her g-spot.

In no time, she's screaming, her whole body shaking as she rides my face until her orgasm consumes her, leaving her boneless. I hold her in place as her body collapses, melting into mine as the last remnants of her orgasm flutter through her body. I continue licking her, lapping up every last drop of her cum until it's all mine. Her body is sensitive, every kiss and lick almost too much for her to handle.

When she lets me fuck her again, we're going to work on that. I'm going to show her just how many orgasms I can give her in one night. I'm going to have her begging me to stop like a good girl. She'll make sure to give me that 'one more.'

Pulling back, I lift her off me and bring her down to lie on top of me. Her eyes flutter closed, a soft smile on her face.

"That was amazing," she murmurs in her sleepy voice, and I love knowing it was me who made her like this. It was my mouth that brought her this pleasure and I'll do it over and over again until she realizes just how much she means to me.

Even though I can't say the words yet, I can show her.

Chapter 26

Cade

Gwen and I have been sitting out on the front porch, the walk we took earlier having worn us both out, especially after our late night last night. It feels good to get some fresh air and tell her stories about growing up in this town.

I know I need to bring up Veronica. It's time to tell Gwen everything. I'm over keeping these secrets from her, even if the thought of reliving everything is almost enough to scare me away... almost. Gwen is worth facing my past.

Right as I'm about to start the conversation, Vince and Kylie come walking out the front door, their usual perky demeanors nowhere to be found. They both seem uncomfortably serious.

"Cade, can we talk to you?" Kylie asks awkwardly, as her gaze keeps flicking back and forth between Gwen and me.

"About what?" I ask, my guard immediately going up. Before anyone can answer, Gwen stands up.

"I'm going to call the hospital and make sure that everything with Kennedy is going well," she says with a smile, but I know she can sense the tension.

Before she can leave, I stop her, not ready for her to walk away. I'm not prepared to face my family without her. She's the only reason I've been strong enough to be here, let alone talk about anything to do with the past. So not knowing what they are going to say, or even what they want to talk to me about, is scary as hell, and I know I want her to stay.

"Are you sure?" Kylie asks nervously.

"Yes, I want her to stay," I answer.

"Okay... then I guess... will you both come inside?"

Standing up, we follow them inside, where we find my parents sitting at the dining room table. They look solemn, like something bad has happened. But we're all accounted for, so I'm confused.

"What's going on?" I ask nervously as we sit down. Thankfully, Gwen takes the spot right next to me. Her hand immediately grips my leg and squeezes once, a silent show of support that means more than she knows.

Intertwining our fingers, I hold her hand in mine, needing to know she's still here. Needing to feel that she's not going to leave.

"Son, we've thought about how to have this conver-

Dirty Play

sation constantly over the years. We've thought about how we could bring it up—how to present it to you in a way that wouldn't have you running for the hills. We never figured out how to do that, and instead, anytime we've tried, we'd lose you for months, if not years. But now, things are different, and we think it's time."

"What are we even talking about?" I say, my stomach twisting and turning into knots as I wait.

My dad and mom get lost in a silent conversation until my mom nods.

"It's time for you to let it go, son. All of it. We've sat back while you've pushed everyone away for years, never let anyone get close enough you were scared. It's time for you to move on, live your life, and stop pushing everyone away. It's been over ten years since we lost your sister, and this entire time, you've blamed yourself. We could never have predicted everything that happened—with you *or* your sister," he says, and I feel Gwen's hand tense on my own. This is her freaking out. This is her sign that she wants to run. If this conversation continues down this path, she'll soon be pulling her hand away from mine completely.

But at this point, I'm so tired. I'm tired of running from the people who claim to love me. I'm tired of running from my past, constantly putting distance between myself and anyone who might care about me. I don't want to do it anymore, especially now that I have Gwen. Even though she doesn't know my whole story... doesn't quite understand why I am the way I am. I feel like I still have one foot out of this whole thing, just in case she leaves me. But right now, she's still here, and that makes me feel stronger—strong enough to handle this conversation.

Besides, if she's going to run, at least she'll do it before I've fallen in love with her.

My whole body freezes and I feel like I can't catch my breath. It hits me like a freight train—the recognition that these feelings might be stronger than I realized.

Am I in love with Gwen?

"Are you even listening to us?" Vince interrupts my thoughts, annoyed by my lack of talking.

Sorry, I can't handle two existential crises at once and realizing I'm in love with one of my best friends definitely qualifies.

Being in love with her is different than enjoying each other's company or giving an orgasm or two while enjoying each other's company.

No, love is more. It's thinking about the future, last names, and where you want to plant your roots. Things I've never considered in my life, but I'm starting to think about now.

Fuck, I'm really not paying attention.

"Yes, I'm listening," I growl, annoyed that I'm not allowed time to process their ambush.

"Look, Cade, sweetie, we don't mean to come at you

Dirty Play

or seem like we're attacking you. We just want to talk to you. To figure out everything we need to be a real family again," my mom says, her eyes welling up.

I feel her emotion like a punch to the gut. I know I put those tears in her eyes. My choices put that sadness in her heart.

"I don't know how. I wouldn't even know where to start," I tell them honestly. "I've spent years trying to protect you, trying to make sure you could all be hap—"

"Protect us? What kind of crap is that? I'm used to your martyr bullshit, but this is a stretch, even for you," Vince scoffs, and I can tell I've pissed him off. He's always headstrong but he doesn't usually come at me like this.

"Yes, protect you. From me."

"Why would we need protection from you?" my mom asks, looking confused.

"I'm the reason Veronica died—we all know that. I'm the reason we lost her, all because I was fucking selfish!" I shout. All the emotions I've pushed down these last ten years bubble to the surface and I feel like I'm going to explode if I keep them in any longer. "She would still be here today if I hadn't gone on that trip. If I hadn't gone snowboarding all to impress a girl, she would still be here. I knew the risk. I knew there was a chance I could get hurt. I was just too cocky to think it could happen to me. A broken arm that required surgery ended up proving me wrong. A perfect fucking kidney sitting inside me and I still couldn't save my fucking sister. *I was a perfect match, and I couldn't do it.*"

My heart is racing, and I feel my body shaking. I'm drowning in emotions, just waiting to be pulled out or swallowed whole. The one thing that's grounding me is that she's still here. Throughout this entire conversation, Gwen hasn't moved her hand from mine, hasn't even flinched or tried to pull away. She's stuck through this with me.

When I look around, I see my sister and mom with tears streaming down their cheeks, they aren't used to me like this. They aren't used to me yelling at them. Hell, they aren't even used to me being around at all, and this just proves why it's better that way. When my gaze finds my dad's, I expect to see anger, maybe the same pain my mother had, but that's not what I see. He looks almost... broken.

"I'm so sorry that you've spent all this time feeling that way," my dad says, leaning forward, looking me square in the eye. "If I had known that's what has kept you from us, why you've refused to come back to us, I'd have kicked your ass ten years ago."

I'm startled by his declaration. My kind, loving father has never laid a finger on any of us, and now he's threatening to kick my ass? Am I in the twilight zone?

"Cade, look at me... and I need you to really listen to me this time. This conversation is long overdue, and while I wish I could be a little more tactful in delivery, you get what you get. Your sister was dying, yes. We knew she had kidney failure, but that's no one's fault. And yes, you were a perfect match, and we were one week away from surgery when you had your accident, but you did nothing wrong by going on that trip. We encouraged you to go, we knew you needed to take your mind off everything. You had an accident, and that wasn't your fault," my dad finishes, looking worn out, his shoulders slumped, eyes sad. I can see how much all of this has been affecting him.

"If I hadn't gone... I would've been able to save her. How can that not be my fault?"

"Because she didn't die from kidney failure, Cade," my mom interjects. "We didn't find out for a while, the damn autopsy took forever, an unfortunate part of small-town life. Your sister... she had a stroke. There was nothing any of us could've done for her, even if she had received your kidney."

My sister didn't die because she didn't get my kidney.

My sister had a stroke.

"Why am I just now hearing about this? Why have I spent years thinking she died from kidney failure?"

"How were we supposed to tell you, Cade?" Vince asks, standing up from the table, his chair sliding back and falling to the ground while everyone around us holds their breath. "Were we supposed to tell you when we came to your games, and you wouldn't show up to visit with us after? Were we supposed to tell you when you declined all of our phone calls, sending everything to a voicemail that you'd never return? Were we supposed to force you to sit down and talk with us? That's not something you just send in a text message and hope for the best. *You* made this choice. *You* left us. We tried hard for years, but there's only so much you can do when someone clearly doesn't want you in their life... and chasing them down to tell them about an autopsy report isn't high on my list."

Vince is shaking, his fists clenched as he unleashes his words on me, letting me know how absent I've been. How impossible I've been since our sister died. How I let my two younger siblings down by running, leaving them to pick up the pieces and hold our parents together afer losing two of their kids. Each word thrown at me feels like a thousand tiny knives stabbing my heart.

How could I have done this to them? How could I have let Vince, Kylie, and my parents handle all of this on their own? Was all of this for nothing? I thought I was protecting them, but was I really just hurting them?

"I—I don't know what to say," I say, gazing downward. Gwen is still holding my hand, her thumb rubbing small circles, a silent sign that she's still here. She's heard all of this and she... she hasn't left.

"I needed you, Cade," Vince says, and I feel like I've been blindsided. A hit that came from out of nowhere with no time to protect myself. My walls crumble, they shatter around me and I'm left feeling like a helpless seventeen-year-old boy who just wants to make it all okay. "I needed my brother, my best friend, and you left me. You left us to deal with everything by ourselves. So fuck you, Cade."

With that, Vince turns and leaves out the back, slamming the door on his way out. None of us say anything as his truck heads down the driveway.

"Fuck!" I shout, slamming my hand into the table. I try to stand up, try to pull my hand from Gwen's, but she doesn't let me. She doesn't let go.

"No. Sit down," she says, her voice is calm yet stern. "No more running, Cade. From any of us. It's time to let it all go and start living your life."

I look down at her. It's hard for my brain to reconcile everything that's happening. Between my family throwing an intervention, my brother screaming at me, finding out it really wasn't my fault that Veronica died... I can't comprehend it all.

It all happened with her sitting right next to me, her hand in mine. Her face is soft like she knows what I'm going through, and she wants to remind me that she's not going anywhere.

I didn't want to believe it before. I didn't want to let my brain figure it out.

But even when we drag our feet, kicking and screaming the entire way, somehow it comes to light.

I'm in love with Gwen Murphy.

I know I need to tell her. The words vibrate

through my body, tingling, just waiting to be released. But first, I need to talk to my family and find my brother. Then, I can tell my girl how I feel.

Because all I can think about is how much I love Gwen Murphy. And how I can't wait to love Gwen Williams.

Chapter 27

Gwen

The last twenty-four hours have been a whirlwind and I keep pinching myself to make sure it's real. I've gone through a huge array of emotions but I'm feeling happy and content for the first time in my life. For once, I feel like I'm exactly where I'm supposed to be. Things have shifted between Cade and I, changing from something we couldn't define to something that's defining itself for us.

It's like the universe decided long ago that Cade's the one for me, and now it's just pulling us together, a million invisible strings leading us right here.

Between him and his family, everyone has been so welcoming and supportive. It's made me understand just how clinical my entire life has been. I've known these people for a few days and they've asked me more personal questions than my own family has throughout my entire life. They've asked me what kind of food I like and don't like, what kinds of things I do in my spare time. You know... questions you ask someone when you want to learn more about them.

Not like the questions my parents ask me about the hospital and my job, or if I'm ready to come work at their hospital yet.

No, here, with Cade and his family, even with the tension, it's been eye-opening. They've shown me what a loving family looks like, how supportive they are of each other, even when the other person fucks up. It's somehow both broken and healed me all at once and I don't ever want to leave.

And after the conversation earlier, I finally feel like I understand Cade so much better. The distance, the grumpiness, the constant pushing away of the people who care about him—it all makes sense. He's been carrying this weight for years.

Now, I see why he does these things, never letting anyone close. Until me.

Bearing the burden of your sister's death is heavy enough, but feeling unworthy of happiness because you blame yourself is harder to push through. And I wish I could tell him that it wasn't his fault. I may not have been there, but I understand the medical side. Regardless whether Veronica passed away because of a stroke or due to complications from kidney failure, it wasn't Cade's fault.

He didn't need to go into a bubble until her surgery.

Dirty Play

He was a seventeen-year-old boy who had his entire life in front of him. He was scared. He went to do something fun for himself and there's nothing wrong with that. It's not his fault that he got injured and couldn't have the surgery. It's also not his fault that his sister got sick right after.

Life is a bitch. There's no other way around it. We all know we aren't getting out of here alive, so we might as well enjoy it while we're still able to. The more I think about it, the more I hope that I get to enjoy it with Cade. With his family.

After Vince left, Cade talked to his family for a while. They were able to clear the air and talk through everything that happened, and honestly, by the end of it, it felt like they understood each other better. It's like they can see the struggle the other faced and love each other even more for it.

I felt like I was intruding, watching Cade's parents hug him like it was the first time. It was a cleansing hug, one that washed away everything, leaving a blank canvas to write their future on, and it was beautiful. Kylie came over and took me by surprise when she gave me a hug, telling me that the only reason any of this has happened is because of me. Because I gave her brother strength. She told me that when you're in love... when you have someone who loves you, it helps you be strong.

But is that what we are? Are we in love?

This is not a thought for right now, though. After

everyone talked, Cade went to look for Vince, leaving us waiting, emotions high because none of us knew how that conversation would go. Based on what everyone here is saying, they're both hot-headed enough that it could end in a fight and with emotions already a mess today, none of us want that.

The only problem is that we have no idea where they went or if they're even together. And of course, neither of them are answering their phones, leaving us just sitting here... waiting.

"I hate this," I groan. "Can't we go look for them?"

"A girl after my own heart," Shelly says, standing up. "I'm over this sitting thing. I'll drive."

She looks over at Kylie and Carson, both sitting there watching us. Carson looks surprised.

"What? I'm not letting these boys do this shit. We've wasted too many years—I don't want to waste even one more day," she says to her husband.

He just nods, shaking his head with a little smirk. "Okay, hun. Let's go find them."

With that, we all pile into their car.

Once we arrived in town, we split up. Carson and Shelly headed in one direction while Kylie and I headed the other way, but so far we've had no luck. We've been going into restaurants, and we even checked the gym.

"Do they have any favorite places in town?" I ask Kylie, not knowing how to help because I don't know this town well.

"No, honestly, I don't know. I know Vince probably went somewhere to cool off and let his anger out, so he could either be somewhere punching a bag or getting drunk."

"Honestly, Cade could be doing the same. Whenever he gets frustrated, he wants to go for a run or grab a beer."

We walk past one of their cafés, and I can't help but notice how cute it is. It's the kind of place you'd just love to get lost in for a day. I can imagine myself sitting there with Cade, drinking a dirty chai, and eating delicious pastries. I smile at the thought, hoping the next time we come to visit, we can do just that.

"Hey, Kylie." I hear a voice from behind us say, and we both turn around quickly. It's not someone I know, but I definitely recognize her for some reason, something I can't quite place. She's probably my parents' age, with blonde hair and a smile that makes her look much younger, and I just know I've seen that smile around.

"Hi, Mrs. Danielson," Kylie says, turning around to give her a hug. "How are you?"

"I'm good, sweetie, just looking for that husband of mine. Who's this young lady? I don't think we've met?" she asks with a warm smile directed at me.

"I'm Gwen," I tell her, offering her my hand, which she graciously shakes. "Gwen Murphy, I'm actually a friend of Cade's."

Her face lights up and I suddenly know exactly

who this woman is. This is Harris' mama. I'd bet my life on it.

"Oh, Ms. Gwen, I know exactly who you are, Harris has told me all about you," she says with a wink, confusing the hell out of me.

"I'm not sure if that's a good thing or not. Harris is a bit of a wildcard." I chuckle, a bit nervous at what he might've told her.

"All good things, sweetie, all good things. Where's Cade?" she asks, looking over my shoulder.

"That's a good question. We've been looking for him and Vince for quite some time now," Kylie says. "They got into a little bit of a disagreement at the house, and we haven't been able to find them since."

"Ah, well I'd check Sally's place right around the corner. When we came into town, I thought I saw Vince's truck there. Maybe Cade found him and they're talking it out?"

"Hopefully talking is all they do. Thanks, Mrs. Danielson."

"Bye, girls. I hope to get to know you properly, Gwen. Maybe I'll tell Harris we should all go out to dinner when I'm in town later this month."

"I would love that." I smile, feeling the sincerity in my words, and it surprises me. I'm not used to agreeing to plans. I prefer to be home in my safe place or at the hospital.

Or with Cade.

But being outgoing? That's not my style.

Dirty Play

Everyone I've met in this town is wonderful. They make me feel like I want to go out and socialize, so I can spend more time with them. That's all I can think about as we head down the street, turning left around the corner where we see both Cade's and Vince's trucks sitting outside Sally's.

"Well, at least we found them. Let's just hope they're sober enough not to be fighting. Sally will kick em' out without question," Kylie says.

After a quick phone call to her parents to let them know we found the boys, we head inside, holding our breath that we aren't walking into a bar fight between two grumpy brothers.

The bar itself is exactly what I'd expect in a small town, dimly lit, lots of cozy booths, and a bunch of pool tables set off to the side so people can still dance in the middle. The booths are covered in the awful red vinyl covers, the ones that make noises anytime you move, even the slightest bit, but it's somehow still inviting.

Looking around the bar and tables for the guys, I'm surprised when we find them at the furthest pool table, each with a glass in one hand and a pool stick in the other. Trying to convince Cade to follow doctor's orders and take it easy, stop doing physical labor, stop trying to fuck your nurse—none of it's working. Proven by what I can only assume is whiskey that he's currently sipping, but I'm picking and choosing my battles.

"Are you fucking kidding me?" Kylie growls, her eyes widening when she sees them, all smiles and joking around like they hadn't just screamed at each other. "We've been worried they're off fighting or making a bigger mess, and here they are, just sitting in a bar, drinking and playing pool? Fucking twats."

Walking over to them, Kylie doesn't miss a beat when she smacks them both upside their heads.

"What the—" Vince starts but smiles when he sees it's Kylie. Cade doesn't say anything, though, because his eyes are on me.

I can feel the heat of his gaze, the intensity in his eyes almost enough to make me want to hightail it out of here... only it's inviting be closer. It's the kind of look that makes me want to jump into his arms and never let go.

I settle on walking to him, though.

The closer I get, the bigger his smile grows, my own following suit, until I'm standing right before him.

He sets his whiskey down, his eyes never leaving mine.

"Tink," he says, his eyes burning with unspoken emotion as he grabs my hand and pulls me into him, his free hand moving to frame my face. "You're here." His voice is hardly a whisper, barely audible in the loud bar, but it's the only thing I hear.

"I never left," I reply, leaning into his hand, loving the way he feels holding me. So much going unsaid but there will be time for that another day. For now, I want to enjoy this moment with him and the way he's holding me. He's not letting me go anywhere.

Leaning in, his mouth meets mine in a slow languid kiss that I can feel all the way in my toes. I fall into him, his arms wrapping around me, and I finally feel home.

This is exactly where I'm supposed to be, here with this man.

My man.

Chapter 28

Cade

HARRIS

How's the trip going? Still breathing?

> Had you asked me this question yesterday, the answer on the breathing part would've been debatable.

HARRIS

Well, at least I have proof of life.

But how is it? How's Gwen?

> Perfect. It's all perfect.

Heading into the day of my parents' party, I'm feeling happier than I've felt in... well, at least ten years. I woke up with Gwen's mouth wrapped around my cock, both of us still naked from the night before. She may not have let me fuck her, but that didn't stop me from spending the entire evening showing her everything I'm feeling, using my body to tell her all the things I'm still too scared to say out loud.

But this morning, it felt like she was trying to tell me the same thing, communicating the only way we know how, with our bodies.

My entire family has been showing me they care—in different ways, obviously—but it's everything to me. Everything is feeling more relaxed. Hell, I'm not even bothered by Kylie's incessant directions or bossy self because I know she's so focused on making sure the celebration for my parents goes well tonight.

I'm actually really excited about the party, which is a far cry from when I wouldn't even agree to come. But now, having cleared the air with my family, I'm excited to be here.

I mean, yes, there have been some tense moments, specifically between Vince and I, but we just needed to hash it out—verbally and slightly physically—but I let him. I knew he needed to unload on me. He's right. I wasn't there for him. He was fourteen when Veronica died, he had so much growing up to do, and I bailed on him. I was supposed to be his protector, his older brother, and I abandoned him.

My brother has looked up to me from the time he was born and when he needed me most, I left. It's going to take a lot for me to forgive myself for everything I've done to my family. All I know is that I'm thankful they're sticking around. At least this way I can spend the rest of my life letting them know I care.

Dirty Play

If everything goes my way, Gwen will be by my side the entire time.

"Are you just going to stand there staring at the lights or are you going to finish hanging them?" Kylie snaps as she walks by with another couple of vases of flowers, some sort of decoration, or whatever, and places it by the table.

Shaking my head, I snap myself out of my thoughts. "Sorry, just keep thinking."

"Care to elaborate?" she asks dryly. "Like, are we talking about Gwen in a roundabout way because you're not ready to admit it... or are we openly talking about how hopelessly in love with that girl you are?"

I'm stunned, not sure how it has taken me so long to realize all of this. I mean, this won't be news to anyone back home. The couple of times I've gotten text messages from the guys, hell even Sawyer texted me once, they all told me not to fuck it up, that this could be it. Sawyer's version was much more colorful and might've included something about cement shoes. She's a little scary.

Just what Rex needs, though.

"I guess we're openly talking about how hopelessly in love with that girl I am," I grumble, but I can't help myself—I smile.

Kylie squeals and gives me a hug like I just told her I got her a puppy, all because I'm in love.

"Have you told her yet?" she asks excitedly. "If not... you have to. That girl is just as in love with you. Gwen's feisty, but her family isn't great. Not a close one, but I'm sure you know all this. Being here with you, she said it's the most at peace she's ever felt. I think you need to make sure she knows you feel the same."

I smile because I know exactly how I'm going to tell her... or at least where I'll tell her.

"I will."

My parents aren't the people who always get dressed up and go out, so we're throwing the party here in the backyard, just making it a black-tie event. They tried to fight it, but even I agreed their fortieth anniversary should be celebrated in style.

Kylie planned this party weeks ago, so I knew I had to bring my tux. Thankfully, when I asked Gwen to come with me, I warned her about it, so she came prepared.

And boy, did she ever. She looks perfect in a flowy, emerald green dress with a slit up the middle. I can see just enough leg to drive me wild. Her teasing touches and seductive glances have me desperate to get her out of here. I made a promise to myself that I would wait until after dessert to sneak off with Gwen, but damn, it's been difficult.

Thankfully, they just passed out cake, and Gwen's heading back from talking with Kylie and my mom. This is the perfect time to sneak off for a bit.

Dirty Play

"You okay?" she asks as she walks back to me with a drink in hand for each of us.

"I am much better now that you're here," I tell her, leaning down and stealing a kiss, loving the soft mewls she makes as my tongue slips between her lips. My cock starts to harden, already craving her. It's been weeks since I've been inside her, and I'm dying to spend the night showing her just how much I love her. I'm desperate to feel her fall apart around me, to make sure she knows she'll always be home when she's with me.

"Slow your roll, Mr. Williams. There are children around." She smiles, but I can see the blush on her cheeks, and by the way she's squeezing her legs together, I can tell she's as affected by me as I am by her.

"About that, can I take you somewhere? I want to show you something," I say to her. My voice sounds more uneasy than I had hoped, but I can't help but be a little nervous.

What if she doesn't feel the same way? What if this is all for show because my family is around, and when we get back home, she breaks my heart? Should I wait until?

No.

It happens tonight.

"Won't people notice?" she asks nervously, but I just laugh.

"Have you looked around? I'm pretty sure everyone

from town is here. My parents won't even notice. And I don't really give a shit if anyone else does," I tell her with a shrug.

Her eyes twinkle as she looks up at me, her tongue darting out to lick those lips I desperately want on mine. But I want to talk to her, I need to tell her, and then hopefully the next time I kiss her, she'll know how much I love her.

"Lead the way," she says as she places her hand in mine.

THE SOUND OF THE RIVER HAS ALWAYS BEEN SOOTHING TO me. Any time I was upset or frustrated when growing up, I would end up coming out here. I would usually just throw rocks into the river, but it was always enough to take my mind off everything and just be.

Some of my best thinking was done in this spot, some of my best listening too.

"What is this place?" Gwen asks, sitting in the back of the 4Runner, her feet dangling as she looks up at me, curiosity filling those dark green eyes.

"When I was younger, I used to come out here. With Veronica. It kind of became our little hideout. She told me that she found this spot one day after she got frustrated with our parents for some reason or another and decided to go on a walk. After that, any time I got frustrated, I would come here."

Dirty Play

"It's beautiful out here, I can see why this would be your peaceful spot," Gwen says as she kicks her legs back and forth, her dress slowly sliding up with each pass until I can see more of her legs and I'm just dying to spread her wide.

Stay focused, Cade.

"It was my spot growing up, but now it's not the only place that I find peace," I tell her, hoping she can feel the sincerity in my words. "Gwen, when I'm with you, I feel the same peace that I felt here growing up, my brain can stop being so loud, and I can actually think, can actually feel." I watch her eyes start to widen at my declaration, but I'm not done.

I won't leave this spot until she knows I'm in love with her.

"You drive me crazy, but before you, I was merely existing. Even before we became *us*, back when we were just friends, you still brought me to life. The time I spent with you would be the highlight of my month. Look... what I'm trying to say is that without you, I'm a shell of a man. With you, I'm alive. I feel like I can breathe for the first time in a long time. I've fallen in love with you, Gwen Murphy, and I'm tired of fighting it."

She lets out a soft whimper as my lips crash into hers for a quick kiss before I drop to my knees in the middle of her dangling legs.

"What are you doing?" she asks, her voice barely a whisper.

"Proving to you in another way how much I love you," I tell her, gripping her panties and sliding them off, putting them in my pocket with a wink. The music from the party can still be heard here, but we're far enough away that I know no one will find us.

Not that I'd exactly care, I just don't want anyone else seeing her like this.

I start pressing kisses up her thighs as my hands adjust her dress, opening the center slit just enough to show me her pretty pussy, bare and glistening. She's already so wet for me.

"Is all of this for me?" I ask, as I slide one finger through her core, dragging her wetness down her thighs. With my tongue, I follow the path, lapping it up as I make my way to her pussy. "Answer me, Tink," I demand.

"Yes… it's all for you," she croaks out as my tongue flattens, sliding from her center all the way to her clit, her screams only pushing me to go harder, rougher, giving her exactly what she needs.

"Good girl," I growl. I turn my head and bite down on her inner thigh, earning me a yelp that morphs into a moan as I press my tongue against her clit.

I make slow movements, my tongue flat as I explore her, taste her, doing everything I can to get her ready. When I think she's close, I stop. Standing up, I unbutton my pants, slide my zipper down, and pull my cock out, precum already glistening at the tip.

I need her.

Dirty Play

"I'm going to fuck you now," I tell her as I take a step closer, sliding the head of my cock through her folds.

"Wait!" she says as I move to reach for my jacket, thrown on the edge of the truck. "I... I don't—do we have to use a condom?"

Not use a condom? I've never done that in my life, never, not even once. I've always been too terrified of a fuck up. The idea of getting someone pregnant has always been enough to scare the shit out of me.

But with Gwen? The idea of one day getting her pregnant and starting a family with her... that doesn't seem so scary. Being able to fuck her with no barrier is a dream come true.

"Are you sure?"

"Yes. I'm on birth control... and I've been tested," Gwen says, as she toys with her lower lip, worrying it between her teeth.

"Me too, Tink. I've never fucked without a condom before," I whisper, one hand sliding up and down my cock. The thought of fucking her like this already has me ready to come.

"Me neither," she says, grabbing my arm and pulling me closer. Lining my cock up with her entrance, I lean forward, kissing her, hoping she can feel how much I love her.

"I love you," I tell her as I slowly slide in.

"I love you too, Cade Williams," Gwen starts, but her words end in a yell. Hearing her say I love you is all it takes for me to lose control, thrusting all the way to the hilt.

The sensation is like nothing I've ever felt before. The feel of her squeezing my cock is so intense I have to hold still.

"Hey, Cade?" Gwen starts cautiously, her breathing ragged.

"Yes?"

"Will you fuck me now?"

Her words set me on fire, and I have to do everything in my control to remember that if I get hurt, if Gwen has to explain to her coworkers that she fucked me and injured me, she'll never forgive me.

I kiss her slowly, my hands gripping her hips as I continue to thrust deep and slow, lifting her hips up enough to hit her in just the right spot to make her toes curl. With every thrust, her moans get louder, her nails biting into my skin as she holds me tight. I smother her cries with my tongue, drinking them in as I've earned each and every one of them.

I can't tell you how long we spend near the river in the back of my truck, but before I know it, we're moving into the truck bed—where, thankfully, I was smart enough to already have pads down, although earlier, I thought they'd be to look at the stars.

I'd prefer to make her see stars.

Laying her down, my cock still buried inside her, she matches me thrust for thrust, her body rubbing small circles against me as I drive into her, over and over. She moves one hand, interlacing it with my own, and in this moment I feel like we are finally, truly understanding each other.

Gwen is mine.

I am hers.

"Don't stop, I'm... I'm so close" she whines, her breathing ragged as she frantically races toward her finish. But her next words push me over the edge. "Finish in me, Cade. Fill me with your cum."

That's all it takes, and with the last few thrusts and a thumb on her clit, we detonate. Her body starts shaking, her cheeks pink, and her pussy clenches down on me, milking every last drop until we lay there, completely spent, in the back of my truck.

It takes us a moment to catch our breaths, neither of us moving as I still inside her.

"That—" I start.

"Was the best fuck of my life," Gwen finishes for me, and I have to chuckle.

Nothing has ever felt like that before, ever.

Maybe because I've never fucked someone who was mine before.

Chapter 29

Gwen

The days after the party went far too quickly, and before we knew it, it was time to head back into the city. After we load up and say our goodbyes—which is the hardest part—we get into Cade's truck and start the drive. Part of me is looking forward to being back home, back in a routine, but there's just one problem.

Home is no longer a place.

Home is a person. An amazing six-foot-four goalie with dark brown eyes and a backwards hat, and fuck, I love him. Even better is the fact that he loves me, too. So now, what the hell am I going to do when we get back to the city? Do we go our separate ways? Back to our own places?

We can't.

I've slept next to him every single night since we've been here, and every single morning I've woken up with his arms wrapped around me. How am I supposed to try and sleep without him now that I've had that?

Dammit.

"Why are you being so quiet?" Cade asks, one hand on the wheel, the other on my thigh.

"I'm sorry," I murmur, realizing I've been zoned out for at least the last fifteen minutes. "I guess it just feels weird going home."

"What do you mean?" he asks as he reaches over and turns down the radio, the sweet sound of Morgan Wallen playing in the background.

"How can I go home when I don't know where that even is anymore? The last two weeks I've felt more at home than I have in my entire life, and that's scary. It's scary because it didn't matter where we were as long as I was with you."

My heart is racing, and I feel anxious, all at the thought of going to my empty apartment, alone. What am I? Sixteen? I'm a grown-ass adult.

"What are you saying?" he asks, his grip on my hand tightening.

"I guess I just hate that you'll be at your place, and I'll be at mine," I tell him. "I guess I'm used to sleeping with you."

The man smirks at me before he starts chuckling. "Aw, Tink. Are you worried you're going to miss me?"

I just glare, folding my arms. I'm sure I look like a

Dirty Play

toddler throwing a tantrum but that's how I feel right now. I don't want to be away from him.

"I hate you," I grumble, earning me a throaty laugh.

"No, you don't, Tink. Which is why, maybe, you don't go back to your place..." he says, his eyes still on the road. "And... if you do... maybe you don't go back alone?"

My heart feels like it's floating, he may not have said the words exactly, but this is the closest to Cade asking me to move in with him that I think I'm going to get, and I'm not even mad about it. I can't help the shit-eating grin that crosses my face, knowing that this man, this big, beautiful man, loves me.

"Are you asking me to move in with you?" I ask, spelling it out for him, and his cheeks immediately redden. "Cade Williams... are you blushing?"

He glances over, his cheeks still red, but this time, he's smiling.

"Yes, I'm asking you to move in with me."

All I can do is smile and nod, immediately excited at the prospect.

"I've never lived with anyone besides my family before," I tell him.

"Me neither, Tink. I guess we can be each other's firsts."

Driving into the city, with all the traffic and the constant hustle and bustle around us, is almost depressing. We've been in this quiet little bubble for the last two weeks, and although it's been a little tense at times, and we've all had to work through things, it's also given us the time to realize just how much we mean to each other.

I don't think I've ever known love like what Cade shows me. He makes me feel cared for, seen, and strong in a way that I've never felt before. Having Cade on my team makes me feel like I can face the world with a smile. As we pull up to my place, I'm grateful for that because I see my parents stepping out of a town car in front of my building.

"What the heck are they doing here?" I grumble.

"Who're they?" Cade asks as he pulls up behind them.

We had already planned that we both needed to get home tonight. I need to get ready for work tomorrow and Cade has a follow-up appointment first thing in the morning, so until we figure out our plan for living together—we'll be separated for at least tonight. It sucks, but it'll make tomorrow easier for us.

"*They* are my parents," I say with a sigh. "Apparently, two world-class surgeons are unable to figure out how a cell phone works. Or just don't care enough to reach out. The worst part is I absolutely don't want to see them right now. After the last two weeks with your family... I'm not ready to get asked by my own parents how the hospital is, what my career plans are, or whatever else they want to ask me about work—never about *me*."

"That's frustrating," Cade says, turning the car off. "As for not wanting to see them, we can always go drop your things off, talk to them for a few, and then head to my place. They don't need to know we aren't going anywhere. Besides, if they didn't give you a heads up when you asked them to, you're not obligated to spend more time with them than you'd like."

I look out the window at my parents, who have grabbed one bag each and are now heading inside, and I realize I really don't want to see them. I'm so frustrated with them that I don't feel like spending any extra time with them, pretending to be someone I'm not—pretending to be okay with their lack of interest in my life.

Plus, I definitely like the idea of being with Cade tonight.

"Are you sure you don't mind if I come over?" I ask nervously, not wanting to overstep. Sometimes when you come home from a trip, you just want to be left alone, and I respect that.

"Tink, if I have it my way, you'd come over tonight and never leave," he says, a smile on his face and sincerity in his eyes, and dammit, I want to say yes.

I don't care if it's moving fast. We've danced around this for so long, all the while these feelings were building deep inside. They were always there—it just took us a while to come to terms with everything. Moving in with Cade feels right because being away from him is no longer an option.

"Don't tease me unless you mean it."

"I mean it."

"Promise?" I ask.

"Pinky promise," he says, extending his pinky to me.

"Then I'm in," I say, wrapping my pinky around his and leaning across the center console to seal it again with a kiss. "Now, let's go grab some of my stuff and piss off my parents."

When we get inside my building, my parents are nowhere to be found. After a quick elevator ride to my floor we find my mom knocking nonstop on my door.

"Gwen!" she says loudly. "Your father and I don't have forever."

"Um, hi?" I say, surprising both of them. "What are you doing here?"

"Don't be silly. I told you weeks ago that we were going to visit. Where have you been, I know you didn't work today."

I hear Cade scoff behind me, my mother is only shocking the first time you meet her. After that, you sort of come to expect her usual bullshit and the fact that she believes the world actually revolves around her. She's not a bad person, though, in fact, she's kind, sweet, and really does love her family a lot. She just doesn't make time to have a relationship with me, and at this point, she just needs to recognize that.

"No, a month ago, you told me you might come visit, and I specifically asked you to let me know before. As for where I was... that's not really any of your business. Now, let's take this inside, I have to get some stuff together, and it'd probably be better to have this conversation somewhere outside of the hallway."

She looks shocked, but agrees, and we all go inside my place.

"We are busy, Gwen, we don't always have time to call," my dad says, settling onto my couch.

"Hello to you, too, dad," I say. "You're not the only ones who are busy. You just think that no one else's lives are as important as your own. It doesn't make you bad people—I'm just not going to plan my life around people who don't plan with me."

When I look at Cade, his lips are turned up, his hand covering his mouth like he's trying not to laugh. I don't think either of us expected this from me—I'm just so over their shit.

"I'll be right back," I tell them all, and my dad uses this time to turn to Cade.

"Hello... you look familiar, have we met before?" my father asks as I slip into my room.

I don't take long. I just need to grab my work clothes for tomorrow and a couple of other changes of clothes because everything else is still packed.

Standing by my door, I can hear the interaction between my parents and Cade.

"Hello, sir," Cade says politely. "I don't believe we've met. I'm Cade Williams."

"Cade Williams? As in the Cyclones goalie?" he asks, a little excitement in his voice.

I've never told my parents that I'm friends with a group of the biggest hockey players in New York. But truthfully, my parents have never even asked the name of one of my friends, so I didn't think they'd care.

"The one and only," he replies.

"It's very nice to meet you. I'm a big fan of yours. How do you know my daughter?"

"Thank you, sir. As for how I know your daughter?" Cade says. "I'm her boyfriend."

The words shouldn't make me so happy, but they do, and butterflies immediately take flight.

Cade Williams just said he's my boyfriend in the proudest voice I've ever heard, and somehow that has me giddier than his I love you.

Walking out of my room with my bag, I smile when they all look my way.

"You ready to go?" I ask Cade, who just nods.

"Are you telling us we need to leave?" my mom says, a look of bewilderment on her face, like she can't believe I'd say such a thing.

"Nope, not at all," I say with a smile. "I'm just letting you know that I am. I have plans with Cade, and had you called to let me know you'd be coming, I could've made different arrangements."

"Well, why can't you change them since we're here? We have a busy schedule these next few months and don't have a lot of time," my dad pipes in, although I can tell he's feeling guilty for not calling.

"With all due respect, why should I change my plans with someone who prioritizes me for people who only spend time with me when it's convenient? I'm not going to bend over backward for you when all I asked for was a heads up," I say with a sigh. "You are busy, I get that. But I'm done playing second fiddle in your life. It sucks to be constantly reminded that I come *after* your jobs."

Looking over at Cade, who has a proud grin on his face, I smile, knowing I probably burned some bridges, but I'm still heading home with him, and that's enough.

"Ready to go?" I ask.

He nods, looking over at my parents. "It was nice to meet you both," he says, shaking both of their hands. My parents just nod, both too stunned to speak.

Grabbing the bag of clothes I tossed together, I give them a quick wave before walking out of my apartment.

It's weird knowing the next time I'm here, it'll be to move my stuff.

Chapter 30

Gwen

"Do you think we still have time to get there before she leaves?" I ask Cade as I get dressed in the kitchen. I was out here cooking waffles before we head to the hospital to meet Kennedy. And apparently, seeing me cook waffles turns Cade on, and he couldn't wait to get me in the bedroom before getting me naked.

Oh well, I guess now I can cross *sex on a kitchen island* off my bingo card.

"Yes, we still have time. She's not being discharged until eleven. That's still two hours away. Then we're going to meet everyone at your place at noon to load up the U-Haul."

Cade has been surprising me ever since we came back from Ivy Falls a couple of weeks ago. He's been putting himself out there with his friends, and I'm so proud that he's working on taking down those walls on his own. He's been spending more time with everyone, including more time on the phone with his family.

They're already planning to visit us sometime this summer, and thankfully, Cade has a three-bedroom apartment, so there will be plenty of room for them to stay. When he told his parents we were going to move the rest of my stuff over, I could hear their excited squeals through the phone. My heart warms, knowing he has so many people who love him. And those people? They've welcomed me with open arms.

It's not that I don't love my family, I do. That's not in question. They don't need the family time and constant connection I've longed for. In the time I've known Cade's family, they've included me, checked in on me, and called just to say hello. And I can't forget the hugs his mom gave me while we were there—more hugs from a mother figure than I've received in my entire life.

Not only has his family noticed the changes in Cade, but our friends have too. He's always been an amazing friend to everyone. He's always the first to offer help, even if the job sucks. But apparently, he's only asked the guys for help *once*—when he was moving and couldn't lift all the furniture by himself, and movers weren't available for two weeks.

But now? He's finally asking others for help, letting them know when he needs something, and they're elated. Which is how they all got roped into moving my entire apartment.

Dirty Play

"Okay, then we need to go. What if she gets discharged early?" I ask. "What if she's already gone?"

"And when, in the history of *ever*, has someone been discharged from the hospital early?" Cade deadpans, probably remembering the day he got discharged, and it took an extra two and a half hours for a doctor to sign off.

"Fair. But we're still leaving now. I want to get a lemon loaf at the hospital. And to do that, I'm gonna need you to put a shirt on."

"You sure about that?" He smirks. "I thought that was against the rules?"

When I moved in, I, sort of... made a rule that if he was home, his shirt needed to be off. I wanted to be able to stare at his arms, with their thick, corded muscles and veins that I want to trace with my tongue. The tattoos covering his body don't hurt either.

"Ugh, you're impossible."

THIRTY MINUTES LATER, WE ARE WALKING DOWN THE hall toward Kennedy's room with a bunch of balloons and flowers. Cade wanted her to feel special and refused to show up empty-handed. I had to stop him from buying her all-new Cyclones gear, telling him there was plenty of time for him to spoil her and her family later.

"Hi, Kennedy," I say as we walk in, smiling at both

her parents, who, for the first time since I've known them, look rested and happy.

A damn near clean bill of health will do that for you.

"Hey! I'm so glad you came," Kennedy says, smiling as she sees Cade walk in, carrying the million balloons he got because I refused to help. "You came, too?"

"Of course I did, little K. Had to come see how that kidney was treating you with my own eyes," Cade says, his smile wide as he sets the balloons and flowers down on her table.

"It's been treating me good enough that they're finally letting me go home." She beams from her hospital bed, although she's wearing real clothes in front of me for probably the first time ever. "I can't wait to finally be home. I miss my dog and my bed."

"I heard, and I'm so excited for you. Although it'll be a bummer not to be able to stop by and say hi. But your parents have my number if you ever want to check in," Cade says, turning to her parents. "Don't forget to let me know whenever you guys want to come to a game. We'll get you set up with a suite and make sure you get the whole experience."

Josh stands up, his arm outstretched to shake Cade's, but when he grabs it, they pull each other in for a bro hug. "Thank you again—for everything. For saving my little girl and trying to make her time here not suck so much. You're an incredible person."

I see the moment Cade almost doesn't believe him,

Dirty Play

his old insecurities rearing their ugly head. But a second later, he pulls his shoulders back. "Thank you, it's been my pleasure. Honestly, this whole experience has helped me as well. It helped me work through some stuff from my past. Guilt I've been dealing with for years that I'm finally able to let go."

We all chat for a few more minutes, knowing when the nurse comes in to get her ready to go home, we'll be leaving, and I'm bummed. I'm obviously not sad that she's getting out of here, but I'm definitely sad I won't be able to sneak her out to get milkshakes in the middle of the night or come in to see what new show they were watching.

"Wait a second," Kennedy says, her eyebrows scrunched in as she looks between Cade and me. "Did you two come here together?"

My cheeks redden immediately, but Cade just chuckles.

"Yes, little K, we did come here together," he says, smiling at her parents, who are laughing as well.

"Does that mean you two are boyfriend and girlfriend now?" she asks curiously, but Cade looks at me to answer this one.

"We are," I tell her.

Without missing a beat, Kennedy turns to her mom with a smirk that I can only imagine means trouble.

"You lose, mama. You owe me fifty bucks."

"Did you two bet on us?"

"Yeah, we were trying to figure out how long it

would take for you two to realize your feelings. Mom thought it would take a while, but I guessed before I left this hospital. So, thanks for stopping by and helping me win that bet."

"Anytime," I reply with a chuckle.

IF I NEVER SEE A MOVING BOX AGAIN IN MY LIFE, IT'LL BE too soon. Who knew that a tiny one-bedroom apartment—in New York City, mind you—could hold so much stuff?

It took all of us hours to finish packing and carry the millions of boxes that Cade and I had already packed down to the U-Haul. I think if I had to do this without all of them, I'd have either died of old age right here in this apartment or sold myself on the streets to afford movers.

Thank God for the six NHL players who have become family to me.

"Is this everything?" Miles asks as he sets down another box in the living room.

The girls have been helping me unpack some of the stuff. Cade basically gave me full rein to put things where I want, change things if I want—pretty much anything as long as I'm happy.

His words, not mine.

"It better be," I grumble, grabbing another box and

bringing it into the bedroom, where the girls are putting clothes away for me.

This apartment really is perfect. Not only does every bedroom have a walk-in closet, but the primary bedroom has two, making this whole process so much easier because he doesn't have to make room for me—it's already there.

"So... now that we're moving your things into Cade's home, would this be an appropriate time to say I told you so?" Sawyer asks with a grin.

"I mean, I can't really think of a more perfect time," I joke. "I did just bring my entire collection of sex toys into his bedroom, so I'd say it's pretty clear you all were right."

Cassie giggles as she grabs her phone. "Can I get that on video? I need evidence of you telling us we were right?"

I flip off the camera, laughing because who knew that all I needed to feel at home was that grumpy man by my side and a group of friends who have always made me feel like family.

Cade walks in, eyeing all of the boxes and clothes spread out, and instead of looking overwhelmed, he just winks. "You ladies and your clothes," he says before walking over to me and leaning down to press a quick kiss on my mouth.

"Embracing the chaos?"

"I've been learning to do that since the day I met

you," Cade says, pressing another quick kiss to my lips before standing up.

It's weird how normal this all feels, like nothing has really changed, but at the same time, everything has. None of our friends have made a big deal about any of it either, minus the little jabs about it taking Cade forever to figure it out, but I approve of that message.

"Don't come at me with that bullshit, acting like us women are the only ones with a lot of clothes," Cassie deadpans. "Have you seen Max's hoodie collection? He has at least a hundred. That's after he lost my favorite sweatshirt from high school to some girl named Candice his freshman year in college."

"Trevor's the same way. That man could live in his hoodies, but that just means there are more for me to steal. Especially now that I'm in my second trimester, I'm no longer in the 'she just looks bloated' stage and am fully in the 'nothing fits' stage," Ellie shrugs before going back to unpacking all of my shoes. "Did you guys get all the kitchen stuff put away?"

Cade nods. "We did. Do you all have plans after this, or would you guys want to stick around for a while?"

The girls all look at each other, eyes wide, having a silent conversation that anyone could hear. Their shock at his invitation is evident.

"Uh, no plans," Cassie finally says, her smile wide.

"We'd love to hang out. We don't have to pick up

the girls for a while, they went over to Rex's parents' house," Ellie says excitedly.

"Good. I was thinking about making a lasagna. Would you like to join us for dinner tonight?"

"You're cooking me dinner? Hell yeah, I'm staying." Sawyer fist pumps.

With a smile that shows me just how far he's come, Cade turns to walk out of the room. Jumping up, I grab his hand before he walks out.

"Wait," I tell him, leaning up to press a kiss against his jaw, my arms wrapping around his neck. "Have I ever told you how amazing you are?"

"Yes, but I'll never tire of hearing it." He grins.

"I love you, Mr. Grumps."

"I love you, too, Tink."

"Promise?"

"Pinky promise."

Chapter 31

Cade

If you'd have asked me last year if I'd be sitting around the dining room table at my house with all of my friends, I'd have told you to lay off the drugs. But here we are, a homemade lasagna completely eaten, empty wine bottles all over the table, and so much laughter it's hard to imagine I'm in my own home.

Gwen gets up from her spot next to me to grab another wine opener and when she returns, I slip a finger through her belt loop and tug. She falls into me, landing in my lap with a laugh. "What was that?" she asks, her eyes playful.

"I want a kiss," I growl, sliding my fingers through her dark hair, I pull her into me until her lips are on mine. What I expect to be a quick, chaste kiss, quickly changes when she moves her tongue along my lips.

"God, is this what we were like when we first got together?" Rex groans.

Gwen pulls back, a big grin on her face as she turns to look at everyone, still sitting in my lap.

"No, you were worse." Cassie smirks.

"Did we make out in a room with all of you?" he asks.

"Yes," Max deadpans. "You also didn't care who was in the office with you... when you did other things. Talk about traumatizing," he says with a fake gag that has everyone laughing.

"Wish I could say I felt bad, little brother," Sawyer says with a smirk as she turns to look at Rex, probably remembering when she hid under his desk while he talked to Max... entertaining herself with the only toys available—his cock.

"Oh well," Max says, slipping his arm around Cassie and pulling her in close. "You got your karma when I fucked your best friend, so I guess we're even."

The two of them are always giving each other shit, but I guess that's what happens when one sibling fucks his sister's best friend and the other fucks her brother's coach. At least there are no awkward introductions at Christmas.

"Did I tell you all that Sawyer and I are going to take a trip next weekend?"

"Really?" Cassie asks, her eyebrows scrunched. "Where?"

"He won't tell me." Sawyer glares, but Rex just

laughs. "Says it's a surprise. Who the hell actually likes surprises nowadays. Instant gratification is where it's at."

Rex just laughs harder. "You'll know when it's time, but for now, I'm enjoying torturing you."

"You can at least tell me," Cassie deadpans.

"You're the last person he can tell if he wants to keep it a secret," Max says with a grin, Cassie sticking her tongue out with a smirk. The girl can't keep a secret to save her life, especially from Sawyer.

I already know where they're going and *why* they're going, but he's right. She'll know when it's time.

"Where did you learn to cook like that?" Ellie asks, looking at me like she's surprised.

"My mom. Growing up with four kids, she would have each one of us pick a night to cook. It stopped a lot of our complaining about what we were having for dinner because we were in control for one night, but it also meant that both my parents were off duty for four nights a week, which I think they loved. In the beginning, she would cook with us, show us some of her favorite recipes, and teach us the basics in the kitchen. After that, we were in full control, getting to make our favorites while she sat back and watched."

"That's amazing. We'll have to do that with Addy when she gets a little older," Ellie says, looking at Trevor.

"She cooks with me sometimes now," Trevor says.

"Eating cookie dough and brownie batter out of the mixer does not count as cooking with you."

He just shrugs.

"Was this one of your favorites?" Ellie asks.

"No. It was Veronica's."

I can feel the vibe in the room change the second I say her name, but where I expect to find sadness or pity on their faces, I find interest and compassion.

"Yeah, Veronica used to make it every single week. My other siblings would complain, but I secretly started to love it too. To this day, I make it whenever I'm missing her—and on her birthday."

Gwen leans back, resting her head on my chest as she looks out toward our friends. The feeling of her body on mine grounds me, giving me the strength to have this conversation without feeling like I'm going to lose a part of myself in the process.

"She was pretty badass in the kitchen. I remember she used to make this cheesecake that I would give my left nut to have another slice of," Harris groans.

"The Oreo one?" I ask, my mouth watering at the memory. I'm not sure what my sister put in this cheesecake, but it never lasted more than an hour in my house. Even less if Harris was over.

"The one and only."

The rest of dinner goes smoothly. We spent the next couple of hours talking. They asked questions about my family and my sister for a while, and instead of feeling uncomfortable or getting upset, I felt excited.

Dirty Play

I'm happy to share stories of my sister, the memories I have growing up with her, and how she was the feistiest person I knew.

Until Gwen, of course.

Obviously, they asked a million questions about Gwen and me. Not a single one of them were shocked about us getting together or even about us moving in together. They just bitched that it took us so long.

The kidney surgery was another story, I get yelled at quite a bit about that one. Harris just sat and laughed since he already got his lecture in.

My favorite part of the night was being close to Gwen. The entire time we talked, the only time Gwen got up was to grab a snack or another glass of wine. Outside of that, she was snuggled in my lap.

By the time everyone leaves, it's after eleven, and we're both exhausted. Being over a month out from surgery has made a huge difference in how I'm feeling. I'm not as weak and tired as I was those first couple of weeks. I was cleared to start working out, so hopefully, I can start getting some of my strength back.

"Are you ready for bed?" Gwen asks from the kitchen, grabbing us each a glass of water.

"I am. I'm worn out," I tell her as I grab my phone and walk over to make sure the door is locked.

"It was a busy day. Luckily, we have one more day before I go back to work. We can spend all day sleeping."

Walking over to her, I take both waters and set them down so I can wrap my arms around her.

"If we're spending all of tomorrow in bed, I can promise you we won't be sleeping," I growl, my teeth nipping her ear.

Turning her face, she presses a long, slow kiss to my mouth, her tongue tangling with mine.

"Pinky promise?" she asks in a whisper.

"Pinky promise."

I used to get sad when I thought about pinky promises because they remind me of Veronica and my broken promise to her. But every time Gwen says it to me, I can't help but feel happy that we're continuing this tradition.

While Gwen grabs the waters again, I turn off the lights. We use the city lights, visible through the windows, to navigate through the living room into my—our bedroom. Gwen grabs one of my t-shirts and lies in bed looking out the window at the city below.

"Your view is crazy," she whispers.

"It's our view, Tink," I reply with a smile as I slip off my shirt and pants, leaving me in a pair of boxer briefs as I slide into bed next to her.

"That's crazy to say... isn't it? I've never lived with anyone before, not someone I was dating. You're my first."

"What's crazy is how right it feels. How normal. I think the only thing crazier is how long it took us to get here," I tell her, holding my arm out for her to slide in.

Dirty Play

Once she's nestled up beside me, our breathing aligns, and her fingers start tracing the patterns of my tattoos.

"Have I ever told you the story about why pinky promises are so important?" I ask quietly.

"No, but I'd love to hear it," she says, looking up at me with curiosity.

So, with her head on my chest and my arms around her, I tell her the story of Veronica and her pinky promises, and I feel another piece fall into place.

It's been years of running, never letting anyone get close enough to care about me, let alone hurt me. But this has shaken me. I never expected Gwen to be the one to knock me on my ass, coming out of left field with a dirty play while I was too far gone, too distracted to stop her from getting through my defenses.

Finding her put all my fucked up, broken pieces back together—her strength and her love holding them all in place. She's helped me be strong, helped me have the hard conversations I've always avoided, and she's helped me remember both the good times and the bad.

She gives me strength, and I am her home.

Epilogue

Gwen

Two Years Later

I'll never get over hockey nights. The lights, the music, the energy—they make for a perfect night of watching hockey. Especially when my man is playing. It's been two years since we finally stopped pretending like we weren't more, and they've easily been the best two years of my life. But tonight?

Tonight, I get to watch *my husband* on the ice for game seven of the Stanley Cup finals.

To say I'm a proud wife would be a gross understatement.

Cade and I have been through a lot in the short time we've been together, but we've made every moment count. Today is no different, as we have a surprise up our sleeves, but that's for after they bring home the cup. I like to think we are packing in as much excitement and as many experiences as quickly as we can to make up for the time we both know we wasted, pretending there was nothing between us.

After Cade and I moved in together, right after we came home from his parents, it was only six months until we were engaged. It was easily one of my favorite days, with my favorite people, ending in forever with my favorite man.

The whole night was magical. I'll never forget seeing Kennedy and her mom crying after watching everything unfold and the hugs they gave both of us. Anyone else watching the New York Cyclones play against the Nashville Firebirds the night before their Christmas break also got to watch our special moment.

After another six months, we were married back at his parents' farm in Ivy Falls. It turned into a much bigger ordeal than I cared for, but that's what I get for letting Cade's mom and sister plan it all. My parents offered to help with the planning—their help just happened to be isolated to financial planning.

At the end of the day, though, they showed up for our wedding and have been working to take more of an interest in my life outside of my career, including showing up to the game tonight to support Cade. That effort alone has helped change my perspective a bit and I am appreciative. Although at the end of the day, I've realized they aren't my only family. I'm surrounded by the family that I chose and who continue to choose

Dirty Play

me every day. We aren't related by blood, but that's okay with me.

"Do you think they'll do it?" Sawyer says from next to me, where she and Rex are standing all decked out in Cyclone's gear. Rex opted to wear one of Trevor's old jerseys, saying now that Trevor wasn't actively playing, it felt less like cheating on his Ice Hawks.

Valid outlook from a coach.

"I hope so," I whisper, holding my breath. Although our news will be exciting either way, it'd be even better to share it with everyone after a win like this.

It's been a couple of weeks since we saw those two pink lines, and every day, I've wanted to announce it to the world. But Cade and I wanted to make it through the playoffs before that was on everyone's mind. I did tell Sawyer, but only because she came over in the middle of an episode of morning sickness and put two and two together.

With just under a minute left in the third period, the Cyclones are up two to one, but the Firebirds are about to go on a power play due to a shitty call. If they can get it down to our end, they'll probably pull their goalie, which would make it six guys against our four. Thankfully, Cade has been on it all night, only letting one puck slip through. He'll be focused on that one, but he's had sixty-three saves so far, so I'd say he's doing just fine.

When the puck drops, my heart stops. My hand

moves to my stomach like I'm grounding myself to him, and I watch with bated breath to see how this plays out. The Cyclones lose the drop and the Firebirds send the puck down towards Cade in the goal. Harris is there and forces their winger to the outside away from the goal. Slamming him into the glass, they battle for the puck, which is stuck between the boards and the other guys skate.

We all hold our breath. Cade's parents, brother, and sister are on one side of me with the rest of our friends behind me. The energy is thick with excitement and anticipation as we watch the seconds tick down.

Miles and Harris are both in the action, their sticks down on the ice trying to break the puck free and get an empty netter to seal the win. With just four seconds left, Harris gets the puck out and makes a quick pass to Miles, who slips the puck through the legs of a Firebird defender, retrieving it on the other side to make a quick shot on goal. Our entire group holds their breath as the puck sails through the net right as the buzzer goes off.

Holy shit.

The Cyclones have won the Stanley Cup.

Everyone hugs and jumps up and down as we celebrate their win, but all I can think about is what we are about to tell the group the second we're all together.

A couple of hours later we're all meeting up with

Dirty Play

Cade outside, both our families surrounding us as I jump into his arms, my legs wrapping around him.

"You did it, baby," I whisper in his ear as he holds me up.

"I can't believe we won," he says, and I can hear the smile in his voice. "Did you tell everyone yet?"

"No—" I start, right as Kylie pipes in.

"Did she tell us what?" Kylie asks as Cade sets me down to stand next to him. His arm pulls me in close as he looks down at me with a smile.

"That this time next year, there will be someone else watching my games," Cade says as everyone watches on, slight confusion on their faces as they try to figure him out, but Sawyer, *and Rex,* look on with smiles, while their kids run around us with Ellie and Trevor's in tow.

"Who?"

"We don't know yet," I finally say with a smile, meeting our families' eyes. "We haven't met them yet, but we know he or she will be proud to support their daddy... and his friends."

"Are you... pregnant?" my mom asks with a smile I didn't expect—she looks absolutely delighted at the idea.

"I love you," Cade whispers as he leans down and places a quick kiss against my lips before turning to face everyone.

"We are... baby Williams is on the way," Cade

finally says, and I'm falling even more in love with this man as he enters his daddy era.

More hugs and excitement are passed around, our parents embracing as they talk about how excited they are to be first-time grandparents. I realize in this moment that not only is this baby bringing Cade and me closer, but they're bringing our families back together, healing our wounds one day at a time.

Epilogue

One Year Later

If you'd have told me ten years ago, hell even five years ago, I'd be sitting here holding a baby, I'd have called you a damn liar. Especially since we're talking about *mine and Gwen's baby.*

But here I am, and I'm the happiest I've ever been.

Also, the most tired.

But I guess that's just what comes with having a newborn... especially when she's a night owl like her daddy. That little fact has quickly become one of my favorite things because I get to do the late nights with Scarlett, spent in her rocking chair. It means I get to spend the middle of the night sharing secrets with my little bestie while she enjoys her bottle, soft music playing in the background until she falls asleep. I usually stay up a bit longer, just holding her. As I watch hockey highlights on my phone, I catch glimpses of her soft little smiles in her sleep, my favorite.

Knowing I'm holding half of my world in my arms gives me a type of peace I want to embrace for as long as I can—at least until my tiny baby isn't so tiny anymore. It's crazy to be living this life, one I always dreamed of but never felt worthy of before Gwen. Now I'm living my dreams, all because this one's mama and I fell in love.

I'll never forget the day we got married. It's a core memory, and damn, it's my favorite.

Everything after the wedding definitely helped solidify it in my mind for life.

Gwen looked like an actual angel as she made her way down the aisle toward me. I felt like everything was finally coming together—the love of my life was marrying me as my family watched on, looking happier than I'd seen them since before Veronica passed. I felt peace like I hadn't known in years.

I will always wish Veronica could've been there with us, but I felt her. I saw her in the rainbow that appeared after a June rainstorm hit mid-reception. I felt her in our vows as we pinky promised to always fight for each other and to love each other forever.

I'll never forget that feeling. It was like seeing the sun for the first time in ten years. I felt happy. I was living in this crazy world where somehow my 'real'

Dirty Play

family meshed with my 'found' family, and they all just became... my family.

That night was even more special because I was surrounded by my best friends, each of them celebrating with the person I knew deep in my bones they were destined to find. It's a crazy thing to watch your friends get picked off by Cupid, one by one. Once you find it yourself, you understand immediately.

The heartbreak. The fear. The unknown.

It all made sense the second I met Gwen.

"Are you ever going to come back to bed, or are you going to sit and ogle our daughter all night again?" Gwen's voice quietly floats through the room as she stands in the doorway, a smirk on her face as she watches us. She loves watching us together, her eyes somehow bright while still sleepy since it's not even five in the morning.

"Eventually," I whisper, smiling up at Gwen. "She's just so cute. I didn't want to put her back in her crib. She might get lonely."

"I know, but at some point, you need to sleep," she says, walking into the nursery and sitting on the ottoman next to us, her hand resting on my thigh. "She's sound asleep and she should be for at least another two hours. Especially since she'll be all warm and cozy after you swaddle her up. But *me*? I'm wide awake, all alone in that big cold bed of ours."

"Is that so?" I whisper, her robe falling open as she leans over toward me. "Mrs. Williams, are you wearing anything under that tiny robe? From my angle, it doesn't look like it."

She just smirks as she looks down at me, her big doe eyes feigning innocence. "Oops, I must've forgotten."

"Tink, if you're not careful, I'm going to put another baby inside of you before your maternity leave is even over."

Her eyes widen at my words, quickly glossing over with desire.

"Put her to bed Cade, and I'll let you do whatever you want," Gwen says before standing, adjusting her robe, and walking to our room.

The second she steps out, I stand up as calmly as possible, swaddle Scarlett and place her in her crib before quickly and quietly making my way to our bedroom. When I walk in, I see her naked on our bed, resting on her elbows, with a look that tells me she knew I wouldn't be long.

Fuck no, not when I know I'm about to spend the rest of tonight buried deep inside of her.

It's been a while since we've been together, and I haven't once pressured her or even insinuated anything more happening between us, so she knew the ball was in her court, when she was ready. This was her way of telling me she's ready, and I'd be a fool not to follow her lead.

It's been a couple of months since I've been inside of her, and I miss that connection. I miss the intimacy that being together brings, knowing that each time we're together, our bond grows stronger. Every single time we're together, I feel another piece of the puzzle fall into place, my heart slowly healing.

"Fucking hell, Tink," I say as I drop my shorts and pull my t-shirt off over my head, leaving me naked in front of her. Her greedy eyes take in every inch of my body, and I'd be lying if I said it didn't stroke my ego a bit. "Keep looking at me like that, and I'll definitely be putting a baby in you tonight. Irish twins sound good to you?"

"Shut up and kiss me, Mr. Williams," she says as I crawl over her body, leaving soft kisses up her leg, across her stomach, and over her breasts until finally I find her lips.

"I'll do more than just kiss you, Mrs. Williams. I'll own every inch of your body, reminding you how much I love having you as my wife."

And I do just that, spending every second we have showing her just how much I love her.

The End

Also by Lexi James

The Empire State Hockey Series

Power Play (Rex and Sawyer's Book)

Puck Princess (Max and Cassie's Book)

Blindside Love (Trevor and Ellie's Book)

Dirty Play (Cade and Gwen's Book)

Delayed Penalty (Harris and Avery's Book) - Fall 2024 (preorder now)

Penalty Kill (Miles and ******'s Book)- Late 2024/ Early 2025 (preorder now)

Acknowledgments

First off I want to thank my readers. I say this every time I release a book, but it will always be true. I wouldn't be doing this without you. Your excitement for these books, for this world, keeps me going, so from the bottom of my heart, thank you, thank you, thank YOU. This community has been so supportive to me as a newer indie author and I'll never be able to express my gratitude fully. Thank you for always dropping in my DM's, sharing edits, and spreading the love.

To My Husband- Thank you for always pushing me to keep going. To keep writing, even when it feels impossible. The way you believe in me keeps me going. You make me feel like I can fly, but safe enough to keep my feet on the ground. Thank you for keeping our lives running smoothly even when I'm off in my own make-believe world. Love you always.

To Candice- Thank you for being the other half of my brain. It's the worst being in different time zones, but you still managed to yank me across the finish line with this book. Thank you for being my person, someone I can bounce ideas off of, helping me with all the behind-the-scenes things because I'm apparently a dinosaur when it comes to technology. Most importantly, thank you for believing in me and these stories. Can't wait to keep on this journey with you! I love you!

To Amanda Mudgett- Not sure where I'd be without you. You cheer me on, keep me on track, and are always offering a helping hand...or a million. Thank you for being wonderful, making the prettiest things, and being funny as hell. Love you!

To my Alpha readers- Candice, Jamie, and Mudge. You helped me mold this story before I'd even typed the first word. Thank you for offering suggestions, talking things out, and helping me get it to where it is now. Love you all!

To my Beta Readers- Ashley, Megan, Andi, Jenn, Sam, Taylor, and Shannon. Thank you for all your feedback and help catching little things that I'd missed and helping make sure it's ready. The unhinged comments will forever be my favorite. Thank you. :)

To my editor, Caroline. Thank you for helping me turn this into something I am so proud of. You're wonderful and thank you for not hating me for my horrible grammar/punctuation.

Thank you Kristen for proofreading this! Your attention to detail is incredible and I'm so thankful you had a part in this book!

To Lexie Woods- Thank you for taking a look at my manuscript and helping me out with some of the medical parts! Thank you for sharing your time and your knowledge!

To my family, thank you for supporting me even though you've been forbidden ever to read my books. You're always so excited about the details I share and I love that. If you've read this, that means you failed. ;)

About the Author

Lexi James lives in Washington with her husband and their two little boys. If she's not at work, you can find her out adventuring with her family, exploring trails, or curled up on the couch with a steamy book. She began reading after the birth of her kids when she needed something 'just for her' and since then she's read every day and found her passion for writing in the process.

She's a daydreamer who always has characters and their has stories running through her mind. With encouragement from her husband and family, she sat down to write a book, giving a voice to her imaginary friends and a place to escape to when life gets crazy.

Printed in Great Britain
by Amazon